Mythic Danger Under the Sea

The sun gave off a dim, sulphurous glow. Everything was suffused with its morbid light. A distant ridge of granite hills bordered the landscape to port. The stretch between consisted of pale, coagulated shapes with the energy of cresting waves. Rough and ropy skeins of stone and simple ovoids gave way to skewed megalithic formations. The terrain was chaotic, sterile and noiseless. There was neither any obvious vegetation—not even a stray leaf—nor any sign of animal life.

For Nolin, the scene conjured up childhood fantasies of his father's adventures with Captain Nemo—wondershot worlds made just for the moment, haunted and beautiful. Every nerve was atwitch with atavistic dread. He climbed onto the submersible. The pain around his eyes continued to pulse. How would he ever find the others? How would they ever get home? He sighed into his chest. The air was thick with dusty death.

An obtrusive crunching and scraping sounded from the temple behind him. This was Apep announcing itself: the serpent slithered out of the temple's shadows, an inexorable grinding, stone on stone, and adopted a striking coil position on the steps. Residual whitespace energy flashed along its length.

Apep tilted its flint-shaped head, curious, then convulsed into a swift stabbing charge...

From *The Divine Drowned*

Other Works in the Nightscape Series

Main Series Books
Early Darkness
Cynopolis
The Dreams of Devils

Double Feature Books
No. 1: The Thousand-Eyed Fear | The Q for Damnation

Short Fiction
Spawn of Cloud & Sword

Comic Books
Entombed

Plays
The Barren Cross

Films
Nightscape (or, Road without End)

Albums
Project Nightscape, *To Sin Against Our Mercies*

NIGHTSCAPE

DOUBLE FEATURE Nº2

The Divine Drowned

Josh Reynolds & David W. Edwards

Forever The Star Finder

Fianna I. Quigg

IMPERIAD
ENTERTAINMENT

Portland, Oregon USA

Imperiad Entertainment
Portland, Oregon USA

First Imperiad Entertainment trade paperback edition September 2018.

For information about special discounts for bulk purchases, please contact Imperiad Entertainment at info@imperiad.com.

Cover art by Isabel McKean
Back cover illustration and interior art for *Forever the Star Finder* by Matthew Nielsen
Designed by Ryan Peinhardt

Manufactured in the United States of America

ISBN 978-0-9897487-5-9

For more on the Nightscape universe, visit www.nightscapeseries.com

NIGHTSCAPE DOUBLE FEATURE NO. 2

The
Divine Drowned

Josh Reynolds and
David W. Edwards

Contents

"Everything is in a state of metamorphosis. Thou thyself art in everlasting change and in corruption to correspond; so is the whole universe."
—Marcus Aurelius, *Meditations. ix. 19.*

Chapter 1

The Heavenly Axis

The Last Cycle of Unmaking
Outskirts of Duah-teh District, Herakleion

Accompanied by her personal guard of baboon-soldiers, Hema crested the spur of carved rock with a nimbleness born of experience. Fingers and toes found familiar cracks in the surface and she summited what had once been a glorious tribute to Ptah, the creator god of the ancient Egyptians. The robed statue was about 100 meters high and set against an uneven ridge. Its right arm bent to a large plinth-like staff. The head had been sheared away by the unstable landscape, leaving only a flattened ledge. Hema situated herself in the center of the bone-white slab and stretched to relieve the tension in her shoulders and upper arms. The bunch-backed simians took up defensive positions around the perimeter, scanning for signs of the enemy. They wore reed and bronze armor and bristled with daggers, sickle swords and handaxes.

Heart-shaped flowers the color of rotted meat sprouted from the statue's cracks and vestigial joints. The captain of the guard, Gapti, offered Hema a short-stemmed blossom with lowered eyes. She breathed in its heady fragrance, tucked it behind an ear and stroked Gapti's wide, scarred muzzle in thanks. He was taller by a half-meter, twice as broad and covered in a thick ruff of white fur. His dog-like face broke into a shy, dagger-toothed smile meant to be encouraging. Then, suddenly self-conscious, he barked a command for vigilance and assumed the post nearest his charge. He'd lived since infancy for Hema and would see no harm done to her, regardless of the blood-price.

From this vantage point, Hema surveyed the twisted and tessellated city of her masters, the Duah-teh priesthood. The city of Herakleion had been subject to increasingly violent mutations in form and arrangement as if malign underground pressures were working their way to the surface. Its structures of pale stone foundered at unnatural angles. Only the buildings closest to the city core—built around the great *atef*-crowned Temple of Osiris—maintained some semblance of their original contours. Given over to Herakleion's wanton metamorphosis, everything else lurched out of kilter. The outlying areas trailed into dense, nearly impassable dreamscapes like vast melts of candlewax.

Herakleion had once towered over the Nile delta, a wondrous and thriving port city modelled partly on the glories of Atlantis. The city no longer rose above the Egyptian coast; instead, it straddled a horizon the length of an eternal moment. Much like smoke drawn up a flue, the city grew increasingly distorted the further it extended from its point of origin toward the blinding light of moment's end. Hema couldn't resist glancing at the pinhole sun that was neither Ra nor Khonsu but some cold unknowable star drafting the city into its ever-expanding maw. She settled on the rock cross-legged and took a few calming breaths to clear the impending threat from her mind. Penetrating the dimensions-spanning dreamtime—what the Duah-teh called the Un-worldly River—required her complete focus.

Her perch helped minimize the mental interference she encountered at ground level. The principle drawback was that it left her especially vulnerable to physical attack. When fully entranced she was insensible to her surroundings and so had to rely on Gapti and his troop to safeguard her from the dangers of a chance shift in surroundings or an assault from the Duah-teh's age-old foes, the Nebwa. The insurgent Nebwa roamed Herakleion's hallucinatory wilds, mounting periodic assaults on the city proper. They were unrepentant zealots for chaos. While her masters struggled to slow and contain the city's corruption, the Nebwa fought to accelerate then loose it on the scarcely-remembered Earth of their ancestors.

A recent spate of psychic shockwaves had spurred the Nebwa to bolder aggressions. Only two solar cycles ago, they'd dared to target the *Ptahkit'b* directly via the old aqueducts. The Duah-teh were counting on Hema to find some advantage in the Unworldly River—a weapon, an artifact, a magickal adept—something to give them lasting hope. Hundreds of attempts had yielded little more than vague premonitions. Hema feared her masters' collective patience was nearly at an end. The flower Gapti proffered might as well have been a funeral token.

Hema closed her eyes and began to settle into her astral mindset by reciting an ancient Sumerian mantra BAB.I.LI ANU.NA.KI (*Ba-bee-lee A-noo-na-key*), one of the last remembrances from her birthplace. The Duah-teh had snatched her out of time as a skinny pre-adolescent in order to nurture and harness her inborn sensitivity to the Unworldly River. Though her body had aged only about twenty years since the kidnapping, her consciousness had accumulated nearly two thousand years of experience. Her wisdom now far surpassed that of her putative masters.

She understood reality as a unified continuum of becoming rather than as an aggregation of discrete, static phenomena. Being and not-being weren't mutually exclusive states; rather, being in its purest form was indeterminate and accordingly, capable of passing into its opposite and vice versa. What unified being and not-being was the process of becoming. The astral realm of the Unworldly River ran through all dimensions and all times. There was no number in this river as there's none in eternity. It allowed her to experience the process of becoming across space-time. The ambit of her consciousness was limited only by her reserves of dream energy.

Most dreamtime adepts perceived the dead as flitting imprints on the astral plane—brief concentrations of memory and dream as transient as footprints in the sand. But Hema had the unique ability to excite their personalities and histories, to return them, however briefly, to a semblance of earthly life.

The murmurs of the dead resounded through her astral self but she paused to gather her dream energy before engaging them. This next part of her task required extra-added effort. Her principal trick for eliciting the dead involved maintaining a delicate mental contradiction. She had to dispense with conscious thought altogether and at once become aware of its absence. The conceit affirmed the nullity of thinking yet was itself thinking. In this way, she became conscious of her own nothingness and invited the dead to approach her as one of their own.

Soon after she completed this transition, several undulating thought-forms began to circle her bleary gold aura. She bent her thinking to their frequency of absence and, in a flashing instant, found herself in the Herakleion-that-was. Memories of the old city broke into her awareness: the vivid Mediterranean sun; a dazzle of red granite towers; the air, warm, briny and shot through with the earthy tang of fresh-ground wheat; a convergence of flat-bottomed boats against the horizon.

One of the orbiting thought-forms manifested an amulet of the hippo-bodied goddess of childbirth and fertility, Taweret. Keying off the amulet, Hema inquired about new things using the thought-glyph of the stork-like Bennu for emphasis. The thought-form bubbled sea-black and wrenched Hema into unexpected depths. The city disappeared under a swirling murk, leaving Hema in a panic of impressions—a bone-chilling ocean—a coral formation attended by wriggling fish—a barnacle-encrusted stele—swift darkness—a deeper cold—then a port hole light: a finned machine—one, two of them—cutting through the down current (like missiles!)—chased by a cloud of sand—hooded red eyes—a serpent (*izft*)—the chaos-bringer, Apep—fear—fervor—fear—in the precious deformed—thundering down—fever-hot—obeyed in pain and moon-bright—BAB.I.LI-b-b-ba-*bwt*—

She gasped back into the Herakleion of the waking world, disoriented and stinging from the prick of a sword-point against her neck. Before her: a baboon-abomination or *ian bwt*. The Nebwa soldier glared at her with red-rimmed eyes. Hema's heart misgave. As the beast prepared to palm-strike the sword into her throat, she rolled back on her shoulders and kicked out. The heels of her leather sandals caught the malformed baboon on the jaw hard enough to give it pause. She rolled aside to evade the beast's follow-on lunge. Then its head spun clean of its body courtesy of Gapti's blade. Hema bobbed her head in stunned gratitude. Her flower was a fitful smear against the rock.

The guard was under concentrated assault from the Nebwa's shock troops—once-sacred baboons ruined by unguided mutations. Bone spurs protruded from her foiled assailant along its shoulders and thighs. Others in the immediate vicinity sported sleek contour feathers, prehensile tails, corkscrewed horns and useless bat-like wings. They were berserk parodies of their former selves and, like their masters, lived for the blood-dream of destruction.

The world flushed red at the periphery of Hema's vision just as the statue began to sway. The granite fractured anew and sections calved into empty air to smash below. Gapti understood the source and enormity of the danger at once. "Ammit," Hema breathed. The Nebwa's giant mutate general Ammit, the Eater of Souls approached. The creature's negative energies tainted the air for some distance and the ground tremored with its every step. Hema could never be sure if Ammit's presence signaled a major offensive or served only as a distraction to draw the Duah-teh from the Nebwa's real objectives.

Gapti barked for a general retreat, slung Hema onto his back and raced on all fours for the platform's edge. He barely gave her time to tighten her grip on his corselet before leaping headlong to a far ledge. Her stomach tumbled after. They skidded across the remnants of Ptah's staff then dropped to a lower outcropping and another lower still. Hema renewed her hold on the baboon. The veins on the backs of her hands stood out. The rest of the guard followed their path, swinging from one cornice or edge to the next, dodging random debris and the occasional spear.

They descended with an untraceable, heart-sinking swiftness. Gapti pushed himself to his limits, grunting in pain at each jolting hand-grab or abrupt shift in direction. These days, he felt his advanced years down to the spent nub. But he refused to slacken his pace—even after the *ian bwt* had abandoned their pursuit—until he and his squad reached the city core and safety.

Hema ruffled the fur along his cheek pouches as much to calm the quickened pulse in her throat as to show her gratitude. She was still reeling from her forced return to the material world. The twin machines from her dreamtime journey portended an inflection point in time, she was sure of it. But when she chased after the meaning of the image it faded into blankness. She closed her eyes a moment to better recapture the sensations of the Unworldly River. The patchy light behind her lids flared and jumped. Then an ominous-sounding word came to mind—something that reminded her of *kontos*, the Byzantine word for cavalry spears. No, not just a word, a name: Lancer.

Chapter 2
No Rest for the Worthy

13 January 1922
Abu Qir Bay, Egypt

Nolin 'Lancer' Quigg fidgeted with his pocket compass as he considered the muted green waters of Abu Quir Bay. The sea was a glazed-over mirror, stingy with its secrets. His cardigan sweater coat fluttered in the brisk winter wind. He stood apart from all the pre-launch bustle around the team's new submersibles. A strange sense of separation and doomed fixity had come over him. Integrand General's mission to explore the supernatural unknown had taken a violent turn of late, giving them an unwanted global profile. The team could expect trouble not only from the usual clutch of apocalyptic cults but also from various government agencies and savvy private interests. It was only a matter of time before they were outnumbered, outgunned, or in Katsuo's parlance, simply ran out of 'divine luck.'

"Thinking about thee-uh loads of discoveries we're bound to make?" Paul 'Shimmy' Weygand, Nolin's childhood friend and 'auxiliary brain' sidled up to him. "Could be a sizeable treasure. Herakleion was thee-uh gateway to the Mediterranean up until it sunk."

Nolin affected a lightheartedness he didn't feel. "And your birthday's coming up, hint, hint." Like Paul, he spoke in an Irish brogue softened by years of foreign travel.

"Well, we did miss the Christmas holidays."

"You got to cross one or two items off your doomsday checklist." Nolin's grin split his short, boxed beard.

"Followed close-on by that damnable Knuckerhole Incident ..." Paul wiped his grease-stained hands on his denim boiler suit then fished out a handkerchief to clean his glasses.

Nolin clicked his compass shut a final time and slid it into his pocket. "Fate of the world, backs against it, sometimes you have to put the hours in."

"Cross off one doomsday artifact, add two ..."

"That's called job security, mate." Nolin clapped Paul on the shoulder. Physically, the two men were a study in contrasts: Nolin was tall and strapping with skin olive-dark enough for him to pass as a local in the proper light; and Paul was half-a-head taller, pale and gangly as a length of rope.

Paul gestured toward the three submersibles mounted on earthworks and launch scaffolding in the frill of surf. He'd designed the four-person vessels after the fashion of Captain Nemo's *Nautilus* using schematics Nolin had inherited from his father. They were spindle-shaped vessels of ribbed steel. "With thee-uh these Kelpies here," Paul said, replacing his glasses on his nose, "we're assured no one can follow us, not even thee-uh Society."

The Society of the Black Sun, headed by a figure known only as the Magian, had dogged them for the past seven-plus weeks—ever since Nolin and company had recovered a bog-preserved papyrus originally thought to be a map to Atlantis. Nolin's translation of the ancient Egyptian record had led the team here. Herakleion had sunk twice and the second, smaller city had been built on the submerged remains of the first. They'd come in search of Herakleion *primus* to secure any dangerous relics.

"I don't know," Nolin said. "They do have those pyrokinetics and that bloody mage."

"There's one to put the wind up me. I'm still trying to figure out how he managed to disappear that castle in Languedoc."

"I think the technical term is 'hand wavium.'"

"Who was your physics tutor again? Winsor McCay?"

"We're all about due for a stretch in Slumberland."

"You most of all," Paul said. Owing to Nolin's superior stamina, he had a terrible habit of taxing himself to show he wasn't above the hard work he assigned others. Paul knew he'd never admit to exhaustion.

"I'm just anxious to know what's down there." Nolin ran a hand through his military-style brush cut. "The Herakleions supposedly took inspiration from the high culture of Atlantis. We might actually find a helpful artifact this time."

"Perhaps if you've a mind to sink something other than your next pint. 'A curious aurora, as if thee-uh the sun-god had set his hand about the city,'" Paul quoted. "When it cleared, Herakleion was gone as if it had never been. It parallels accounts of Atlantis, Ville d'Ys, Rocabarra...*Nuair a thig Rocabarra ris, is dual gun tèid an saoghal a sgrios.*" His voice was aquiver with the rush of ideas. He stuttered as a consequence of trying to catch up to his thoughts. "When Rocabarra returns, thee-uh the world will likely come to be destroyed."

"You sure know how to cheer me up." Nolin's eyes shadowed over. The specter of cataclysm prodded him to share the awful secret of his prodigious strength and near invulnerability. He'd come close on countless occasions but each year that passed in silence made the prospect of it more daunting. At this point, Nolin feared Paul would take his admission as a decisive gut-punch betrayal. He curtailed the worst effects of his daimon blood through meditation and exercise. But there was always the chance he'd lose control and undergo a version of Cú Chulainn's *ríastrad* or warp-spasm. "Paul," he said, forcing down the old anxiety, "we've known—"

Nolin stopped short at the sight of the team's British liaison, Captain Abercrombie Gilcott, rounding the launch area. When some of his old friends at Whitehall had gotten wind of his plans to explore Herakleion they'd decided to stick their oar in, ostensibly in the spirit of discovery. Since the Great War, Nolin's attitude toward the British government had grown increasingly skeptical. He'd tapped his family fortune to purchase Egger Island off the coast of Greenland so he could establish a base of operations for Integrand General free from government interference. Nolin hoped he wasn't building a bunker amid a world destined for ruin.

Gilcott saluted Nolin in recognition of the younger man's distinguished service in the Royal Irish Lancers. "Sir." The Englishman was spare-bodied with a scooped face and eyes like conkers. He wore his khaki uniform as if he'd known no other attire and stood with one hand on the service revolver on his hip. Old scars flensed one weathered cheek. Shrapnel, Nolin thought. Or, given what he knew of Gilcott, an indignant woman's fingernails.

"Captain." Nolin nodded. "Everything ready?"

"Snug as houses, sir. Fellahs are a bit restless, what? Then, these days when are they not?" Gilcott's tone betrayed an easy condescension. He'd been in Egypt for most of the war and had a low opinion of the locals. "They ain't keen on the thought of us being here."

"Here in particular or in general?" Paul asked. He cast a wary look at the closest knot of laborers. A mix of Egyptians, Indians and Tunisians had been brought in to help erect the launch-frames for the submersibles. A susurrus of dialects hummed in the background below the gas generators and construction noises.

"Take your pick, Mr. Weyland. It's all the same to them, I expect. Can't trust them, you know. Turn on a chap soon as look at him. Even Lawrence, bless him, said that." Gilcott dabbed at his sunburnt neck with a handkerchief. "We got word from headquarters to be on the twitch, so to speak. Lots of babble from the usual suspects."

"The nationalists?" Nolin asked.

"Who else? Damn Fellahs. Happier with the Turks, I shouldn't think. They're staging demonstrations in Alexandria and Abu Qir today. Probably hoping that bugger Zaghloul will show on a white horse." Gilcott sniffed at the name of the nationalist spokesman, Saad Zaghloul, whose recent deportation had inspired violent clashes between police and protestors in Cairo, Alexandria and even provincial towns like Zifta and Abu Qir. "Ask me, exiling him to the Seychelles was too good for him."

Nolin kept his opinion to himself. Zaghloul was a stalwart hero to the Egyptians and for good reason. The country's halting independence was due primarily to his tireless efforts. Nolin exchanged a knowing look with Paul before turning back to Gilcott. "You anticipating trouble, Captain?"

"Always. We're due some violence, I expect."

No surprise there: Nothing could ever quash the simple human need for recognition, to say, I too am here, even if doing so meant jail, serious injury or death. Nolin wondered what would follow the protectorate's inevitable demise. Broken nations tended to break the world in turn. "I'd like to make a test-run of our subs before we lose the light."

"Do as you like, Mr. Quigg. We're here to make sure the Fellahs don't get rowdy with His Majesty's boffins." Gilcott gave a lazy salute and started away. Before he'd gone two steps, however, a tremendous explosion knocked him flat on his backside.

Nolin whirled, scanning the camp for the source. Blue-black smoke billowed over the tented neighborhood past the launch area.

"Gammon and spinach, what the devil was that?" Paul slipped his Schofield single action revolver from its holster.

"Damn nationalists!" Gilcott spat as Nolin hoisted him to his feet.

"Whatever it is," Nolin said, "we'd best get those subs clear. Might be more than a local—" A second thunderous discharge rent the air, followed by a third and a fourth. This last detonation toppled the makeshift guard tower where Prince J was stationed. Nolin's heart gave a painful stab at the crash.

Gilcott shoved away, shouting orders to the few squaddies within earshot.

Nolin gripped Paul by the elbow. "You see the guard tower come down? Grab Katsuo and the others then get to the Kelpies. I'm going for Joey." The dull, persistent pain in his chest threatened to flare up.

"The cussedness of the universe tends to the maximum..."

"Don't be all day about it," Nolin snapped.

Paul frowned at the edge to Nolin's voice then hurried in the direction of the command tent. Obscured by a pall of smoke and dust, the tent camp appeared suspended in a dream.

Nolin rushed toward the burning remnants of the tower, sickened by the prospect of losing Prince J and so senselessly. The Brooklyn-born sharpshooter and skilled mechanic had been a friend and indispensable aide since the war, never once disputing an order. Though barely 21 years old, Nolin knew that kind of trust was an inestimable rarity. He needed to prove to himself here, now, alive to the aching question, that he deserved it.

Chapter 3

Black Sun Barrage

John Hodge, popularly known as 'Dixie,' threw up his hands in exasperation. He'd been bickering with his sometime girlfriend for the better part of a half-hour—time they could've spent canoodling. He tried to trace events back to the argument's source and, failing to come up with anything, figured he'd made a thoughtless remark or offended her in some other way without his knowing. "Jus tell me what I gotta apologize for already."

"What? So you can get it over with?" Babette *'Pétard'* Labrecque pushed away from a folding table littered with powder, blasting caps and safety fuses. The small livid scars on her throat and cheek pinked up.

"You know it ain't like that. How long I been carryin a torch for you, *mon petit chou*?" Dixie eschewed the word love. He feared its implications of promise. Beyond the considerable demands of Integrand General, Babette was the one limiting factor in his life. The thought had compelled him to give her up periodically on the slim chance another girl might reveal some fresh range of potential. But no alternate paramour—no matter how gorgeous, wild or distracting—had ever felt as authentic. He and Babette had an irresistible history dating back to the Great War. He'd come to the dark understanding that a life without her would likely exhaust him before his time.

"It's *chou*—like 'shoe' not 'chow.' That would be Italian for goodbye." Babette shook her tawny flapper's bob in disappointment. "And it seems to me you're only talking serious now because I'm spending so much time with Paul." Her pursed-lipped disdain was like a starlet's—cool and exquisite.

The charge disarmed Dixie. It had never occurred to him she might have a motive for seeing Paul other than to improve her knowledge of chemistry and associated bomb-making skills. Paul was so dithering and, well, sapless—hardly a match for Babette's take-charge temperament. Once introduced, however, the idea seemed inescapable. *Oppo-*

sites do attract... "T'chaw. The only things got his innerest is books and machines and you ain't got the parts for neither." His magnified Tennessee accent gave the lie to his nonchalance.

"He's still a man—smart, worldly and *plein de vie.*"

"If that's a dry stick," he said, meaning humorless, "I agree."

"Don't play dumb." She softened her hard, finely featured face with a mocking smile.

Dixie gave the brim of his flat cap a nervous tug. She was the only one who could make him feel self-conscious about his lack of refinement and what he dismissed as 'artificial schoolin.' "I'm guessin that sounds better in French."

Before Babette could reply, an echoey blast tremored the earth. She gestured to the unassembled munitions. "Don't look at me."

Dixie drew his s&w M1917 revolver. "For whatever's goin on outside, mind." His stomach tightened in anticipation of a fight.

A more distant explosion sounded as the smoke from the first started to waft through the tent's center column netting. "Some big metaphor, yes?" Babette asked.

"That's it—sting me with the spellin bee words." Dixie waited at the tent flap for Babette to arm herself.

She scooped some stray ammo from the table into a trouser pocket then yanked a Luger from her hip holster. "I pray to God I don't somehow come down with telepathy." She waited for a third detonation to dissipate before rounding off her comment: "I couldn't stand to know for sure your head is full of lint."

"Maybe that's the problem: head," he pointed at her, "and heart," he said, cocking a thumb at his chest.

"If so," she said, throwing the flap aside, "that would mean you have at least two undersized muscles."

Dixie followed her into the smoky confusion as a fourth eruption sent sand and splintered wood into the sky. He covered his mouth with his free hand at the uprush of dust. The camp was a riot of noise—gunshots, curses, panicky bleating. Men in cotton *thawb* and *keffiyeh* raced in all directions. Some fled in wild distress while others moved with purpose, bobbing up on their toes at the glimpse of a British uniform. "What ya think? Them nationalists?"

Babette indicated a man wielding a curved knife. The robed figure vanished into the acrid haze. "You don't accessorize like that without looking for trouble."

A bruising blow between the shoulder blades sent Dixie flying. The thrown axe spun away having hit him handle-on. Babette turned and downed the attacker with a brace of lead. "You're too stubborn to die, *j'imagine*," she muttered, advancing on a wave of Egyptian miscreants.

Flat on his stomach, Dixie lacked the wind to object. He stretched to retrieve his gun when a boot heel stomped it into the sand. The blur of a hook-ended pry bar loomed above him. He rolled out of its punishing arc and got to his feet. His assailant stooped to claim the gun. Dixie scrabbled for the axe. The Egyptian's guttural swearing told him he would've been too late. But sand had apparently stifled the gun's firing pin. Dixie grabbed up the axe and, with a backcountry whoop, let it fly. The weapon smashed his target in the chest flat-end first. The man gave a plosive wheeze and slammed to the ground as if dropped from a great height. Dixie recovered the gun, holstered it and joined Babette with the axe. "Two blunt strikes in a row so this thing ain't magick."

"*Plus ça change.*" Babette reloaded her Luger. A score of foes bled into the sand. Her uncanny air of decorum remained unperturbed. She cut a prim and elegant figure in a short-waisted jacket and jodhpurs. The only ungainly thing about her were the men's All Star sport shoes she wore for comfort. "I can hold here. There's another revolver in the tent if you want to arm yourself properly."

Dixie started back inside when he saw Paul emerge from the ashy smoke. He spun on his heel, narrowly avoiding an unseen knife attack from around the tent. The squinty-eyed saboteur lunged for his ribcage. Off-balance, Dixie managed only a glancing parry with the axe handle. The saboteur redirected the blade. The upthrust edge made for the soft flesh under Dixie's chin. A staggering guncrack. Dixie could've sworn he felt the heated air against the helix of his ear. A sibilant spurt of throat-blood. The saboteur collapsed in a liquid gasp. His face took on a watered-down color as he bled air. Dixie shot Babette a sour look. "You wouldn't a been aimin at me now?"

"Are you hit?"

"Cause it ain't like I need savin by ..." Dixie swallowed the rest hoping she wouldn't notice the incriminating preposition.

She took a couple of threatening steps. "Finish that sentence and you will."

Dixie suspected Babette could see straight to his doubts. He visualized his insides exposed as in one of Paul's mechanical cutaway diagrams. "I don't mean to be insultin."

"Oh, you can't help yourself then." Her voice perked at Paul's arrival.

Dixie ignored the stoop-shouldered Irishman as he came to a halt between them. "Anyways, I don't gotta worry bout gettin hit I'm so fulla lint, right?"

"Can you two please not argue while I'm in thee-uh the middle," Paul said.

Babette shrugged off Dixie's comment. "I'm not arguing. He's not a serious enough person to argue with."

"No," Dixie said, "problem is we're not serious bout the same things—cept shootin evil in the face and loudness." He tipped her to a man approaching at a run from behind, sickle sword raised.

She swiveled and dropped the would-be assassin with a single shot then added: "You forgot being in the right."

"Oh, a course. Jus took that one for granted."

"Among other things."

"Uh, we've got orders," Paul interjected. "Grab whatever gear you can muster then rendezvous at thee-uh launch." He looked over the heap of bodies muddying the sand. "Where's Katsuo?"

"Far as I know he was over at the guard tower with Prince J," Dixie said.

"Let's go," Babette said to Paul on the hustle then, glancing back at Dixie, asked: "Pack my things, will you *mon cher*? Oh, and don't forget my handbag. I've my old trench club in it."

"Course you do." Dixie watched her disappear into the murk. Did she put a hand on Paul's back? Disappointment upon disappointment unfolded in his mind's eye. The French bayonet, he thought, should've been called Babette instead of Rosalie.

"Okay, Joey-san?" Katsuo 'Kei' Fukai extended a hand to a woozy Prince J. The explosion had taken out the ten-foot guard tower at the base, throwing them free. Except for whacking his upper-thigh on the perimeter railing, Katsuo had tumbled to the sand unharmed. It looked like a timbered fragment had caught Prince J just above the brow line. Nothing serious as far as Katsuo could tell. They'd been lucky to survive—again.

Blinking blood out of his left eye, Prince J took the proffered hand and levered himself to his feet. His khaki shirt and flat, high-waisted pants were dusted with ash and sand. He screwed up his small bright eyes. "Seen my rifle?" He pulled a handkerchief from his trousers to stanch the wound.

Shots rang out from the cluster of smoke-enshrouded tents. Katsuo drew a 9mm Astra pistol from his shoulder holster. The haze billowing across the collapsed tower was impenetrable. Drifting ash forced him to lower his eyes. They were effectively blind to the dangers in camp. "Good to move? We should find others, yes? That a lot blood."

"Must be why it hurts." Joseph Jenkins, a.k.a., Prince J, examined the crimsoned handkerchief with disgust. "Like to find my rifle first if we can." He had a much-teased attachment to the M1903 Springfield he credited with getting him through the war.

Katsuo started to pick through the immediate wreckage when an agonized shriek prompted him to whirl into a defensive crouch. Prince J followed suit and unholstered a ten-shot pistol. The smoke thinned out on the wind enough for them to discern a couple of men locked in close-combat. One of them was tossed aside, leg bent at an unnatural angle, leaving Nolin's unmistakable silhouette. Katsuo signaled him with a curt wave. Self-conscious about his beginner's English, he substituted gestures for speech as much as possible.

"Good to see you lads on this fine, rich day," Nolin called.

Katsuo closed the gap at a run. He was a small man with a wide face and narrow body. His untucked, collarless shirt fluttered between suspender straps. As he neared Nolin, he slowed to snug the shirt into light tweed pants. "Four bomb at cardinal point. Feint make us think camp surround?"

"Possibly," Nolin said. "But I'm going to take it as our signal to leave."

"Jeep or—"

"By Kelpie I mean."

Prince J joined them, his vision reduced to one eye by the handkerchief pressed to his forehead. "I hear that right? We abandoning camp?"

Nolin nodded. "You in working order?"

"No, not really." Prince J scowled. "Missing my Springfield something fierce."

"I'm sure we'll find you a worthy replacement."

Another concussive report shuddered the air, this time from the water's edge. Katsuo raised his eyes to the source. Plumes of hot gas and alloyed metal debris blitzed the shoreline. One of the Kelpies was gone—smithereened into scrap. The supporting launch was engulfed in flames and swayed unsteadily around the apex. A figure in a patchwork of black stood at the launch's foundation, arms outstretched. Katsuo's heart pounded in his throat. He knew the man from the Knuckerhole Incident. The pyrokinetic had set a burning farmhouse alight in an effort to dispose of the team.

"Recognize that bugger in black, don't you?" Nolin gave a wry smile. "I'd say it's time for his comeuppance. Distract him for me, will you?" He set off at a phenomenal sprint.

Katsuo got down on his stomach a few meters from Prince J. The magicked heat around the pyrokinetic made him nearly invulnerable to bullets. But that's all they had in the way of distraction. Out of habit, Katsuo made silent obeisance to the *sai no kami* (deity of luck).

The pyrokinetic spun in Nolin's direction.

"You've tried to kill my friends," Prince J said as if holding a conversation with the Society agent. "You've tried to kill me." He discarded the handkerchief so he could balance his shooting hand. "You made me lose my favorite rifle." He huffed in frustration. "You've gone too damn far."

He pulled the trigger, Katsuo joined in and together, they unleashed a steady on-target fusillade. The pyrokinetic staggered at the opening salvo but soon recovered. Eerie light rippled away from each point of impact. Nolin churned up the sand. Making threatening gestures, the firebug advanced to meet him.

Clickety-cli-click. Guns emptied all too soon, Katsuo and Joey looked askance at each other. Nolin had at least another 50 meters to go. He'd likely crumple into a burning heap before he made half that distance. Katsuo prayed on Nolin's behalf, worried luck chose people like words chose poets and no amount of pleading could change things.

The heat began as a series of scattered pinpricks then surged through Nolin white-hot, confusing his senses. He struggled to focus, narrow his energies, press on. The pyrokinetic flickered and faltered in his vision. The sand put up greater resistance. Bolts of cramp shot through him. His clothes crisped and blackened. His eyes watered. His blood fired. His daimon-half bellowed for release. *No, not now, not here.* He stumbled. The pyrokinetic wavered at a hopeless distance. He felt himself surrendering to the searing pain, withering up. Better that than manifest his worst secret.

The world reeled away from him. Then the panicked, overcrowded moment passed in a strangely muted barrage of gunfire. *Paul, Babette...*

He heard Paul above the dulled booms: "Finish him, Lancer!"

The heat began to dissipate. Nolin's thoughts became his own again—reasoned. He gathered himself up. His sense of himself returned with the effort and he arrowed toward the pyrokinetic at full pelt. Paul and Babette maintained their desperate assault to give him a chance. In his peripheral vision, Paul started to smolder. Nolin redoubled his power. Dark eyes widened in surprise. The firebug risked a bullet to vent a hellstorm. Nolin bulled forward, arms crossed over his face. The flames frenzied over him. No time for finesse. He slammed into the cultist, driving them into the tottering launch scaffolding.

Scorching fingers groped for his face, but Nolin's hands snapped up, catching hold of his foe's wrists. His grip tightened, shattering bone until he could almost make a fist. The char-black flesh was a sutured-together hide. The pyrokinetic's open-mouthed writhing revealed a burnt-stump of a tongue. Pathetic noises issued from the back of his throat.

Nolin jerked him into a decisive head-butt. The heat whooshed into nothingness. Then several burning timbers gave way and the entire scaffolding crashed down with a tremendous roar and flurry of sand. Nolin hunched over the unconscious firebug, arms wide, bearing the full force of the onslaught. He pitied the saboteur for the apparent cruelty of his origins.

When the air cleared somewhat, Nolin dragged his captive out of the rubble and dropped him at Paul's feet. His friend sported a wing of frizzed hair and a few blackened patches of denim but his eyes looked solid—resolved. Babette had an arm around the small of his back for support. She'd emerged from the ordeal as prim and unmussed as ever.

"Thanks for that bit of encouragement." Nolin stripped off the burnt tatters of his sweater coat.

"Well," Paul said, "I started to feel my gut juices boil."

"What say we make this dive before any more show up?"

"At least I didn't get shot this time—like at Killarney."

"You weren't the only one." Nolin started for the nearest submersible.

"Same difference." Paul snorted. "I swear it was a ricochet from you."

"Growing up, I never would've guessed how many times I'd have to apologize for being bulletproof." Nolin shook his head, grinning. He was relieved to see Prince J and Katsuo almost at the launch and, some distance behind them, Dixie, burdened by rifles and gear bags.

Sporadic gunfire still flashed from the camp. They weren't out of danger yet.

Chapter 4

The White Depths

As Nolin set the last of the gauges and primed the rebreather systems, Katsuo climbed into the Kelpie behind him, a rifle slung over one shoulder and a gear bag in hand. Babette paused a couple of rungs down laden with her own bag. "How many more times I gotta say I'm sorry?" came Dixie's voice from somewhere on the launch platform.

Babette scoffed. "Depends on how much longer we live." She slammed the hatch shut, ensuring the last word. Three bucket seats on swivel-pivots occupied the forward area while the back was filled with equipment, including replacement parts for the most sensitive internal systems. A cargo-web storage area separated the two sections. Babette avoided Nolin's concerned look while she stowed her gear.

"Should I be worried?" Nolin asked from the pilot's seat when she came forward.

She settled in front of the communications console. "For him maybe."

"That's what I meant."

The radio squealed to staticky life. "He has his American bluff and charm to protect him."

"Oh, is that what you call it?" Nolin cycled up the main engine. No matter the personal snags and small resistances that afflicted the team from time to time, he could rely on everyone to band together when it counted. "Katsuo?"

"I have not the words." Bullets pinged against the hull.

"No, not that. You ready?" He twisted around in his seat to confirm Katsuo was secured.

"I hear shooting," Katsuo said.

"Good enough." The hull's metal plating was designed to withstand the immense pressures of the ocean floor, not concentrated gunfire. Nolin peered through the reinforced viewport and the expanse of Abu Qir Bay at the foot of the massive ramp. The drop looked awfully intimidating. He wished again they'd had time for more than a single shakedown cruise. "Babette, let Paul know we're on a quick countdown."

The radio hiss resolved to Paul's quavery voice: *...an you read me, Lancer?*

Babette activated the broadcast unit so the crews could communicate across their parallel launches. Each station had an independent switch for broadcasting.

"Roger that, Paul," Nolin said. "Ready?" Another volley of small arms fire underscored his question.

Ready. How are we doing thee-uh this?

"On the jump."

And into thee-uh deep then.

Nolin smiled and reached for the release. One pull would loosen the mooring clamp and set the submersible to rocking on its platform. He tugged the handle back and, with a dull *ka-thunk*, the Kelpie began to wobble. He heard the crunch of the chocks giving way then the vessel gave a lurch. "Hold on."

The upper-scaffold shot away from them at speed and a parachute-drop queasiness took over. Nolin gripped the control wheel as the Kelpie screeched down the ramp. The gyroscopic equalizer kept the submersible generally on level but its speed and weight were taking their toll. The landscape blurred past—smears of brown and white. The din of stressed metal assumed a dizzying intensity. Nolin increased the pressure flowing through the hoses and pumps. It was all a matter of timing. Open the fins too slowly and the Kelpie would sink like a flat iron; too fast and the vessel would surge to the surface. He laughed as the Mediterranean rose up to meet them. The rush of seawater jounced him in his harness. The Kelpie's frame groaned as the bay swallowed it whole.

"Everybody shipshape?" Nolin put the guidance fins in motion and checked the depth gauge. With a hiss of air, the submersible's trajectory smoothed.

"I don't know," Babette said. "My head hasn't caught up with my stomach yet."

Katsuo put a finger to his bloodied lip. "Maybe—what you say?—bite sticks next time."

"Consider it done." Nolin confirmed the rebreather system was working at full capacity then switched on the forward diving lamps. Twin beams of pale light cut through the ocean murk. They were fast-approaching the shelf where the bay deepened and he expected to find the ruins of Herakleion. "Babette, let's see how the others came through."

She opened the radio link and queried: "Kelpie One to Kelpie Two, do you copy? Over."

After a moment of static, Paul's voice came through: Roger that, Kelpie One. That was some rough fun.

"The only upside is we're watchdog-free," Nolin said. "If we hadn't been forced into an early departure, Gilcott would've tagged along." He tried to rationalize the cost of their escape as wartime collateral. Because this *is* war, he thought, albeit baffling and covert. "How'd your Kelpie hold up?"

Seems nearly enough. You?

"Between the jigs and reels, ourselves." The Kelpie's fins waggled a bit as it left the shallows behind. "Stay close now. We're on the descent." The depth gauge fluctuated. Nolin tapped it, frowning. "Katsuo, check the pumps. We still getting enough pressure?"

"Yes, but gauge…hesitant."

"You mean uncertain?"

"Yes, sorry."

"No need. You've done a damn sight better on your English than any of us would've done with Japanese."

Babette harrumphed in protest. Since the war she'd become fluent in six languages and was currently teaching herself Farsi.

We're dropping down now.

"You're dawdling some behind us then," Babette informed him.

If Herodotus wasn't telling porkpies, Herakleion was actually two cities. Thee-uh the second, Herakleion-Thonis, is the one we'll likely see first. Herakleion primus vanished after a light rose from thee-uh waters or fell from the sky and swallowed it up. Th-the second city was built on whatever was left.

Nolin theorized Herakleion proper was destroyed by one of the earliest recorded whitespace events. These miraculous events occurred in places where extradimensional 'whitespace' energies intersected with our world. By cross-referencing various occult and historical sources, Nolin and his team had mapped many of these hot spots of preternatural activity. They called them terror zones. Integrand General's overarching aim, in part, was to wreck them, seal them up or otherwise preclude access to them. Otherwise, there was no telling what sort of unearthly disasters might ensue. Herakleion's watery doom was only one compelling illustrative.

The Kelpie's lamps swept over a half-buried stele or stone slab, followed by a titanic statue—a robed, baboon-headed figure with a lengthy headdress. "Hapi!" Katsuo lifted off his seat in excitement. "Not feeling, god of Nile flood, fertility..." He'd taken to surveying the world's mythologies for suggestive cross-cultural patterns and so was familiar with most of the major deities. "From Con—Conopic?—part of river. Big time new to world." He corkscrewed around to watch the backside of the statue slide from view.

"Lancer?" Babette strained to see anything of substance. "Does the sea look odd to you? There's a ...*Je ne sais pas*, a kind of folded darkness..."

Now that he looked past the proximate ruins, Nolin detected a strange diffusion to the water. It seemed to spiral in on itself. He clicked the radio. "Paul, you lot seeing this?"

We are, though I'm a mite too distracted to make a study of it.

"What's happening?"

Dixie thinks a bullet hit something vital. Probably a leaving present from the Society. We're losing internal pressure and leaking oxygen into the water. I've got bubbles clustering on my view screen. I'm going to try— The transmission dissolved into static.

"Paul? Dixie?" Babette asked in a hushed voice.

Nolin struggled for a calming tone. Panic was useless. "Paul, if you can hear me, try the ballast release. Get to the surface and head for shore. Gilcott's probably got things in hand and if he doesn't, well, he could use your help."

Babette leaned in Nolin's direction. "We can't leave them behind."

"Don't worry. We'll make short work of it—just a cursory survey before we—bloody hell..." A sinuous shadow undulated in and out view.

Then the Kelpie rattled down to its rivets and juddered sideways from a portside shockwave. The standby compass shattered. A pressure line near Katsuo sprouted a pinhole leak. Nolin manhandled the control wheel to prevent the Kelpie from spinning. His whole upper-body tremored from the tension. Until the vessel settled, engines flooded or otherwise compromised. The hull-lights sparked and flickered in the abyssal dark.

Nolin's ears popped at an unexpected change in pressure. "Status?" He swiveled around to face the others.

"*Que se passe-t-il?*" Babette muttered.

Nolin followed her gaze back to the main viewport. Two red crystalline lights in the distance—eyes?—gave the darkness a coiled shape. Then, silhouetted by a blaze of light, a rock-ribbed serpent hurtled past at incredible speed, tumbling them toward the sprawling ruins of Heraklieon and the seabed below.

"The ballast release done jammed." By way of demonstration, Dixie gave the lever a last half-hearted kick. "Must've been damaged on the ramp or maybe hittin the water." A hose burst behind him, venting steam. "Don't tell me," he said to Paul, "you put this thing together with library paste."

"This is thee-uh devil's own luck and no mistake." Paul pounded the control wheel with the flats of his palms. The vessel resisted his attempts to guide it and something—or someone—had rendered the radio useless.

Prince J snatched up a tin of liquid rubber sealant for Dixie. "Think we can make it back to shallow water?"

"Not with thee-uh the current the way it is," Paul said. "We're being pulled deeper." The term 'current' was a necessary simplification. The Kelpie's swift descent wasn't consistent with standard undersea flows. Whirlpool effect? Localized gravity well? The possibilities—each more esoteric than the last—fascinated and frightened him.

"How bout we jus pop the hatch and take our chances?" Dixie paused to unscrew the lid from the sealant tin. "Can't be any worse

than suffocatin."

"Drowning, suffocating—same difference really." Prince J muscled a wrench around a stress-loosened nut on the oil distributor. The jug-shaped tank was under pressure at about ten pounds per square inch. The indicator showed the pressure increasing steadily…

Dixie braced himself against the vessel's juddering descent. "Shimmy, now'd be the time for one a your bright suggestions."

The hull-lights fuzzed and faded, making a spooky dimness of the sea. Paul could scarcely see beyond the bubbles obscuring the view port. He white-knuckled the control wheel against the ocean's pull. The engine whined and belched oil smoke into the compartment. The leaks indicated the outer hull was deflating, putting pressure on tanks and pipes. He scanned the essential gauges, pushing down the incipient panic. The Kelpie's depth was around 107 meters (351 feet). The estimated crush depth—little more than an educated guess given the limited shakedown period—was 150 meters (492 feet). At that point, the outer hull would shatter, followed by the fuel and air tanks and then the wafer-thin inner hull. The vessel would implode as if it were a telescoping spyglass collapsed of a sudden. They'd be compacted into jellied skinsacks in a matter of moments.

Through sheer force, Paul managed to arrest the submersible's descent but for how long? The electric motors were almost at their limit and, once they burned out, regardless of how he adjusted the rudder angle, the sub would sink to a fatal depth in seconds. He lamented not insisting on a drop emergency keel, regardless of the construction delay. The space behind his eyes ached. He could see the contours of their dilemma but not all of its constituent variables. If only it could be reduced to a geometric proof: *Solve for the saving angle within the pressurized shape…*

Blank horror at the prospect of failure seized Paul. His whole idea of himself depended on his mental brio. When anything can happen, went his private motto, the only way to survive is to know everything. Had he merely deluded himself about his intelligence? Or was he an outright fraud? What did he actually know of use here? His da, a part-time merchant seaman and full-time drunk, had perished at sea. Paul remembered the strange pattern of emotion he'd experienced as a young lad on learning of it—wonder and love coupled at once with petulant anger. There was a bleak harmony to sharing the same sort of untraceable death.

When Dixie started in again, Paul held up a hand for silence. He had the makings of a possible solution: venting their entire compressed air supply into the aft compartment might create enough of a pressure imbalance to shoot them to the surface. Even if the gambit worked, however, they lacked a dedicated oxygen supply and a means to control their ascent. They could easily suffocate or cripple up in the attempt. High, low, Jack and win, what was he missing to improve the odds? The black logic of the situation kept overwhelming his efforts to think past the obvious: uncontrolled descent/ascent = death …

"C'mon, what ya got?" Dixie asked.

"That thee-uh maths suggest we're about done for," Paul said over his shoulder. "Happy?" He immediately regretted how he sounded. He'd let his own frustrations foul his tone.

"Well, that's a poor attitude."

"No sense in giving false hope."

Dixie pointed with the brush-end of the sealant lid. "Scratch that out on the viewport there 'n' it can be your gravestone sayin." There was an uncharacteristic edge to his words.

The control wheel shook free of Paul's grasp. "Flaming Norah!" The staccato growl of the engines whined to nothing and the vessel plunged toward the bottom faster than before. Dixie snagged the cargo netting for balance and trapped the sliding tin of sealant with a boot heel. Whatever force was dragging them down seemed intractable. "Joey, ready the blowtorch," Paul ordered. The ballast system was their last chance for survival. Given the failure of the release valve, Paul was willing to risk cutting through the main and variable ballast tanks to drain them of water then sealing them back up in hopes they could regain enough positive buoyancy to—

"God almighty!" Joey gestured toward the viewport, stunned. Distant, crackling white dots spirited into a disordering blast. "There's a Lucifer light I ever saw one," he said then added from the popular wartime marching song: "Smile boys, that's the style."

The air escaped through Paul's lips and it was a long moment before he could eke out the word at the tip of his tongue: "Whitespace."

Forking through the sea like a lightning storm, the concentration of whitespace energy enveloped the vessel. Paul shaded his eyes from the consuming radiance. The energy broke over them, zizzing against the hull and sparking up the instrument panels. He gripped the arms of his chair. A previously hidden shape sprang from the center of the sublime light—serpentine—with eyes as brilliant and cold as heart-blood rubies. "Hold on, lads!"

The lashing end of the creature's tail struck the Kelpie with a hollow tolling sound. The submersible slewed away from the whitespace horizon, its dimmed lights playing crazily over the surging length of the serpent.

"Some kinda OT Leviathan?" Dixie asked as the vessel recovered an even keel.

"Whatever it is, it's comin about," Joey said.

The monster's looping coils shadowed over them and constricted, screwing them into near-darkness. Rivets twitched in their housings and cracks exploded along the reinforced glass. Paul's heart battered in his chest. Water beaded on the viewport's interior curve. He buttressed himself against the inevitable rush of cold, pitch-dark sea. Shock after fearful shock to the fleeting last. He could hear his mam chiding him now, "Off in thought's goin to set you on a no good road."

The cabin lights flared to full strength and the engines whirred to life as the submersible careened free of the whitespace effect. Nolin zero bubbled the vessel then reversed course to pursue the serpent.

"Apep," Katsuo said. "Also, Apophis and Rerek. The snake-god. Egyptian spirit of evil, darkness, enemy of sun-god, Ra."

"Saboteurs, fire magicks, Egyptian gods—*zut alors*," Babette said, "I think my head is going to explode."

Nolin said, "Not on the controls, please."

Katsuo peered ahead. The ragged glow of the whitespace phenomenon overran the portside edge of the screen. The serpent was a streak of earthen colors. "We after it now?"

Nolin grunted in assent, focused on maximizing the vessel's forward power. The serpent and the other Kelpie gradually hove into view. A frenzied pang made a hollow of Nolin's chest. Apep spooled its rough, granite-faced coils around the de-powered sub, clearly positioning itself for attack, then kinked into a knotted up ball. The Kelpie's guide fins buckled at the whip-fast contraction. Nolin despaired of watching Paul and the others mashed past all recognition. "Man the pneumatic guns," he barked. "We're going to play scissors to this thing's paper."

The guns were another invention of Nemo's. An ingenious system of pressure pumps and hoses enabled them to fire at high velocity underwater. The slender lengths of treated steel used as ammo were designed for breaking up ice packs or reef beds but could serve as missiles in a pinch.

Hurry now, Nolin thought as the pneumatic cylinders cycled up. The stubby guns were set at opposite angles along either side of the Kelpie's prow. They didn't have much in the way of range or movement, which meant he had to get close.

The Kelpie buzzed past the serpent's giant triangular head. Snakes bearing that head-shape, Nolin knew, tended to be venomous. Apep tracked the submersible's orbit, jaws wide. Red light limned the sundry gaps and fissures in its body. The water boiled in its wake. Nolin could just make out the Kelpie trapped inside the coiled tangle. He spun the control wheel, putting the submersible between the creature and the whitespace field. The vessel moaned in protest at the maneuver.

"Now," he said. "Let's see him off with all due haste." Katsuo gave a shout and hauled back on the protruding console trigger. Babette followed suit, mouthing French curses. The pneumatic guns fft-fft-flitted through the water to batter the creature's skull. Bits of granite splintered into the dark.

Apep reared back in what Nolin took to be surprise rather than pain. He doubted their weapons could ever penetrate to its raw nerves—provided it had them. "Keep up the salvo," he said, swinging them around for another pass. A worrying staccato chug from the engine compartment compelled him to ease the throttle. They might well get swallowed up this time. The guns continued to chuff as the snake-god lanced toward them. The monster's unhinged jaws gaped open, expectant. Its gullet was an endless cavern.

Nolin wondered if he might somehow survive the impending crash while the rest of the team—woefully mortal—shattered into sunk oblivion. The serpent recoiled from their barrage then twisted away only to arch and surge again. Now, Nolin told himself. He wrenched on the control wheel to aim them at the whitespace field and its unknown horizon.

Released but powerless, the wrecked Kelpie plummeted closer to its crush threshold. The depth indicator read 128 meters (420 feet) and falling. Paul waved Dixie to the back of the vessel. "Thee-uh hand crank—quickly!" Through the fractured and leaking viewport, he discerned the tail-end of the leviathan. "They've broken it up some. Look at thee-uh the way its trailing debris."

"Too bad the guns are useless—crushed," Prince J said. "We're nuthin but an outsized sounding lead."

Dixie tugged on the restart crank, gradually building momentum. "Guess we gotta use the disintegrator ray."

"What disintegrator ray?" Paul asked.

"Another serious design flaw."

The incandescent lamps flickered and settled at dim. Dixie threw his weight against the crank and the electric engines stuttered. Paul toggled some air valves to bring the shrieking engines down to a continuous whir. The Kelpie wobbled forward, gaining speed. Water trickled through the ruptured glass. There wasn't much time. He revved the engines as high as he dared without exacerbating the leak. "Take a seat, Dixie." The leviathan strained after Lancer's Kelpie, leaving itself undefended from the flank.

"Oh. Oh, no, Paul, no," Prince J intoned.

"What?" Dixie asked, securing his harness.

"He's going to ram it."

"Waitaminute," Dixie said. "That's my kinda thinkin. How come it sounds stupid when somebody else says it?"

"Lancer's chipped a flaw in it," Paul assured them.

Dixie made a dismissive gesture. "No worse'n ours, I bet. Gonna be like peltin it with a chickadee egg."

The speed indicator showed seven knots. Paul figured that was about the vessel's new top speed as the damaged engines couldn't produce more than 70HP. "Don't worry over it," he said. "We'll never catch them."

The first Kelpie disappeared from view against the dazzle of whitespace. "Why would he head into it?" Prince J asked. "They could end up anywhere, right?"

"Could be thee-uh they're compromised as well," Paul said.

"Or maybe Lancer's jus in a mood," Dixie said.

"Always looking ahead to posterity, he is." Paul watched in mounting horror as Lancer's vessel reappeared, momentarily suspended in the whitespace field, then eee-looon-gaaat-ed like a drive belt stretched taut and vanished. The serpent shot after its quarry, rippling into the blinding nothingness. "Well, lads…"

"No choice, right?" Dixie asked. "Gotta go after em…"

Prince J nodded his assent.

"Right then: set controls for unreality and hope the home front holds out." Paul could feel the Kelpie's engines struggling as he eked out every last erg of power.

Whitespace energy caromed off the misshapen hull. Joey swore and Dixie added his brand of hills-n-holler invective.

The gauges burst their housings and the rudders went slack. Paul relinquished the control wheel. They were caught in the whitespace flow now and plunging at an immeasurable rate. Committed. His heart thrashed against his ribs. The viewport shattered from the pressure. Icy seawater cascaded into the vessel. Paul barely got in a held breath before the illuminated ocean rushed over him. He sensed strange immensities behind it. *Masks within masks and more besides…* He would drown, eyes closed, full of frustrated wants and winnowed from the truth of things.

Then the static in his head nearly burst him from the inside
and the fulminating white was everything
and nothing
at once

Chapter 5
What Lies Beyond

The Last Cycle of Unmaking
Kekw D'srt, the Chaos Desert, Herakleion

Hissing steam flooded the crashed submersible. The world outside the exploded viewport came through in misted glimpses—a livid sky, some stony abstractions...Jörmungandr, the world serpent, Nolin thought. Jörmungandr, Jörmungandr, Jörmungandr, Jörmungandr. There were starburst aches around his eyes. He brushed slivers of glass from his coveralls. "Is...is everyone...?" he croaked, fumbling at his restraint-straps. The sound of the buckles falling away seemed overloud. He stood up, steadying himself with a hand on the piloting console. The Kelpie, heeled over to one side, creaked and shifted in its crater.

Katsuo gave a desultory wave. "Safe, yes." He unbuckled his harness and shook it off. His face had a distinctly gray tinge.

Closest to the source of the steam, Babette strained for unheated air. "Damn straps—tangled." She drew a utility knife from her belt and cut herself free.

"Sorry for the hard landing," Nolin said.

Katsuo shrugged. "Like always."

Babette's laugh sputtered into a silent grimace.

"You hurt?" Nolin asked.

"Only when I laugh." She took a tentative step in his direction and winced. "Or move." Nolin offered his arm. She declined it with a firm pat. "From the tension, I think—a cramp?—nothing serious."

Nolin surveyed their position. The Kelpie had come to rest in the lee of a tree-fingered projection. To starboard, a wide expanse of stone steps led to a cobbled tower or temple. It was all lines and angles and non-Euclidean geometry, replete with massive hieroglyphics. Even the shadows were somehow rich in inscriptions.

"Where is the snake-god?" Katsuo asked.

"And the others?" Babette added. "Think they followed us?"

"If they could…Their sub…" Nolin's heart clenched. *Paul, Joey, Dixie—lost, drowned…?* The words stopped themselves. "They might be anywhere. Whitespace events transcend our understanding of physics. Time, space—the standard laws don't apply. Even if they landed here, they might've arrived days, maybe even years, before or after us." A line that characterizes a number of deaths in *The Iliad* came back to him: *and he lost the day of his home-returning.*

Babette gestured toward the viewport edged in sharded glass. "Where are we?"

"Someplace we breathe," Katsuo said.

"There's that at least." Nolin stepped past him and onto the ladder for the topside hatch. "Let's grab our gear and get the lay of the land." While the others gathered their supplies, he muscled the hatch open and poked his head out. The Kelpie was pitched at a lazy angle, caught in a coral-like outgrowth. A series of intermittent furrows in the stony ground described the vessel's headlong descent. Nolin had only just recovered his senses when they were ejected from the whitespace field. Katsuo could mark their survival in the good luck column of his mental ledger.

The sun gave off a dim, sulphurous glow. Everything was suffused with its morbid light. A distant ridge of granite hills bordered the landscape to port. The stretch between consisted of pale, coagulated shapes with the energy of cresting waves. Rough and ropy skeins of stone and simple ovoids gave way to skewed megalithic formations. The terrain was chaotic, sterile and noiseless. There was neither any obvious vegetation—not even a stray leaf—nor any sign of animal life.

For Nolin, the scene conjured up childhood fantasies of his father's adventures with Captain Nemo—wondershot worlds made just for the moment, haunted and beautiful. Every nerve was atwitch with atavistic dread. He climbed onto the submersible. The pain around his eyes continued to pulse. How would he ever find the others? How would they ever get home? He sighed into his chest. The air was thick with dusty death.

An obtrusive crunching and scraping sounded from the temple behind him. This was Apep announcing itself: the serpent slithered out of the temple's shadows, an inexorable grinding, stone on stone, and adopted a striking coil position on the steps. Residual whitespace energy flashed along its length.

Without taking his eyes from the monster, Nolin bent to the open hatch to warn the others away: "Stay in the sub." He considered the best line of attack. The pneumatic guns had blasted an irregular gouge around the serpent's frontal groove. Hitting that weak spot, however, would require a head-on lunge—right over the fangs.

He grasped the top hatch by the locking wheel and, with a grunt of effort, ripped the door from its hinges. Katsuo and Babette stared up at him. "What is happening?" Katsuo asked. Nolin deflected the question with an open hand and took a step aft, raising the hatch to his shoulder like a hoplon shield.

Apep tilted its flint-shaped head, curious, then convulsed into a swift stabbing charge. Nolin blunted the attack with the door, tucking and rolling over the serpent's pitted nostrils. The jaws snapped empty air. Nolin raced for the sought-after wound. The broken granite showed fleshy pink beneath. The monster squirmed out from under him, intending to catch his flailing body in its recurved teeth. Nolin gathered himself up behind the hatch and descended like a catapulted projectile. He cracked against a fang and tumbled hard onto the temple steps. The snake-god withdrew in hurt surprise, eyes hooded and fierce.

Getting to his feet, Nolin risked a glance back at the submersible. Pains jolted up his spine. Babette emerged from the hatch and extended her Luger. "Bugger and blast," he muttered, motioning for her to stand down. Apep elevated its head in preparation for another joust. Nolin had no choice. He stumbled forward—shield first—to draw the monster away from the Kelpie. The serpent's lancing drive was too fast for him to follow. He collapsed on his back against its tongue sheathe and curled up under the raised hatch. The damaged fang splintered against the door and the serpent spasmed in pain, fearing to close its mouth. Nolin took advantage of this hesitation to roll clear. The serpent's black tongue lathered the top of his head as he flopped onto the steps.

He settled into an unsteady crouch. Apep resumed an s-shaped crook and launched into him, twisting its mouth to give its intact fang the largest possible target. The serpent closed on the hatch, nearly piercing Nolin's forearm, and pushed him toward the temple in a violent arc. The heat from the monster prickled his skin. The steps crumbled around his heels. Dust billowed upwards, enveloping them.

Though Nolin slowed the monster's push before he could be forced against the gloomy recesses of the temple, his strength was near to giving out. His limbs strained with every ceded step. Acidic ichors dripped from Apep's fang onto his arm and bubbled through his coveralls. The fumes stung his nostrils and lungs. He was reminded of the trenches—clouds of suffocating mustard gas roiling through the troops. His unique physiology seemed to protect him from the venom's worst effects. But the hatch began to soften and warp. He pivoted and dropped to the ground, discarding his makeshift shield. The serpent's inertia carried it into the temple wall like a kinked whip. The wall collapsed in a tumult of perspectives. Unthinkable geometries caved-in on each other in obsidian tones. Shimmering planes of negative space buried the serpent in darkness while taking up no room at all.

Nolin clambered to his feet, unable to top his lungs with air. The skin on his forearm flared hot where the ichor had stained him. A line from the Edda streaked crazily through his mind: *nine paces fares the son of Fjorgyn, and slain by the serpent, fearless he sinks.* The taste of pitch was on his tongue. He fumbled uselessly at his collar. The world flickered and yawed to a shuddering drop. He felt centuried dust against his cheek. Muffled voices called for him across the debris. Black came over his eyes. Behind the ridge of his brow the line from the Edda went on and on.

"Nine paces," he breathed.

Then with a final wracking cough he surrendered to the consuming dark.

Neter-Khert, the Domed Bog, Herakleion

Prince J leapt from the wrecked Kelpie with a watertight gear bag at his hip and a pistol in hand. The floatable bag of supplies was secured by a strap across his chest. He splashed into the brackish water up to his waist, eliciting concentric flickers through the faintly luminous algae. The muddy bottom snagged at his boots. He adopted an exaggerated stride, shifting his weight from one leg to the next to gain enough traction to pull free of the muck.

Ahead some ten meters, Paul dragged an addled Dixie toward a hummock of dirt and sedge-like grasses. "C'mon," Paul said, "at the double soldier!" The high-ceilinged dome enclosing the bog amplified his voice. "Getting your legs yet?" He was struggling to both shoulder a heavy gear bag and help Dixie along.

"Why?" Dixie gave the supportive hand around his waist a squeeze. "You f-f-fixin to slooow daaance?" he asked in a worrying slur. The Tennessean had jerked halfway out of his harness and smacked his head on an instrument panel in the corkscrew crash. A tourniquet banded his skull from forehead to nape.

Paul yanked him onward. "Shame your sense of humor survived."

"Raaather lose my witsss thaaan my w-wit."

"You Americans—always mistaking wisecracks for cleverness."

The sick-green algae around Prince J stirred in a new circular pattern. The unnatural drift quickly bubbled into a current. The vitalized water pulled at his thighs. He glanced behind him. The quickening whirlpool centered on the submersible. The smashed Kelpie pitched to and fro. Prince J barreled after the others, planting each step with renewed urgency. "Faster! Faster!" he warned above the screech of stressed metal. He stumbled and dipped the semi-automatic in the mossy water. The vortex threatened to unfoot him for good. He was compelled to stop and square his shoulders against it.

Paul shouted something to him he couldn't hear above the din of warping metal. The ground beneath his feet dribbled away. He cycled his legs to keep upright, holding out on the margins of the undertow. Grasping flagellates burst from the bog and netted the Kelpie, tightening around its dorsal spine and mangled guide fins. A colorless creature like an unshelled oyster appeared just below the surface. The creature contracted its flagellates and crimped the vessel's shell. The starboard portholes popped their frames. Prince J winced with every squeal. "Three months of work," he muttered.

The water whipped into a dirty froth. Prince J crouched to better keep his balance. His stuttering heart sounded at the base of his throat. Here he was, a sharp-eyed Negro from Brooklyn, contending with an alien bog monster. His aged father, skeptical of anything he didn't read in the black-owned *New York Amsterdam News*, would never believe it. He backpedaled against the vortex to no avail. The current edged him closer and closer to the creature's swelled mantle. He tried to steady the M1921 "Bolo" Mauser to get in a decent shot or two before he went under.

The creature ballooned above the surface, revealing a fringe of serrated bone. Prince J anticipated breaking against it, gone, gone at last…He fired wildly in the creature's direction. Then the submersible buckled and snapped and sploshed into its unseen bowels. Must stretch under the bog itself, Joey thought, envisioning a fluted creature with its posterior snugged deep in the mud. Then another, more terrifying possibility struck him: What if it were the base of the muddy bottom itself? As in: all of it?

Though a tangle of flagellates remained active—twining and elongating—the whirlpool abated, releasing him from its arresting turbulence. Ah, a blessed reprieve…He about-faced and scrambled for the hump of earth some 25 meters distant where Paul and Dixie had taken refuge. The malign ugliness of the monster spurred him on. He set a more determined pace this time, swinging his arms front to back, elbows tight. The blood rose in his face.

Paul bent over the water and waved him on. The iridescent algae gave the Irishman a ghastly pallor. "Had us worried for a minute thee-uh there!" he called.

Prince J slacked his jaw to reply when an outthrust of mud and peat rippled under him, throwing him forward. He tread water for a suspended instant, gun raised, until he touched bottom again. The source of the disturbance crested a short distance ahead and exploded into a spray of undulating flagellates. The bog monster appeared to be a liquid-filled cavity with a roving orifice. Prince J shook his head, bemused and distraught. The absurdity of the situation confirmed his Christian faith. Only the Biblical God would go to such pains to make a confused and comedic test of his life. A wry smile crossed his lips as he shot at the base of the flagellates.

"Lighter!" Paul shouted through the snarl of tendrils. "Ligh-ter!"

It took Prince J a moment to realize Paul was asking for his ciga-rette lighter. He'd recently acquired a semi-automatic flint lighter in Germany. Curiously, the brass device was engraved with WATSON'S SCOTCH WHISKY. He transferred the gun to his left hand and felt in his breast pocket for the lighter. It was cool to the touch. He reared back for a Burleigh Grimes curveball. The flagellates descended in a knot and seized him at the wrist and elbow. He relinquished his gun to the bog and flipped the lighter into his left hand for a hasty underhand lob. The glint of metal skimmed the surface of the bog and redounded from the monster to *shlup* into the water.

Straining against the wiry flagellates—now around his neck and torso—Prince J saw Paul drop to his knees at the hummock's edge then retreat to higher ground and Dixie's side. Tears of pain blurred the rest of the action. The creature lashed him tight. His tensed limbs pled for relief. The pulse at his temple seethed.

A crazed southern yawp went up. Followed by a throw of sparks—dynamite!—and a concussive clap. An eye-shuttering blast of foul wa-ter and sludge and jellied bog monster spilled Prince J into the murk. The racket—God almighty. The painful vibration in his eardrums car-ried underwater. He landed his toes on the bottom and pushed back to the surface, gasping and sputtering for air. Paul was wading toward him, calling out above the afternoise. The creature was nowhere to be seen, shocked into dormancy. "Alright. Not like I took a wound under the fifth rib," he said, referencing Abner's murder in 2 *Samuel*. "Just some ringing in my ears."

Paul grasped him around the shoulders. "Sorry you've been trou-bled."

"And the smell." Prince J brushed a swirl of algae from a cheek. "Yeah and I lost another gun."

Huddled near the verge, Dixie waved him onto the hummock with an unlit stick of dynamite. "Ain't nuthin nowhere can beat the Good Lord and gunpowder." His head bobbled a bit unsteadily but his words cohered now.

Prince J clambered up the grassy hummock sopping wet. His wa-terlogged boots punctuated his movements. "Thanks for the help." He unzipped his gear bag looking for his traveling towel. "This is actually my life, right? Fighting off otherworld nasties?"

"Yeah, ain't it great?" Dixie tossed him the lighter. There was a worrying streak of blood across the whites of his left eye.

"You know how these things go. Let's hope you didn't save me for something worse." Prince J indicated their similar wounds. "How's the head feel? Looks like you could use some sticking plaster. Now Paul's the only one without a dent in his noggin." He pulled out a T-shirt and swabbed his face, careful not to dislodge the bandage above his brow.

"He's already so doolally, how'd we even know different?"

"Hey," Paul said, "right here, mind." His tight, papery expression, however, suggested a distant focus.

"Mournin yer wreck? I toldja not to name them things. That's when you start feelin attached. Which one was that?"

"Destiny. Or *Destin* as Babette called it."

"Any idea where we are? Where they are?" Prince J asked. "We were right on their tail…"

"Hard to say with thee-uh these whitespace fields. We—they—thee-uh the both of us—could be anywhere." Paul pointed to the oblique hole they'd punched in an upper portion of the dome on entry. "From what little I saw, looked like a ruined city outside…There must be a hatch or ventilating shaft somewhere. Grab me an electric torch, will you?"

Prince J retrieved a metal diving torch from his kit. Paul switched it on. "That's more like it." He aimed the beam toward the Kelpie's final resting place. The light skimmed over the bog to wash across featureless stone. "Looks solid in—"

The hummock jolted in the opposite direction as if on a rail. Paul snatched a handful of grass for balance.

Dixie got to his feet and started toward the summit. "Don't tell me we been restin on that monster's gonads now…"

When they reached the top, Paul flashed the torch toward their inexorable destination: a small pier occupied by a troop of simian nightmares. The white-furred monsters brandished sickle swords and Persian-style war hammers. They shaded their eyes from the torch's glare, baring their teeth in dismay or anger. A particularly large specimen beat his misaligned wings in warning. "Looks like God rummaged them up from the parts bin."

Prince J and Dixie exchanged grim looks. "You the one mentioned worse," Dixie said, throwing up his hands.

Paul diverted the torch so as not to further annoy their welcoming party. "Chins up and guns at thee-uh ready, lads. Make sure they know we're forthright in our intentions."

"Which are?" Dixie asked.

"Whatever's necessary to get us all home for a proper tea."

Forwards and backwards, Prince J cast his thoughts. No matter what strange shape the world took, his first duty was to prove himself worthy to his companions and his God. *Walk in a manner worthy of the calling to which you have been called…* He couldn't say what would be asked of him this time. But the appearance of a tall, poised black woman amid the baboon-things suggested something altogether new.

Chapter 6

Armaments & Artifacts

Kekw D'srt, the Chaos Desert

Time seemed an elastic torment to Babette, alternately too slow and too fast. The sun, edged in faint inkblot spirals, was fixed in the bleak sky. Nothing stirred across the oppressive mineral plain or, insofar as she could tell, in the many-angled temple. According to her watch, over two hours had passed since the crash. Katsuo's watch, however, attested to about 45 minutes. Regardless, Nolin's condition was unchanged. He was stretched between them on a wool blanket, unconscious and fever-hot. Babette had treated his acid-burned forearm with iodine then applied a dressing greased with Carron oil, a mixture of olive oil and lime-water. The skin was unbroken, leading her to believe he'd somehow absorbed the venom. Or perhaps, inhaled its fumes in the course of his struggle.

"How can he be poisoned?" she wondered aloud. "The treatments his parents gave him as a child—they should have protected him, no?"

Katsuo continued cataloging the supplies from the gear bags he'd dumped on the temple steps. He held a Japanese-designed respirator in his open palm. The demand valve was operated by the diver's teeth. "Protect from earth poison, yes. But this …?" He shrugged.

The corner of Nolin's mouth twitched as if he were dreaming. Babette put a hand to his cheek. His uncertain state brought to mind the fraught moment she'd found her mother in the bowels of a German military compound, comatose and beaded in sweat. She owed Nolin for her mother's rescue and for the few lovely post-war months they'd spent at home before she'd been forced to send her *maman* to the Vaucluse asylum. The trauma of her mother's captivity had proven too much. There was nothing Babette could've done in that instance. But she'd never forgive herself if Nolin perished for lack of trying.

"We shouldn't wait any longer," she said, glancing back at the temple. Its shimmering, maze-like facade was like a series of abutments exposed by lightning. "That serpent could return. Judging from the architecture—those stairs look a good imitation of the National Assembly—there must be people here who can help. We can use some supports from the wreck and the cargo netting to make a, hmm, *la civière*?" She mimicked pulling a stretcher to ensure Katsuo understood.

"Ah, where to go?" He gestured toward the numbing distance and the far bordering hills. "The desert flat—it look bare, a wildness ... *Gambatte ne.*"

"I know. But he's feverish and weak and, *enfin*, not getting better."

"He said one time, he said, 'Greek thought all tragedy—all bad luck—fate.' Like Oedipus ... Life too much absurd not be fate."

"Yes, I'm sure Lancer would appreciate dying after the fashion of his vaunted Greeks. *C'est la guerre.* But not now ..."

From his shirt pocket, Katsuo removed a band of pink-tinged paper with faded red kanji characters printed across it. "This *o-mikuji*—paper-strip fortune. You get from temple. This one carry great blessing. *Negaigoto*: like wish. You hold weeks, months—until you feel luck run out. Bring me good fortune. Maybe do same ..." He leaned over Nolin and placed it in the chest pocket of the senseless man's coveralls.

Babette felt for Nolin's pulse at the neck. Her fingertips registered a coagulated rhythm. "Afraid to say Lancer might be the clue its luck is over." She smiled at Katsuo with the grim humor of the defeated. "Did you get it on leave back home?"

"I have also *omomari*." He held up a gray silk pouch tied to his belt. "This for ward off evil."

"I don't want to think about what we would've fought lately without it."

"Haw. So small a charm. Maybe Greek get wrong. Fate just adding up small a charm."

The phrase 'small charm' recalled her comment about Dixie in the submersible. What was it? Something about his backwoods charm as a form of protection. Yes, a charm depending on adolescent intensities and impatience. She could admire those qualities in the moment, especially because so-called 'monster hunting' required them to live on the run much of the time. But was that enough on which to base a future, however long it lasted?

The same impulsiveness also accounted for his unremarked-upon 'escapades.' Though hurtful, she could understand his impulse to stray as a form of growing up. "You're like a blind man making one mistake after another teaching himself to see," she'd once told him. What she couldn't countenance was the presumption she'd take up with him again whenever he had the urge. She had her own wants and needs—intellectual, aesthetic, cultural—many of which he'd never help realize. There was an 'I' holding its breath somewhere inside, waiting to be sustained before it ran out of air. She'd always been the decisive one, the—

"See," Katsuo said. "See there?" He rose to his feet and pointed to an approaching smudge in the sky.

As Babette followed his gaze, the smudge became a fluttering w. Then the w became a vaguely gull-shaped animal. Its wingspan was daunting.

Katsuo broke into a tenuous grin. "Some crazy monster land."

Babette unholstered her Luger. "The whitespace field could have sent us anywhere, no?" She quickly confirmed her gun was fully loaded. "Why couldn't it have been Paris at the height of *La Belle Époque*?"

"What would we shoot there?" Katsuo shouldered a Swedish Army rendition of the M1918 Browning Automatic Rifle (BAR). It sported a pistol grip and a 20-round detachable magazine of 6.55×55mm "Swedish Mauser" cartridges. He sighted the prospective target. "Range on outside one-four-zero-zero meters."

"What are you thinking? Lay down a preemptive fire?"

"Could be friend."

"You trust that silk pouch enough to risk it?"

"You want make it mad before we sure?"

"Your call, sergeant." She took aim, feeling small against the vast consuming strangeness of this place. There seemed no shortage of possible misfortunes: hunger, terror, pursuit, madness, abandonment and, *en fin de compte*, death …

The smooth, speckled-gray animal was the size of a Réseau autobus. It rounded the temple, flapping large, triangular wings not unlike the pectoral fins of a manta ray. The head was broad and flat and topped with feathery antennae. Babette tracked the creature with her gun, half-expecting it to spew fire or launch chitinous spikes. The attribute that gave the animal its gull-like profile was a semi-translucent air sac or bubble. The air sac deflated into a fleshy wattle as the animal descended to the temple forecourt. Suckerless tentacles extended from its underbody to cushion its landing. The animal emitted a low seashell drone.

Stone dust whisked into the air from the updraft confused Babette's vision. She spit to clear the grit lodged between her teeth. Neither she nor Katsuo lowered their guns. The droner bowed its seemingly eyeless head to reveal two riders saddled side by side: a young woman with a shaved head, lithe and black and bearing a bronze-tipped staff; and an albino baboon with belted hand-weapons. Babette started in wonder at this pairing.

The baboon dismounted first, sliding down a crease in the droner's skull that ran as far as the corner of its ribbed mouth. On noting the guns raised against it, the baboon drew an axe. The woman alighted on the stone in a similar fashion, staff in hand, and assumed her full height. She was draped in a sleeveless sheathe dress of sun-bleached linen. Her gait was measured, deliberate. With her free hand extended, palm up, she said, "Hail, newcomers from the waters of heaven. Be not afraid." Her voice was a melodious calm. "I am Hema, servant of the Duah-teh and former upworlder like yourselves. Ptah, god of justice, has seen fit to bring us here, together, to join in a worthy purpose."

Katsuo relaxed his hold on the rifle and gave Babette a triumphant smile. "Katsuo—no accident name in Japanese sound like word 'to win.'"

Babette rolled her eyes then took a few steps toward Hema, the Luger free at her side. Despite the woman's welcoming mien, she was light-headed with anxiety. How many times had she been lured into danger by magickal illusions? Katsuo lingered behind, a check on any sudden movements. The stranger cut a striking figure: oval-faced with deep, almond-shaped eyes, a slightly tilted nose and high cheekbones accented in red ochre. Her skin was an oiled, sun-kissed brown. Babette wondered if she were royalty and Duah-teh her patron god. She gave a slight bow. "Babette Labrecque. And this," she said, gesturing for clarity, "is Sergeant Katsuo Fukai. I'm—I have to say, shocked—relieved but shocked—to hear you speak English."

"The land has willed it so we hear in our own tongues." Hema inclined the butt-end of her staff toward Nolin. The spheroid crystal at its tail emitted a spectral iridescence. "I must be quick if he's to have any chance of surviving." She advanced on Nolan with swift efficiency.

Katsuo moved to intercept her and the extra-large baboon bounded forward to counter him.

Hema fixed Babette with her shrewd brown eyes. "I am here only to heal. I have no falsehood in my breast. My heart is pure and my hands also."

"How do you even know what's wrong with him?" Babette asked.

"I witnessed your arrival in my waking sleep—the missile from the sun, Apep and its chaos-poison ..."

"Then you know the dreamtime?"

"We call it the Unworldly River." Hema bent to Nolin's stricken body. "Besides the primal gods, he's the only one to ever face Apep and live. Even now, he undergoes endless tortures of the mind. Have you not wondered why nothing else abides in this place? This is the rebel-serpent's domain alone. It lives on souls, being provided with their power." She put a palm on Nolin's chest. Incipient tears worried her eyes. "We must hurry—for him and our own sakes." She raised the staff from the blade-end to anoint him with its crystalline fitting and paused, waiting on Babette's permission.

"Parmatmar crystal," Katsuo said in astonishment.

At this, Babette's skepticism abated somewhat. She recognized the crystal from the team's wartime encounter with the alien Mimirodat and the samples in Paul's lab. Looking at it more closely, she could see the gold moderating fluid at its center. Such crystals had the potential to render and magnify dreamtime effects in the material world. If anything could restore Nolin to health it would be this sort of otherworldly magick.

Hema touched the crystal to Nolin's damp brow. The crystal sparked and flashed, leaving indecipherable imprints in the air. Nolin seized up, arching his back. The muscles in his neck strained. Hema reclined on her heels and closed her eyes. "O favored of heaven," she began, "O lord of the corpse which rests in Heliopolis, protect him as you protected Osiris against Set…"

Babette gradually relaxed the grip on her holstered weapon and followed the woman's hushed ministrations with a growing sense of confidence. Hema was a rare type, she thought, earnest, mediumistic and attuned to the manifold layers of the world. There was something bright at the core of her—an aura, a charge like a strong gift for life. Babette wasn't spiritual enough to know the exact quality. But she wouldn't have been surprised if Hema sprouted wings of her own.

Neter-Khert, the Domed Bog

"Fear not, upworlders," the woman at the end of the pier said, arms outstretched in welcome. "We are here to protect and watch over you as the lord of life who rests in Dedet." The whites of her eyes shone out from her dark face.

As soon as the hummock came to a stuttering halt, Paul stepped onto the crumbly-edged pier, followed by his compatriots. The woman was slender and shapely in her pleated gold dress and nearly as tall as him. Her conical *atef* crown accentuated her height. A small light blue cape covered her shoulders. She held the retinue of agitated baboon-things in abeyance with a look.

He was compelled to avert his gaze from her elegance. "I'm Paul— Paul Weygand—and thee-uh these are my companions, Dixie and Joey." The number and variety of questions that came to the fore dizzied him. He had the feeling of trying to stand upright in an unstable canoe. This woman and her mutated apes, the hummock, the bog monster, the possibility of finding Nolin and the others—which first? "I'm sorry, how is it you're able to understand us and vice versa?"

"It is not what I speak but what you hear." Her voice was throaty and pleasing. "You breathe an atmosphere of sleep. It filters speech as we might dream it." She put a teasing finger to his lips. "As in the flux of dreaming, the boundaries between things—between people—dissolve in the air."

"Where *is* here, exactly?" Prince J asked, dropping a gear bag.

"Ah, my upworld brother, this is Herakleion in its twilight cycle." Her lips thinned into a wistful smile.

"And—I'm sorry for all thee-uh questions—but, um, what was that?" Paul pointed to the hummock shuddering back to its original location. "How did—?"

"I made it so. Like a dreamer aware she is dreaming. The land responds to directed thought—within limits, of course." Her kohl-accented eyes fell on Paul. "You may call me Nicandra. I am the *shemshw nehw* or leader-protector of the southern horizon. You are honored guests of my people, the Nebwa, and under my aegis now." With a wave, she prompted the baboon-things to put away their weapons. "Do not mind these changelings. Their aspects may be fearsome but they were once like us and retain their human hearts."

Paul responded in kind, holstering his weapon and signaled Dixie and Joey to follow suit.

Nicandra gestured toward the bog. "I suspect even that creature—the translated population of a small village—still has dim feelings like our own."

"You mean that bog monster used to be people?" Dixie asked. "I gotta say this for the war—at least we knew who we was shootin at most a the time."

Prince J said, "That was before we figured out reality's held together by mystery string."

"Sad to think them might be the good ol' days."

Paul ignored the exchange, more intent on understanding this world and its supernatural laws. "Translated?" he asked Nicandra. "You mean transformed?" He pushed his black-rimmed glasses up on his nose. "Is there some disease we should be aware of?"

"Our enemies, the Duah-teh, call it corruption and try against fate to withhold it. We, however, consider it *swadjet* or psychogenesis. It is like the Eye of Horus that refreshes the heart." She led them down the pier to a large inset door. The baboon-things surrounded her in a pack. "The city will make it clear."

Paul shouldered one of the gear bags.

"You ready to trust this Nicondaroga?" Dixie asked in a low voice.

"Nicandra," Paul corrected.

Dixie gathered up his own share of supplies. "Right. What did I say?"

Paul shrugged off the misunderstanding. "For now—as long as that door doesn't open on thee-uh the larder."

"I'm jus sayin upfront, I don't care if we gotta carboy a moonshine waitin for us…" Dixie indicated the changelings in their primitive armor waddling after Nicandra. "No way I'm wearin boiled leather and bronze."

"Great," Prince J chimed in. "Now I have to hope she has the magick to remove that picture from my head."

"Actually," Paul said, "we should be careful about thee-uh that—what we're thinking. She's telekinetic. No reason she couldn't be telepathic too."

The vault-like door ahead of them clanged open, ushering in a dingy watercolor light. Nicandra beckoned them forward.

"If'n Babette's right, I should be good either way." Dixie set off in a huff.

At Paul's inquiring look, Prince J said, "No idea."

They followed Nicandra and her guard through the exit and onto a pitted city center avenue. The otherwise empty street and the jumble of structures around it consisted of the same pale stone. On bursting into the air above the city, Paul had thought it collapsed by age or earthquake. He could see now that it wasn't in disrepair so much as deformed. The avenue's colonnades figured in complicated knots as though untrellised vines. Towers and belfries had warped into shapes impossible for regular quarried materials to maintain. Stone hung in columns dotted by empty space like the tracks of stray electrons. Connecting arches described cheeky squiggles. If not for the wan, sobering light, the city might have drifted out of a child's pleasant dream.

Paul smiled to himself at this unforeseen bonanza. How differently his life had turned out from what he'd envisioned as a precocious schoolboy. The most he'd dared hope for then, listening to mice race along the bedroom curtain rail, was to be a Dublin-based mechanical engineer or black robed professor. The River Liffey was about as far as his fantasies tended. What a testament to God's secret geometries to find himself here—some extradimensional vestige of Herakleion *primus*—surrounded by untold wonders. Nothing less than this kind of life would've ever satisfied his intellectual appetites.

"Our city is on the brink of transcendence," Nicandra said. "Every-thing—the land, its plants and people—are in a divine state of in be-tween." She pointed to a misshapen obelisk as they walked past. The pinnacle was a blazon of energy vectors. "Our final forms are yet to be decided. For now, we are changing, becoming, like Kheper, the beetle that gives birth to itself."

Herakleion's instability could explain the advent of the whitespace field and that bloody serpent, Paul thought. The light source in the sky appeared to be more of a swirling void than a sun. Like a pinhole revealing a greater brilliance beyond. It's possible the city was enclosed in an increasingly volatile whitespace bubble. "Do you know how you got here?" he asked. "This is *the* Herakleion—the Egyptian port city that sunk between 3 and 2 BCE?"

Nicandra nodded. "The story of how we came to be here, separated from the upper-world, however, is confounded by myth and specu-lation. It happened during a psychic war among gods and daimons and souls. Some artifacts remain that give proof to it, among them, an oracle, the decapitated head of Osiris. We've long-since lost it to the Duah-teh and they, in turn, have lost it to psychogenesis—buried." She put a hand on Paul's elbow. "There's another, more important artifact—*the* most important: *Ptahkit'b*."

"What is it?" Paul glanced back to confirm Dixie and Prince J were alert and following at a prudent distance. Joey assured him of their watchfulness with a look.

"To all appearances, a book."

"Like a grimoire?" he asked, distracted by a tower ribboned like peeled fruit and suspended in air. The place was a tantalizing spectacle he ached to research and catalog. The alabaster stone could well be the fabled *prima materia* itself—nature blasted down to its very funda-ment. But he had to focus on discovering a way home. He returned his attentions to Nicandra. "A book of spellcraft?" he clarified.

"*Ptahkit'b* is the source of our unmaking. I believe it to be the heart of Osiris, king of the living. I will show you through the living altar."

"So you have it?"

"No." Her mouth twisted into a grimace. "I mean only to share my scattered memories of it. The Duah-teh have claimed the book for their own. But I am hopeful you and your companions will help us recover it."

Paul considered potential replies. Given the possibility she could read his mind, he decided on a half-truth: "I'm afraid we, uh, have a policy of non-interference in these situations. I appreciate thee-uh rescue and your hospitality but meddling in tribal matters..." He shook his head. "At thee-uh moment, my first priority is to find another group of friends—if, indeed, they landed here—and then return upworld, as you call it."

"It may already be too late for them." Nicandra adjusted the hang of her cape around one shoulder. "They've been taken by the Duah-teh."

"How do you know this?"

"I previsioned their arrival just as I did yours."

"So you knew where to find us..." The avenue narrowed under the influence of some woozy bridgeworks, forcing Paul to duck under a massive support. The changelings dropped to their palms and bounded ahead, scabbards clattering on the paving stones. Dry echoes filtered through the surrounding debris. "Are they safe? Unharmed?" he asked to the back of Nicandra's head.

She waited for Paul to join her on the other side of the obstruction, shoulders squared. Her expression was solemn, imposing. "The bearded one suffers the chaos-poison of Apep. If he survives, the Duah-teh will doubtless turn him against us. Their victory would mean the cataclysmic end of Herakleion. Even the serpent, last among the primal gods, would perish. The book is our only sure defense." Her soft brown eyes gloomed over. "So you see, Paul of upworld: this is no mere tribal matter."

Chapter 7

New World / No World

Seshtah Weben, the Mysterious Overflow

One of the Nebwa's messenger birds took a manic interest in Dixie's discarded helmet of bandages, chirruping the find to its brood-mates. The bird was about the size of a large fowl but with longer and narrower wings. Its lustrous dun plumage more closely resembled scales than true feathers. Clawing up the gauze, the bird emitted a rude booming note. Dixie had dubbed the creatures 'honkers' for this bothersome habit. He made a half-playful lunge at the bird with a mechanical pencil, shrilling his annoyance. The honker fluttered a short distance out of range. Its wings assumed a flickering transparency in flight. "Yeah, yeah," Dixie warned, "keep on like that I'm gonna wring your neck and wear ya for a hat."

"Don't get the natives riled up now," Prince J said from behind a whorl of cigarette smoke. He jutted his chin in the direction of a nearby pair of baboon-things. They'd bristled at Dixie's outburst and were slow to resume dragging a wicket of tree branches to their cooking fire. The faded gold leaves were like draped cloth. Against Paul's demurrals, Nicandra had insisted on preparing an honorary feast.

Dixie shrugged off the changelings' hard looks and took in the stone garden camp from his low-rise perch on the terrace. To the left, mineral water trickled down the rock terrace into a gently curved basin. Oil bloom colors ringed the central pool. An elastic mass of stilt-rooted trees bordered the far side of the sunken garden. The rest of the lunar surface was dotted with odd amoeboid forms and giant, vertically-creased tubers the baboon-things used for shelter. The huts struck Dixie as overgrown Tennessee spinning gourds. *Just another day in this weird army.*

He hunched over the blank page torn from Paul's moleskin notebook again, still unsure of what to write Babette but cheerful in his cussed survival. Sure, he'd banged his head a bit but he'd made it through another harrowing crash into irreality. The dark future had risen up to meet him then retreated. No telling how much longer that would go on. But he asked only for a little while longer and a mite longer yet. "I tell you what, pal," he said, "we eatin these birds, I don't care if'n they taste like offal, I'm gonna chew em with great vigor."

Prince J smiled around his hand-rolled cigarette. "Can't be any worse than buckshot pheasant and I know you've had your share of that down home." He took a meditative drag as he cleaned the loading gate on his new rifle of choice—a 1921 Winchester .30-30.

"Buckshot's a damn sight safer to swallow I'd wager."

"Me, I'd just like a decent shower after that bog. There ain't enough rolling paper in the world to cover my stink permanent."

Dixie shivered a scrap of unlined paper free of white dust. "Ask that Nicuyahoga. Bet she got a lavender bath here somewhere."

"Nicandra," Paul said from behind him. He was up one level, examining a peculiar rock that stretched several stories in a broken line. Small pearly growths gleamed out from it like disembodied eyes.

"Bless you."

"Stop fooling with her name. That's an order."

The snap resort to rank got Dixie's hackles up. "Don't tell me you're sweet on that monkey-mad dame," he said in a wheedling voice. Excepting the urgency of reuniting the team, how could he take the situation seriously? The somber sky and chalk-white desert, the husks of biomorphic plants, the honkers and baboon-things—it was like the backlot of that kooky French moon film Babette had made him watch. He half-expected the surrounding rocks to be made of Camembert and the *ian bwt* to reveal themselves as midget actors in costume.

"Upset her," Paul said, "and she's liable to think up an earthquake to swallow you whole."

"I could make do with that and some chopped straw for a billet. How do we know these squash huts they're fixin up for us ain't fulla alien lice?"

His concentration broken, Paul abandoned his study and advanced on Dixie, twisting and clenching his lanky frame as if hobbled by some inner tension. "You're really starting to get on my wick. What's gotten into you? You've been whinging and carping at me since thee-uh launch."

"Have not." Dixie raised his defiant eyes to Paul. "Whatever the hell whinging is…"

"My mistake," Paul said, clearly unconvinced. He clambered down to the same level and took a seat, chin resting on his hands.

"But with you takin that tone, now I'm whing-y." Dixie gestured with the pencil for emphasis. "Satisfied?"

Paul ignored the incitement to extend their spat. "Let's just hope this won't take long and we can get to finding Lancer and the others. Nicandra will guide thee-uh messenger bird via telepathy to wherever they are. We can at least let them know we're here and alright. I guess in easier times that's how thee-uh the two tribes communicated." He glanced at the blank sheet of notebook paper. "At a loss there?"

"What would you know about it?" Dixie's voice sounded too loud even to his own ears. Sometimes he let his trouble with Babette dull his sense of other people. He couldn't help it. Despite himself, he had a panicky affection for her.

"You and Babette? Nothing besides what you've shouted mid-gun-fight."

Dixie pictured her in the heat of battle, scented and serene. He pointed his chin toward Paul in challenge but with the secret intent to make an impression on the hard angular face in his imagination. "She's never, you know, in private, said anything about her feelings…" His throat stoppered on him and he cleared it to start his question over: "She's never gotten close to you to admit or confide or …"

"What're you getting at?" Paul raised his head from his steepled fingers. "You think Babette and I…?" His eyes gleamed with suppressed laughter. "Spinach and gammon! No, mate, no."

"What?" Dixie colored up at the ease of Paul's denial. "She not good enough for you?"

"Please, Dixie. No offense but she's hardly my type."

"She seemed plenty insulted when *I* said that." The joke helped quell the heat in his cheeks.

"Frankly," Prince J chimed in, "I don't know if she's *your* type either. Sure a high-strung Frenchie's the best match? Not like you can apply for the soldier's wife's grant."

"I don't know." Dixie sighed in relief. "She's like her nickname—*Pétard.*"

"Firecracker. Sounds better in American. Beautiful at a distance but get too close and she blows up in your face."

"I tend to look at these things in terms of magnetic draw," Paul said. His tone suggested the opening to a lecture.

"Smartually," Dixie said.

"What?"

"Smartually. Like 'naturally' but with a book-learner's smart-ass spin."

Paul choked back a rejoinder, eager to pursue his pet theory. "As I was saying—magnetic draw occurs between positive or negative polar opposites: night and day, yin, yang. With magnets, a positively charged pole bonds tight to a negatively charged pole. Thee-uh same thing occurs in chemistry—with particles instead of poles. There, polarity results from thee-uh uneven partial charge distribution of atoms in a molecule." He paused to gauge whether Dixie was following his line of thought. "Some atoms, like oxygen, are more electronegative; others, like carbon, are either neutral or have partial positive charges. Thee-uh molecules with charges aren't symmetrical in their arrangement of atoms, meaning there's some instability in their attraction. You could say the same for couples—thee-uh molecule in this analogy—in cases where one person has a stronger personality than the other." Sensing Dixie's impatience, he cut the explanation short. "Look, you keep coming back to her, right? That's a sure sign of magnetic draw in action. You just need to be aware of thee-uh innate imbalance caused by—"

"I'll keep that in mind next time I build up a head of static electricity." Dixie directed Paul's attention to the camp below. Nicandra was gesturing for Paul to join her. The skeleton of a crocodile-like lower jaw was draped around her shoulders. The bone-strand was encrusted with lapis lazuli and bezel-set gold plate. "Better not keep her waitin on ya, what with the chance a earthquakes and all."

"You want an escort?" Prince J asked, getting to his feet.

Paul waved him off as he started down the terrace. "Not necessary, thanks. It's just a book."

Dixie took up the pencil again only to suffer a debilitating blue numbness. He'd feigned ignorance in the moment but knew what he'd done to hurt Babette. His last dalliance had gone on too long and been too obvious. He would have to express remorse and mean it—in writing—always a daunting proposition for him under the best circumstances.

When Paul was safely out of earshot, Prince J asked, "Just a book, he says. That's what got us here in the first place. Think we should follow anyway?"

"Aw, let im go. He's the brains carrier a this outfit. He oughta know what he's doin." Dixie didn't simply dislike book learning—he distrusted it. He believed the five senses alone were sufficient in themselves to know the world and through them, the paths of God.

Prince J dropped down next to Dixie. "You alright, man?" He stubbed his cigarette on the rock. "Just between me and the Good Lord, I mean." He'd developed a camaraderie with Dixie over the years founded on soldiery and faith.

"Yeah, we bristle and spar like brothers."

"No, not Paul—Babette."

"You know, it's jus…The heart ain't no simple valentine." Dixie had persisted in living in the moment as though moments were all there were. The notepaper asked him to reconceive the future as something more than a nebulous small town ideal. Whatever he wrote would imply new obligations. His chest tightened at the thought. He'd feigned ambivalence these past four-five years from a boyish fear of losing some essential freedom. But maybe that's what he needed: a thread around his middle binding him to real life. The idea of that everyday tension seemed a chastening and at once, a necessary test of maturity. Hell 'n' hullaballoo, he thought. There was nothing for it but to risk getting hurt.

"I'm not sayin I can't live without her," he said in a low voice. "But…" He shook his head as if to throw off any vestigial doubts. "The way I'm feelin, though, why take the chance?" It was as much of a confession of love as he had the strength to make.

"Well then," Prince J said, "write that down and see what it do."

The Temple of Osiris, Lord of the Underworld

The upworlder lay unconscious under a linen sheet in a dusty, long-vacant antechamber. Hema worried over him with a compress, checking the gelatinous *ikm 'm ankh* covering his nose and mouth for signs of residual chaos-poison. If any were found, the creature would expel the venom as a diffuse and harmless gas into its waste-stalk—assuming her cleansing ritual had sufficiently diluted the venom. Her insides still ached from her dreamtime labors. She recalled them as a razor-edged eternity, a painful now with nothing behind it and nothing ahead. Her sympathetic magick had exposed her to a divine conflagration of the soul. She'd felt her skin char and flake away, her muscles wither, her bones come clean...At one point, she'd expected to emerge an osseous relic, forsaken and, with the exception of Gapti, disregarded. Praise to Osiris, lord of the horns, for giving her the strength to outlast the agony.

The ritual had also revived forgotten and disquieting emotions. For a monotonous age, her life had centered on her masters and the *Ptahkit'b*. She'd lived a rigid existence, alternating between mundane duties and dangerous forays into the Unworldly River. Tending the courtyard gardens. Feeding the menagerie and mucking out the cages. Preparing the meals. Making and mending garments. Dusting the statuary. Sweeping the floors and shaking the rugs. All done virtually alone and in funeral silence. Few Duah-teh could be spared for anything other than manning the Chamber of Osiris, where they deflected, absorbed and periodically directed the energies of the *Ptahkit'b*. Preoccupied as they were with shielding Herakleion from the full force of the book, her masters had wizened into remote and unfeeling pharaohs. Only the faithful Gapti allowed her some measure of everyday feeling.

Now, the unavoidable intimacies of the cleansing ritual had renewed the promise of ordinary human contact. How long had it been since she'd shared the subtleties of surprise, anticipation, joy, even of disgust and fear? She missed how something as transient as a laugh could lift her spirits and looked forward to taking an illicit pleasure in high emotion. The Duah-teh would doubtless be on guard against a breakdown in discipline. They demanded she manipulate the upworlder with dispassion. She'd have to be mindful of their invisible oversight.

As she lifted the compress from his head, he twitched and snapped awake. His pale blue eyes went wide at the *ikm 'm ankh*. She flung an arm across his chest to prevent him from mulching the creature in a claw-fingered squeeze. "Stay, upworlder. Calm yourself." She gripped the jelly-like organism by the nerve bundle under its posterior hood. "This creature means you no harm." She gathered the oxygenating tendrils in her free hand and slowly removed the creature to its standup tank next to the bed. The *ikm 'm ankh* relaxed its feelers in the buoying gases.

Once separated from the creature, the upworlder instantly seized up and spewed a thin iridescent mucus. He wiped his chin on the dirtied linen, bleary-eyed and embarrassed. The bed's supporting leather straps creaked under his shifting weight.

"I apologize," Hema said, a hand on the carved headboard. Her knees had almost faltered with relief at his recovery. "It's a bit unpleasant, I know, but the *ikm 'm ankh* was scouring out the poison." Uncertain of the proper courtesies, she gave a shy smile. "I am Hema, servant of the Duah-teh, the keepers of the book."

"The others—my friends?" the upworlder choked out.

"Safe in a nearby apartment and resting after their ordeal." She offered him a cup of milky water from a side table. "Thirsty?"

"Yes, thank you." He accepted the ceramic cup and took a tentative sip before downing its contents. "How long?" His voice had been roughened under the *ikm 'm ankh*'s care.

"Time has been a madness here ever since Apep arrested the barque of Ra in the sky. The snake-god set the sun on us and now we live in perpetual day."

He ran a hand over his cropped head. "Are we near the crash site or...?"

"Some distance away—in the protected city of the Duah-teh."

"Protected from what?" He pushed up on his elbows, squinting in the direction of the balcony and the stretch of mingled ruins beyond.

"The *kekw wahhhw* or chaos wave. This is the only place in all of Herakleion free of its destructive influence." She marveled at his resilience, though wary of its suprahuman source. His double nature was no secret from her. She'd pierced his quickened soul.

He swung his legs from the angled bedframe and tried his weight. She rushed to put a steadying arm around him. He was a brute mass against her petite figure but she bore him up without undue effort. He gave off an unfamiliar, though not unpleasant, musk of sleep. "Careful now …" She had an impish whim to blurt his name just to watch his reaction.

"Thanks—for everything." He took a trial step and found his balance, though his mouth trembled when he smiled. "I owe my life to you. I remember that much."

"I was duty-bound," she said, looking askance from modesty. She was afraid she'd gone too far in grasping him around the middle. The Duah-teh expected her to be poised and never flinching. She had to be perfect. But again and again, she found herself looking into his pale eyes in hopes of catching herself in them—a dark glint in a watery mirror. "There is a great need for your help in defending the *Ptahkit'b.*"

He made his way to the balcony as though exercising newly-grown limbs. "I'm sorry. What's the translation? The Book of …?

"Unmaking."

"And how long have *you* been here?"

Her eyes almost welled up at the question. It was the first time in recent memory someone had asked about her origins and by extension, her place in the larger world. "I cannot say for certain. I was a skinny child when the Duah-teh took me. They had the power then to draw periodically from the upworld. I've been their novitiate and servant ever since—centuries inhumed in a moment."

"I'm sorry for that." His brow puckered in concern. "Your childhood—it must've been full of real fears, life or death choices, not the pretend and niggling fears of an ordinary growing-up." He bobbed his head as if recollecting something hurtful then headed onto the balcony. She knew of his adolescent pains through their dreamtime communion: the trials he'd endured to attain his unbreakable skin; the undead plague he'd suffered as a sea-going youth; the early and unforgivable loss of his father; his keen sense of loneliness; the Great War and its haunting atrocities ...

Leaning on the edge of the balcony, he surveyed the rubbled district controlled by the Duah-teh. Her chest tightened at the scene below—the clench of a useless life. She remembered when the boulevards were unbroken and the towers abounding and unbent. Everything save the temple had decayed into a disorienting barrens. If only resuscitating the upworlder would restore the city and redeem the wasted ages. Was it too much to hope?

"All this," he asked, "is from the chaos wave?"

She found it hard to swallow and answered with a nod. Standing next to him, the first upworlder she'd ever touched in this reality, she felt more keenly than ever a sense of lost time.

"I can see the vestiges of large, fortifying outworks." He pointed to a series of pitched and sagging walls. "The city had a star-shaped design once, am I right?" He batted at the air as if to seize the concept whole. "By the 17th century, this design—derived from the Golden Section—was considered the ideal defense. Saarlouis, Neuf-Brisach, a number of other European cities, adopted it. Looks like you anticipated its usefulness centuries in advance. The problem with it is: the more you entrench yourself, the more you end up on your heels."

While they looked out on the pulled-apart city, a distant temple shrieked in descending keys as its compound dome buckled and split. "Is that it—the chaos wave?" he asked.

"Either that or a psychic attack by the Nebwa."

"Psychic ... Is that how we're able to talk to each other? You're reading my mind?"

"No," she explained. "It is an effect of the air itself. More and more Herakleion becomes the dream foretold in the *Ptahkit'b*." In dreams, she thought, we see the veil of truth through the truth of the veil.

"What do your master's think I can do against these Nebwa if they have telekinetic powers on this scale? I'm no dreamtime adept."

"If you feel up to walking into the adjoining chamber, I can show you." Hema led him from the antechamber into an airy, unfurnished room with bipartite windows on two sides. The milky sunglow barely tinted the walls. Hema waited in the shadowed chamber for the upworlder to amble closer to the center, heart drumming against her ribs. How many times had she visualized this moment, now in hope, now in despair? He approached at a measured gait. Close enough, she decided, and adjusted a crystalline wall sconce to flood the chamber in ghostly light.

The upworlder gaped in stunned recognition at the ancient mural on the facing wall. The identity of the chief figure was unmistakable: it was him—Lancer—in daimon form. His horned image protected Ma'at, the winged goddess of cosmic order and truth, from an unseen danger. In one hand, he held the Eye of Horus, the most potent symbol of protection against evil and by some accounts, the moon; and in the other, a rod crowned by a sun disk, a symbol of kingship. Hema had traced the plaster braille for untold years, wondering if she'd be blessed enough to witness the scene firsthand. Her pulse raced at this first inkling of its realization. The fate of Herakleion would soon break clear. "The Nebwa have a daimon general, Ammit, the Eater of Souls," she said. "The Duah-teh want a daimon of their own as counterbalance."

The upworlder's breathing shallowed. "I don't understand," he muttered. "How is this possible?"

"The Oracle of Osiris previsioned your coming many cycles past. There is a prophecy…" She relished the chance to try his name on her tongue. The painted daimon had been known only as the Judge Foretold. Up until the cleansing ritual she hadn't understood the mythical figure and the upworlder were one and the same. Her masters were eager to test him. The prospect excited a needling anxiety. "You are to be known as Lancer, the Blade of Change."

He gathered himself up against the evident burden of this pronouncement. "And what am I prophesied to do?"

"To destroy our enemies and end this twilight cycle for all time."

Seshtah Weben, the Mysterious Overflow

Despite Nicandra's assurances, the living altar *ib peshedj* made Paul uneasy. It was a colorless plant extruding from a waist-high slab of Parmatmar crystal. Several of the plant's wriggling stalks ended in blushing, toothed hoods. Nicandra had placed one on her shaved head by way of demonstration. "On the heart belonging to my spirit," she said, "I promise no harm will come to you. The *ib peshedj* will conform to your upworld mind and calm you. It is a conduit for psychic exchange, nothing more."

Paul put a hand on the back of a shiny hardshell couch to steady himself and, with Lancer's predicament in mind, thrust his chin forward. The proffered hood reeked of what might be charitably termed eau d' fermented dog. It closed around his skull, tickling him with its fine trigger hairs before establishing a suction grip. A pleasant warmth coursed from his crown to the tail of his spine. Nicandra motioned for him to lay on the couch—one of five arrayed in a star pattern around the altar. He clambered into it with a nervous intake of breath. The jellied interior oozed around his boiler suit like a second skin, leaving only his face and chest and the tops of his limbs exposed.

Nicandra assumed a comparable position in the couch directly behind him. They were now aligned back-to-back, connected by the *ib peshedj*. She began to pray: "O Wepwawet, Opener of the Way, bless your coming and going: the sky encloses the stars, *hequa* encloses its settlements, my mind encloses the *hequa* that is in it …"

Hequa was one of the few Egyptian words Paul knew. It meant magick. The base of the Parmatmar crystal dashed the hut with scintillant fractals. "Feel yourself settle in your body," Nicandra instructed. "Close your eyes and sigh into your chest. See how the redness behind your lids twists and takes shape under my influence. When next we speak, O Pa-ul, it will be in the language of dreams."

The rational side of Paul refused to let go even as the inchoate patterns before him fanned into a shimmering black. Though a firm deist after the mathematician and physical scientist Carl Friedrich Gauss, Paul resisted the supernatural aspects of his vocation. The notion of reality as magickal at its core offended his cast of mind. So in situations like this—exposed and vulnerable to forces beyond logic—he tended to abstract himself from them as if he were only an attentive observer.

Here, careering into someone else's dream, he recalled the mechanistic dream theory of Lydiard Horton. According to this theory, dreams can be usefully considered in terms of discrete stimuli that, routinized over time, create lasting nerve channels. Bizarre imagery and disorientation result when new stimuli surface from the unconscious that run counter or otherwise don't fit these established arterials. Like the fantastic imagery spooking Paul now: an endless surge of dark water; a thin emergent crest—the moon? no, a mountaintop—and rising from its peak, a shadow giant with two plumes on its head…The kinetoscopic whirl of impressions overwhelmed his mental defenses. He lost the conceptual diagram he'd begun to trace from the stimulus-idea in Nicandra's head through the living altar and into his conscious brain as an active neurogram. Stimulus-idea, automatic precepts, trial apperception—the terms vanished in the hurly-burly of the shared dream.

Yes, be at ease, Nicandra thought. *Let the Unworldly River wash over you and the void assume form.*

Much to his chagrin, Paul discovered he'd been holding his breath and made a point of exhaling. A pinprick of light rayed out to bleach the shadow giant away. He flinched at the starburst, afraid his panicky thoughts constituted an inadvertent assault on Nicandra.

In their original state, the gods could not be distinguished one from the other as they were composed entirely of starlight, she intoned in his head.

The hallucinatory whiteness faded into airy and overlapping depictions of various Egyptian deities: Osiris, typified by his black-green skin; his wife, Isis, in her throne-shaped headdress; his treacherous brother, Set, bearing a peculiar aardvark snout…*We believed they would descend from the heavens in their individuated forms to awaken the god-nature in us.* The figure of Osiris took on cut-glass edges. He towered over Herakleion *primus* at its zenith on Abu Quir Bay. Paul had learned from Katsuo that the Egyptian gods were represented by largely human guises to show they possessed human consciousness among their many attributes. Animal parts, on the other hand, were thought to denote higher functions like telepathy and astral sight.

Nicandra narrated successive images of Osiris and Set as if they were manifestations of the deities but Paul suspected they were actually extradimensional visitors. The ancient Egyptians had founded every

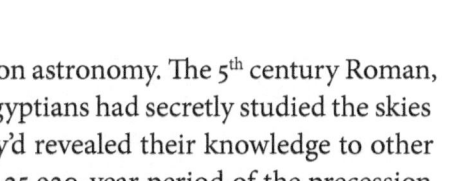

major aspect of their civilization on astronomy. The 5th century Roman, Martianus Capella, figured the Egyptians had secretly studied the skies for over 40,000 years before they'd revealed their knowledge to other cultures. They were aware of the 25,920-year period of the precession of the equinoxes. The siting and architecture of the temples along the Nile geometrically represented the music of the spheres. And hadn't Katsuo said something about the Pyramid Texts referring to Osiris as a being made from 'celestial metal?' What followed seemed to confirm his hypothesis.

They came not to bestow a sense of divinity, Nicandra continued. *Instead, they re-enacted the war from the beginning of time, Osiris against Set, with Herakleion caught between. Our city was cast into this realm of perpetual day and in the end, as before, Set won out over his brother. He then seeded the land with parts from his murdered brother before forsaking us altogether.*

A restless excitement almost broke Paul out of his waxy dream-state. Nicandra's story described a secret history that surpassed imagining. He wanted to slow her down, get his notebook, probe for more. Important details were slipping past him without comment or time for explanation. *You mentioned something about this—the head of Osiris.*

Our former oracle. The gods contain the whole of Creation. We believe the Ptahkit'b *to be the heart of Osiris and of possibility itself. But the Duah-teh consider it a plague-weapon.* In Nicandra's transmission, the book lay on a crystal altar not unlike the *ib peshedj.* Its cover was a spectral shear of light, unreadable yet eerily familiar. *When the* Ptahkit'b *was discovered, Herakleion was one city, one people. Then the Duah-teh opened the book, beginning the cycle of* swadjet *or psychogenesis. First, written language warped out of recognition, rendering our accounts and histories useless. Other things soon underwent the same wasting change: farm tools, our crops and cattle, our streets, our towers, the untamed beasts, our people, the land under our feet...The Duah-teh marshalled their psychic powers and for ages attenuated these effects. But as the priesthood aged and weakened and its numbers dwindled, the book reasserted its power.* Ptahkit'b *seeks to rewrite the world in dream and, in the process, translate us out of it—as gods ourselves.*

Drawn to the image of the book, Paul registered her words as a muted ramble. It appeared immeasurably thin, almost gossamer. He speculated that the book might be an alien communication device gone awry, a dimensional projector, a whitespace magnet drawing energy from adjacent universes, a fully-realized mimetic equation ... Yes, a formula for reductive change, he thought, forgetting Nicandra in the moment. *An infinite number of points make up a line. Infinite lines make a plane. Infinite planes equal volume—this volume, this hypervolume...*

You recognize it? Nicandra asked.

Paul discontinued his ad hoc mantra, embarrassed. *Not exactly, no.*

It opens itself to some people. Perhaps you are one of those it favors.

I did seem to read into its nature there for a second.

Then you know its purpose lies unfulfilled. The Duah-teh—their psychic priesthood constrains it unnaturally. They mistake the book for a curse on Herakleion, as if it were a primal blight like the rebel-serpent Apep. Circumscribed by their waning power, it confirms their fears, deforming and depleting our land, bleeding the light from the sky, degrading the order of things. If they only relaxed their hold, it would open the holy roads for us. At this, representative changelings materialized from out of the book's dreamglow—ghosts of generations past. *We were the people's hope against these usurpers. Time and again we Nebwa fought to release the* Ptahkit'b *from its psychic fetters. But the human among us were comparatively few and harried, outcasts forced into camps like this and the wilds beyond. We can no longer access the energies of the book at a distance. To protect us, we have only our own meagre powers through the Unworldly River and a lone daimon.*

A shudder of anxiety worried the edges of Paul's consciousness. *You cannot know the depths of our desolation, to know hour-to-hour, day-to-day that your world is dying while you are powerless to arrest its decline, no matter how much you give up in the attempt, what joys and aspirations—your very humanity.*

The projected dream shifted to a weirwood of gnarled stone. Paul shrunk inside at the vast and monolithic ugliness. *We could be gods in the Field of Offerings, Field of Rushes, vibrant and new, yet for the Duah-teh. For them, the past has the force of law and must ever and always overrule the future.* Through the living altar, Paul could feel as well as hear Nicandra's thoughts. He recognized the natural passion for liberty in her words, the grasping after a self-determined dream. It seemed a recurring plight for the Egyptians, whether upworld or no.

Your life is defined by thousands, possibly millions, of incremental decisions made and unmade. Inspired by Nicandra's dream-imagery, Paul saw his entire allotment as a sequence of numbered doors. He contemplated each in turn knowing the book was behind one of them and only one. His palms itched to hold it. *Ptahkit'b* promised universal insight. He was certain of it, though he couldn't say how. Questions he'd asked himself repeatedly—about whitespace field dynamics, the origins of the dreamtime, cosmic teleology—and others he hadn't even formulated properly due to sheer bloody ignorance would be answered at last and in full. This feeling could be a lunatic faith or some darker, slanted impulse to hasten cataclysm; regardless, he was in for it.

He concentrated on articulating his next thought so as not to be misunderstood: *What would you have us do?*

The Temple of Osiris, Lord of the Underworld

The mess of cityscape below whispered with chalky dust. It reminded Babette of post-war France—the cratered avenues, the heaped and gutted buildings...She tapped the stone parapet with an index finger. What had the Allies really accomplished outside of avoiding the worst consequences—foreign conquest and totalitarianism? The Versailles Peace Treaty was a guarantee of ongoing instability, German nationalism was on the rise and, as evinced by the Russo-Polish War, any number of borders were subject to violent dispute. Instead of a new world made safe for democracy, the Allies had secured an old world still engaged in traditional—and dangerous—power politics.

The futility of the war had, in part, prompted Babette to sign on with the borderless Integrand General. She found real meaning in Nolin's quest to rid the world of supernatural menaces and, in the process, learn, invent, explore and yes, occasionally make a ruckus. The pressing question now was: could she do this with Dixie and be happy? The ambiguity of their status had begun to frustrate her need to make

sense of things.

Pointing toward the horizon, she said, "Looks like the Great War all over again."

Katsuo paused in his fidgety card shuffling at a nearby table. Given that Lancer was in a near-coma and the rest of the team's whereabouts were uncertain, they hadn't been able to sustain any interest in playing manille. Katsuo set the cards aside and joined her at the edge of the balcony. "What Hema say, sound like never-ending war."

"Not much different than our life up top, I guess. This could be our own otherworldly fight accelerated into the future." The idea conjured up unwanted memories of her mother at Vaucluse asylum. Her *maman* had recently developed the habit of keeping a bent nail in her mouth. She thought it a charm against divulging national secrets under torture by the Boche or some other imagined enemy. Babette caught Katsuo's eye. "You volunteered for Lancer's unit during the war, yes? I don't think I've ever heard you say why."

Katsuo looked askance but humored her question. "In beginning idea was adventure, honor ancestors. My home—Honjima—old base for Shiwaku-suigun. You would say pirate. Later, they become navy. But long time past. Men only fish today, no more warrior. I thought to show different. The emperor, too, I want honor. Now…" He bit his lower lip, deliberating how best to explain. "I am loyal to heart. I have, *etto*, family feeling? For you, Lancer, everyone." He broke into a quizzical smile.

Babette assured him with a gentle hand on his shoulder. "Might as well be a family, no? None of us seem to be able to leave this madness behind." She considered her own sense of loyalty to the team a kind of compulsion. Since the war, she'd suspected that, no matter what, in the end, you're on your own. She'd hoped the members of Integrand General and, Dixie especially, would prove her wrong. She beamed at Katsuo, eager to encourage his honesty. "It's good to hear you say that."

"In Japan, feeling not so free. No one say 'I love you' in real life. Only—what you say?—legend, romance story."

"Who knows? We might be honored someday with our own *chansons de geste*—heroic song. Like the ones about the medieval knight Guillaume d'Orange." She recalled the strange thrill of riding the droner through the impressionistic wash of sky and tried to envision how the scene might be rendered in the style of an illuminated Old French manuscript.

A baboon-soldier loped onto the balcony bearing a hammered metal supper tray. Its swaying tail helped it balance on its hind legs. Babette bent down to accept the food and drink. The baboon smacked its lips and narrowed its eyes at her. She was surprised to see its upper eyelids were flesh-pink. "*Merci.*"

Katsuo relieved her of the tray as the baboon cantered out through the apartment on all fours.

"They're like apes got up for the Opéra Comique," Babette said.

"Baboon sacred animal in ancient time." Katsuo carried the tray to the table. The smoking meat gave off a wretched stench. "Thought to be dead ancestor. First-born son of Osiris, Babi, he baboon. Also, Hapi, son of Horus."

Babette examined the bronze plates of flat bread, winged, small-boned meat and vegetable mash. She recognized lentils, leeks and cucumbers among the mashed herbs.

"Look like *tatsutaage*—tang-fried chicken—under sauce." Katsuo's eyebrows twitched.

"We should be so lucky." Babette had seen worse. During the German occupation of Cambrai, she'd lived on dog and horse meat pâté.

Katsuo put a finger into the cherry-colored meat sauce and gave it an experimental lick. His face puckered up. "Taste rot," he choked.

"And with all this apparent magick in the air, saying grace might well resurrect it." Babette plucked up a bronze drinking cup and smelled its clouded contents. She set it back down without a taste. "You want to purify your—beer I guess it is? I don't know if they separate their dead from their water supply." From a utility pouch on her belt she removed a small jar of Halazone. It was a white crystalline powder made from a chlorine compound. She pinched some into her drinking cup and swished the beer to speed its dissolution. "I have a—"

With a startling flutter of wings, a bird alighted on the parapet close to Katsuo. "*Ehhhhhh,*" he uttered, taking a step back.

"*Merde!* It's after the food." Babette unholstered her Luger, took aim at the bird then shrugged off the thought of shooting it. She was afraid it might be a presentiment of bad fortune. "*Bof*, so long as it leaves the beer alone, I don't care."

The bird had a small bare head and a sharply hooked bill. The feathers resembled scales more than typical plumage.

"Maybe we eat kind uncle," Katsuo said.

"Or it's this world's equivalent of Poe's raven."

"You see?" Katsuo pointed to what looked like a message canister attached to one of the bird's chicken-like legs. "Message for us, you think?" He reached out for it with a wary eye on the creature's beak. The bird cocked its head in his direction but allowed him to pass his hands under its pebbly-scaled belly.

"Careful." Babette moved to get a straight shot at the bird over his shoulder.

Katsuo untied the canister by feel and slowly backed away. On closer inspection, the canister was revealed to be a large-caliber shell casing. He stuck a pinkie into it and twisted out a couple of sheets of rolled notepaper. "*Maji?*" He recognized Paul's precise script on the first sheet. The second one was addressed to Babette and in an unfamiliar hand.

"Don't tell me: another of your paper-strip fortunes." Babette holstered her gun and sidled up to Katsuo to have a look.

"Haw. Deliver by Tengu, birdman trickster."

"It's for us—from Paul—and, *enfin*, this one's private." She plucked the note intended for her from Katsuo's grasp and removed away to read it. Her heart spiked in her chest at the salutation.

Mon Petit Chou,

I don't know if I got much call anymore to greet you like that. The last thing I want is to offend you (again). But I thought I should at least try for some friendly feeling from the start.

Our native contact says you come through the whitespace field okay. I hope that means you got no injuries or aches. Me—I got a bit a the trembles after the crash but nothing serious. My only worries now are getting back to you and then home.

There's not much room to write everything I want to say so I'll just get to it. Regret. It's damn near a way a life for me. I have a bad habit a not knowing how good things are as I'm living them.

In my growing up days, Granny Iva used to set us a late winter task of finding the first budded dandelion. She always said the warm spring days would be coming shortly oncet we found it. I was never one for learning flowers but you know I never been more at home than in the open air. So I played along with her and my sisters. Gave me a excuse to put off homework for the mud and forests a the holler.

Funny how those days are some a my favorite and best remembered. Not for what I was doing so much as what I felt. Traipsing around with my sisters (onery as they are) made me feel rooted to plain life with all its randomness and ugliness and quiet joys. (Tumbling in the grass is the best kind a prayer.) And I come to realize you give me the same sense a color and peace.

You'd think we'd be sick of each other, working side by side the day long, either holed up in that unfinished cave base or out in some Godforsaken wilderness (like this desert fairydom). But I miss you all the same and would be sore hurt if you was to leave.

For whatever reason—pride, nerves, impatience—I been reluctant to put myself in your hands for good. I want you to know that dithering is over. We're soldiers at heart and that means we'd probly learn to live without the other if it came to it. But with the way we feel, why try until we have to?

With love and promise,
Dixie
PS
Write back if your able. Paul says the honker bird will wait.

Babette gazed out over the monotonous ruins stretching to the horizon, her throat tight with feeling. The shock of the note was hard to take. She'd mistaken Dixie's rough mannerisms and dearth of self-awareness for an incapacity for refined emotion. Her error made her teasing provocations seem cruel in hindsight. She still resented the casual, unapologetic air with which he'd described his downtime escapades. He didn't seem guilty about them per se, only about how they made her feel. But she could believe for the first time that he was trying to remedy his lapses and doing it for her sake. The effort suggested she might yet ameliorate his most galling weaknesses, if only just enough to ensure he was reliable.

That wouldn't resolve her other qualms—his restlessness and occasional crudity, his disdain for high culture—traits bound to frustrate her. But she was at ease enough in her own skin, alone, to pursue her interests without his aid or encouragement. Dixie had never presented himself as anything other than what he was: a natural born fighter, alive with a simple pathos and a sure instinct for survival. Who's to say what someone ought to know or enjoy? They had other interests in common and years of shared adventures few, if any, outside the team could ever grasp. She couldn't guess how Lancer and the others would find commensurate matches.

Nolin—Lancer— as much as Babette admired him, he'd never inspired any lasting romantic feelings. He was monastic in his service to history and seemingly too self-contained to be well and truly needed. Excellence is its own distancing mantle. No, for all his faults—or rather, because of them—Dixie better complemented her nerve and wry humor and penchant for unsparing honesty. She could help defuse his wayward energies, act as touchstone or lightning rod, whichever was required. She was the stable one, after all, always focused and composed, even in her anger. She would simply have to trust Dixie had the humility to acknowledge it.

"Paul—he have big time doubt on Duah-teh." Katsuo noticed the bird remained perched on the balcony wall, expectant. "This other, rebel tribe he like. Stay low, he say, and they come for us."

Babette slipped the note into a trouser pocket as she returned to the table with a renewed sense of decisiveness. She tipped her drinking cup to Katsuo before downing it. In the absence of any hop bitterness, the malty brew had lingering notes of date and honey—surprising in its sweetness but not unpleasant. "That's supper then."

Katsuo deposited Paul's note into her open palm. She scanned it for essential details: …*The Nebwa describe the Duah-teh as a dangerous priesthood. They sound like fanatical theocrats…Watch out for the* Book of Unmaking, *where it's located, how it's protected…I don't know the details of our plan, but we'll set off shortly for you...* She wondered if the Nebwa had coached Paul in what to write, seeking some psychological advantage. It was hard to believe Hema could be so wrong or deceiving about the Duah-teh's enemies. "We should get back to Lancer. If he's conscious, he needs to see this."

Katsuo hefted his gear bag. "Leave or take?"

"*Nous reviendrons,*" Babette whispered to the bird.

There was a slap of sandals in the open apartment. The bird gave a discordant honk then fluttered into the sky. The near-invisibility of its wings in flight reminded Babette of the camouflaged observation planes from the war.

Hema rushed onto the balcony at the bird's noisy retreat. "What did it say?"

"Say?" Babette stalled. "Nothing. It was begging for food and we chased it off." She hoped against hope Hema couldn't see her thoughts.

"*Yappari!*" Katsuo hurried to a doddering Nolin. "Yes, I knew it." He clasped Nolin's forearm.

"Oh, thank God." Babette broke Katsuo's hold on Nolin as she hugged him to her. He smelled of light sweat and linen. His acid-frayed coveralls had been replaced with a plain tunic and pleated calf-length kilt. When she pulled back, she noticed how pallid and drawn he looked, the flaky skin around his mouth and nose. This was Nolin at his weakest. "I feared we'd lost you."

"There was a light," Nolin said in a scratchy voice, "but I didn't see any of you lot in it, so ..."

Katsuo favored him with a broad smile. "Stop snake-god might make you king now."

"If you're able," Hema said, touching Nolin's elbow, "the Duah-teh wait for us."

"All of us then?"

Hema nodded, lips tight.

"Are you sure you're up to it?" Babette wanted to delay the meeting until she'd shared Paul's missive. There might even be a code in it known only to Nolin. But she couldn't figure out how to get him alone without arousing suspicion. The bird seemed to have put Hema on alert.

"Fine." Nolin hunched his shoulders. "I've had worse."

"Exactly what I'm afraid of." Babette patted the Luger holstered at her waist. "We have a bad habit of going from one dark ruckus to another."

Chapter 8

By the Grace of the Damned

The Temple of Osiris, Lord of the Underworld

The temple's main tower was a vast, unnerving mind-twister. Corridors ribboned into blank walls or empty air. Stairways recurved on themselves. Flat planes morphed into three dimensions and back again. The spaces between various tiled glyphs formed their own recognizable shapes. Nolin trudged down a hovering staircase, joints protesting every jolt. The chaos-poison had taken more out of him than he'd let on. Under the pounding of his skull, his thoughts ran to fever. One moment of dizzied fascination and he might pitch into the abyssal dark. He focused on the backs of Hema's sandals.

A wall covered in scarab glyphs blurred foreground and background, giving the illusion of insect-patterned windows. Katsuo held a hand up to it. "Hard to focus here. Like seven cup of sake then bottle hitting you in head."

"Been palling around with Dixie, have you?" Babette pulled up short at the unexpected end of the steps.

Hema ushered her onto a floating stone platform. "This passage has all the reason of a dream. It was one of the first purposes to which my masters put the energies of the *Ptahkit'b.*"

"So this place has a function," Nolin mused. "Other than to frustrate any Nebwa that make it this far …"

"Disorder inhibits the reach of the *Ptahkit'b.* Once, these passages and alcoves were peopled by the mad and raving. The atmosphere of delirium helped check the book's corruptions. We break the whole to make the whole." Hema extended her arms protectively. Her touch reminded Nolin of the psychic intimacies they'd shared in the cleansing ritual. She knew him down to the deep unconscious. Gapti drew his lips back in annoyance at the contact. Hema pretended not to notice. "Do not be alarmed by the sudden change in direction."

The tiled platform dropped a few meters then flipped perpendicular to the unseen bottom. They might have been suspended over the rim of the world. On reflex, Nolin grabbed up Babette and Katsuo. There was an awkward intermingling of heads and arms. But some mysterious force held them level against gravity. Nolin released his companions, amazed and embarrassed.

Babette flashed a teasing smile. "Worried I'd see up your skirt?" The chasm turned her jibe into an ominous echo.

They crossed to a wide granite corridor that should logically have been a straight plunge. Crystalline wall sconces affixed to its one enclosed side lit their way. The opposite side revealed more of the crazytechture they'd spanned earlier. The negative space around a suspended beehive shape resolved into the positive image of a *wadjet* eye.

As Nolin started after Hema, he heard Babette whisper in French and Katsuo laugh. He glared back at them. "Quiet, you yokes." Babette smirked and blew him a kiss. Katsuo's face was as placid as the moon but Nolin read amusement in his eyes. Nolin shook his head and redoubled his pace.

Gapti reared up on his hind legs at Nolin's approach, earning a reproachful look from Hema. The baboon ducked his head in obeisance.

"Wish I had some Necco Wafers or something on me," Nolin said. "Your bodyguard might like me better." Hema looked at him blankly. "It's a, uh, sugary treat," he added, forming an illustrative circle with thumb and index finger.

A glint of understanding shone in her eyes. "A sweet, yes." She broke into a knowing smile. "He senses our heightened connection."

Nolin acknowledged it with a sheepish nod. He remembered almost nothing of his hours wracked by the chaos-poison except for scattered images of Hema's calming astral presence. He suspected she was responsible for his merciful forgetfulness. He'd come away from the experience sore and bone-weary but with a lasting sense of abundance. "What we talked about back in the chamber with the mural..." Recovering from the shock of the prophecy, Nolin had impressed on Hema the fact he'd kept his daimonic blood a secret. He glanced over his shoulder to make sure the others weren't following their conversation.

"I know not what my masters will do," Hema said, "other than try to persuade you to our cause."

"But you grasp my dilemma here?" Nolin asked this, in part, to coax an assurance out of her he could remember with clarity.

"I understand more than you know." Hema shifted her healing-staff into her left hand so it was no longer a distraction between them. "I, too, have voices inside—the small, breathless voices of the dead. I hear them awake or asleep—rising from somewhere in the back of my un-sleeping mind."

"The unconscious, psychologists call it," Nolin said. "The part of the mind we're not fully aware of." He noted the shapeless button of a birthmark below her right ear.

"The unconscious, yes." She fit the word to her experience. "I seem fated to suffer their pleas and cries for attention, their curses and lost wishes, their regrets, the abstract tailings of thought … I try to imagine silence but have not heard it in ages—not since early childhood—and never paid attention to it then. Why should I have?"

"I'm sorry," Nolin said, reflecting on his own peripheral haunting.

"I am used to their choric shifts and cycles." Hema held out her hand and, unthinkingly, Nolin took it. Her touch opened up a faint, pro-tean sound verging on the human in its oscillations. The susurrus grew louder and more insistent until it crested through him like a wave.

"It is a constant reminder," Hema said, smiling sadly.

"A reminder?" Nolin asked, still holding her hand. It pulsed with a generous warmth.

"These voices—they are existence itself." She flushed under his gaze. "And also, a persistent reminder that death—Anubis—awaits. When I meet the Golden Jackal, I expect the voices will finally quit me."

"Perhaps," Nolin sighed, daring himself to go on, "we'll have a chance to help each other." He saw in Hema's personal tragedy the ruinous flaws of ancient Egyptian culture in general. They inverted the right order of things, he thought, giving precedence to death and the spirit over life and the intellect. In contrast to the ancient Greeks, they made monuments of tombs rather than temples or theaters. Their priesthood imposed strict limits on citizenship, leaving personal hap-piness for the afterlife; whereas the Hellenic Greeks, honoring reason, spurned priestly ultimatums and considered happiness 'the exercise of vital powers, along lines of excellence, in a life affording them scope.' This idea and its implication that Man was, in essence, a reasoning animal, had sustained Nolin through some of his darkest days. Whenever he grew susceptible to daimonic whispers of 'what if,' he recalled the anonymous phrase. It would gladden his heart to share it with Hema.

Gapti barked and Hema jerked her hand away. "We near the threshold to the sacred chamber. You see the radiance of the *Ptahkit'b*?" A shaft of ethereal light cut across the corridor ahead. She motioned for Babette and Katsuo to gather round. "I will take you before the Greatest of Seers, the Wer-Mauu. His visage may be fearsome, covered as he is in metal skin, but you can depend on his wisdom. Know also: your thoughts may be traced like butterflies in flight." She drew them on, slower than before and silent.

Each step forward put increasing pressure on Nolin's heart. His secret had long ago taken a body—a so-called shadow self. As a child, he'd taken it to bed with him every night, fearing the *ríastrad* or warp-spasm that would unleash it on the outer world. He could feel it now, heavy and dumb, straining against the breakable cage of his ribs. Babette looked at him, concerned, but he dismissed her unspoken question with a shake of his head. He needed to gather himself, remember his training in self-control, keep the monster at bay. You have power over your mind, not outside events, he told himself. *Realize this and you will find strength.*

They followed Hema through an archway manned by stern baboon-soldiers and into a catacomb worthy of the gods in dimension and design. Even after the labyrinthine netherspace that had come before, Nolin could scarce believe the scale of it. A countless array of anthropoid coffins studded the circular chamber's pale stone walls. The painted coffins bore identical embellishments: gilded faces and bands of gold over a base of green—a color symbolic of Osiris and resurrection. The massive walls had no discernable hard surface peak; instead, they rose up and up to vanish in a hazy photo-negative of the Milky Way. The source of the starry projection was the chamber's focal point: a golden plate on a squat, jagged plinth of Parmatmar crystal. The canted plate (or book as Nolin assumed), emitted a mesmeric light. Vague strands of shadow twisted within its beams like infusoria or animalcules.

The crystalline plinth was encircled by a ring of robed, mummified bodies hunched in the lotus position. They were shriveled, gray like aged garden statues. Katsuo pointed demurely to the bronze base of the plinth—a circle with a straight tangent to it. "Shape is shen ring. Mean eternal protect." Despite his whispering, the words ricocheted from unseen angles to return in a distorted tongue. Katsuo apologized with his eyes.

Hema brought the group to a halt about ten meters from the plinth. She knelt, head bowed over interlaced fingers. Nolin signaled his companions to do the same. "My masters, the Duah-teh," Hema said, indicating the galactic vista above. "They have become like the stars themselves in the drowned body of Osiris. Their psychic wall is all that prevents the *Ptahkit'b* from corrupting Herakleion to its essence."

We defend the rightness of things—Ma'at. The voice came from everywhere and nowhere.

The stone floor tremored once, twice, then in a more or less steady rhythm. Babette put a hand on her holstered weapon. Given the ambient power in the room, Nolin signed for her to belay drawing it. A mechanical giant emerged from behind the plinth. Or more accurately, a withered Egyptian encased in a three-meter tall exo-suit. The reinforced armature was broad and massy with multiple points of articulation. Nolin figured its weight at a minimum of twenty metric tons or about two and a half times the weight of an African bush elephant. Movements were slaved to those of the operator. The legs twitched periodically at the knees, indicating loose bearings or a faulty actuating motor. Sections of the suit had lost their original shielding. The exposed mechanisms looked dull and weathered. When the apparatus came to a noisy halt, Nolin saw engine sludge on the chassis' counterbalance.

Only the operator's head and skeletal arms were visible. A roll cage adorned in gilded wings concealed the rest of him. He was crowned in the tri-cone headdress of Osiris. Below it, three metal spindles protruded from his forehead. Whitespace energy arced from tip to tip. His eyes were poor slits, altogether blank, and the rest of his face was a fierce mask of puckered flesh. Blind and all-seeing, Nolin thought.

"Praise to you, Wer-Mauu, the Greatest of Seers and Governor of the Balance," Hema said in the giant's shadow. "You are the master spirit in my body."

Fitful motors lifted the exo-suit's ponderous metal arms in a gesture of deterrence or protection. One arm ended in a vise-like grip; the other in a large-barreled weapon. The Wer-Mauu spoke again inside their heads: *Long have we watched the dwindling horizon for your arrival. It is a pity you come so late. Herakleion has long passed its zenith. Our greatest monuments and inventions are become as dust. The light of Ra wanes and the earth rebels. You see us now a broken and ossified people—the last shadows against the corrupting radiance.*

"You mean the *Ptahkit'b*?" Nolin asked. "Hema has given us hints but what is it in essence?" The artifact looked to be a singular marvel. Not even the Mimirodat, he suspected, could match its extradimensional power. He could sense its disorienting radiation insinuating itself.

It is a relic from the gods, whether weapon or learning tool or something else, we know not. It consists of a single leaf of reality—one page that contains every history, past or future, real or imagined, in every variation. The Ptahkit'b *is the divine cosmos itself.*

Nolin thought of the book as a manifestation of Plato's five solids from *Timaeus*. In that dialogue, Plato posits the universe is comprised of a handful of geometric shapes out of which all others are derived. He pairs four of the shapes with the terrestrial elements of old (earth, air, fire and water) and the fifth with heaven to balance his schema. His particular mapping of geometrical ideals to the physical universe is clearly wrong but Nolin believed the underlying idea was right. In seeking the mysterious laws of the subatomic realm, he knew many physicists had turned, like Plato, to symmetry as their guide.

We opened the book in ignorance and, to our everlasting horror, it has consumed us and everything we have ever known or loved. In resisting it, we have lost everything of value—generations on generations—and for what, you may ask? To preserve the rightness of things.

To show he was unafraid, Nolin met the Wer-Mauu's vacant eyes. "I'm sorry. I'm not familiar with that phrase."

It is our governing principle. It comes from sacred texts like The Book of Coming Forth by Day. *We refer to it as* Ma'at. *In ancient days, it was a physical concept. You would call it straightness or levelness as suggested by its wedge-shaped glyph. When our wisdom was in its fullness,* Ma'at *became a principle of moral fitness, meaning truth, justice, the rightness of things. To live into the promise of* Ma'at *is to live in harmony with the ordered whole.*

"A matter a million times true," Hema intoned.

It can also mean the 'knowledge of true being.' Some especially sensitive to its radiance dared touch it and lo became as Thoth in their understanding. I am the last of these chosen beings, active in the world only through half-remembered artifacts like this machine. Having trapped the book in a moment stretched taut between past and future, we curtail its worst effects. But now our powers flicker and fade and its corruption proceeds apace…

"What will happen when your psychic defenses fail?" Nolin asked.

The seal on Herakleion will burst from within and the corruption will find new purchase upworld. You see? We have damned ourselves for your sake, for Ma'at.

Nolin flashed on the implications: a smashed and barren Earth as if an ancient sea had receded into nothingness and left behind a desolate globe, its lifeforms trapped in dusty sediment or fossilized instantly on exposure to a poisonous atmosphere. The horrific scope of the vision made Nolin sick at heart.

"What about the Nebwa?" Babette asked. "From what I understand, they believe the book means liberty and a chance at paradise."

The Wer-Mauu answered in a 'voice' as harsh as a shrike's. *Liberty? If by liberty you mean anarchy without end then yes. Their thinking is untrustworthy, distorted as it is by the unprotected wilds of Herakleion. It was not so long ago they made a ritual of eating their first-born to supplement their psychic reserves. Thankfully, their kind is near-gone and you—Lan-cer, the Blade of Change—will deliver them unto Anubis for final judgment.*

"I'll do what I can, of course, to protect the upworld." Nolin recalled his portrayal in the mural as he added, "But on my own terms." He'd long dreaded the notion of being a figure of destiny. The very term seemed an unreasoning presentiment—a feeling likely arising from his immersion in the heroic epics of ancient Greece. In Homer, destiny

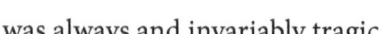

was always and invariably tragic.

I—we—sense resistance. Why turn away from your true strength? It comes with a face out of our own pantheon. Come, show us the visage foreseen by Osiris.

Nolin's chest hitched and he stiffened against the feared warp-spasm. He lived in the panting of his breast, eyes shut and teeth gritted, his languid strength concentrated in preserving his quivering reason. No, no, please, not here, he begged. He felt his daimon blood pooling to the center of his gravity.

Gapti drew his sickle-sword and interposed himself between Nolin and a dismayed Hema. The baboon yawned wide, revealing his barbed canines.

"Lancer? Lancer, what is it?" Babette asked. "Are you under attack?" The insult of scars along her throat colored up.

She started for his side but he waved her off, fighting a bestial snarl. His chest seethed with icy heat. He struggled to recite one of his calming mantras; instead, he seized on an old folktale about a boy with a fox in his belly, how the animal had chewed its way free...

There: we have your soul in hand. Resign yourself to our collective fate.

Nolin caught Hema's eye and she drew away, chin trembling, a brief sympathetic brightness in the shadowy depths of his own thinking. She alone knew the nature of his struggle and his undying shame. The daimon blood thundered through his veins and up the thrust of his jugular to the neural fringe beyond. Panicky gibberish overrode his intellect: *Like a man invested remote... where monsters do live and regions on old maps discrete unto himself... antecedent to the known world...* His fingers contracted into fists made heavy. He bellowed through his teeth, convulsing into an involuntary bow. Confused shouts and gunfire dimly penetrated the blood-noise in his head. Through misted eyes, he saw Katsuo rush the Wer-Mauu, firing at all risk.

Hold, miscreants! The Wer-Mauu's command shook the upworlders to the seat of their being.

The force of it hurled Katsuo backwards into the air. Despite the pain, Nolin lurched upright to snag his elbow. Flailing, Katsuo twisted out of his grasp to sprawl across the stone, bruised but conscious. Babette gave a yelp and dropped her Luger as if it had scalded her.

A crippling psychic blast returned Nolin to hands and knees—the Wer-Mauu reinforced by others of his priesthood. Nolin strained against a slew of unreason: *Blood legatees…alchemically out of hail…concocted with a plague…*It was no use in his spent condition. He was slipping into a berserker delirium one vague and wayward thought at a time. *Laying there grinning in the east…brother sun a rising mouth…*His heated skin began to harden over, his brow thicken.

You are as brazen as the Bird-Fly or mantis in attacking creatures larger than yourself. But we assure you: there is no Fly of Valor for defying us.

The whitespace energy ringing the Wer-Mauu's head flared into a diamond-shaped star and his pupil-less eyes became the entirety of Nolin's sight—an infinite and inescapable void. Nolin grabbed at empty air, stupefied, while the last of his human ideals evaporated. He got to his feet a new creature, the Judge Foretold, red-eyed and great-horned, with nothing under his skin but boiling blood. Amid subdued cries of grief and despair, he announced in a brute growl: "I am that I am." This unpitying self was all—this torment, this now, this forever …

Seshtah Weben, the Mysterious Overflow

"See—the city," Nicandra said. At her touch, the ground bubbled like volcanic mud and spilled upwards, shaping itself into a rough approximation of the Duah-teh district. The other Nebwa murmured appreciatively.

Paul dipped his shoulder, allowing Dixie and Prince J to view the facsimile. "Fascinating," he murmured. The city spread outward like a splatter of paint. A film of moisture on his glasses dimmed his eyes. "And where's the temple?"

"Here. The route is defended by the *hequa* of its priests." Nicandra molded the air with her hands, causing the mud to adopt the contours of the temple. "Wherever they hold territory, they have set their living-dead minds to hold back the waters of the Unworldly River." Her fingers teased out the ruins around the stronghold. She'd proposed a two-pronged strategy for securing the *Ptahkit'b* which involved a concentrated assault on the city's outskirts and a concurrent raid on its central temple. The first offensive, generaled by Nicandra herself, would serve as a distraction while Paul and the others seized the book.

Two unusual items figured prominently in the stealth attack. One was a repurposed relic for safely transporting the *Ptahkit'b*. For this, Nicandra led them from the grounds just outside her shelter to a clay funerary cone near the pond. A pair of servile baboon-things rolled the hollow cone from its base.

"We gonna play three card monte?" Dixie asked, leaning against a gnarled tree root.

Hidden beneath the cone was a large chipped metal disc about a half-meter in diameter and a hand's width thick. Paul marveled at the advanced materials. More support for his theory that Herakleion had been snatched away by alien gods. The center of the convex disc was sheeted in dirty glass. On bended knee, he could discern an accordioned gray-blue mass inside. The lump of organic matter made him both giddy and queasy. He generally preferred the smooth geometries of machines to messy flesh. "This really a slice of brain?" he asked, eager to demonstrate his deductive powers. "At least it looks like thee-uh the cortical folding in our own cerebrum."

Nicandra rewarded him with a smile. "Sampled from the fallen god Osiris. We thieved it from his cut-off head before the Duah-teh decided it was too dangerous to preserve. It is a powerful psychic weapon, though only at close range."

The crowd of Nebwa murmured in awe at the artifact. Paul glanced around, studying the pinched, hungry faces, the determined gazes. There were fewer than two dozen of them, though Nicandra assured him this outpost was only one of many and she'd be mustering their scattered forces for her part of the operation.

"What's it feel like Paul?" Dixie asked. "Not bein' the biggest brain around?"

"I'm sure you could tell me."

"So what are we using it for?" Prince J asked Nicandra, quick to prevent an argument. "You said we could transport the book in this—what? Underneath? And it's a weapon?"

"The *Ptahkit'b* infuses everything with its psychic energy," Nicandra said. "That is why the land, our animals, even the serpent Apep are susceptible to directed thought. Only the brain of a god can possibly survive it unchanged." Her gestures were precise and supple as if she were enacting hand magick. She always returned to a position with her hands at chest level, palms out and elbows pressed to her sides. It suggested an attitude of openness to the world, or perhaps, a regal sense of ownership. "If you fail to acquire the *Ptahkit'b*, this relic can still be of use. Break the center with a sword or axe and its death-throes will produce a kind of mental static, depriving any Duah-teh in the area of their powers and disrupting their protections around the book. There is no telling how long the effect will last but their abrupt mental silence will alert me to your plight."

At first, Paul was inclined to doubt the disc's utility as a weapon. Nicandra's claims reminded him of the ridiculous healing powers attributed to martyrs' bones in the high middle ages. How could a fragment of brain matter retain any substantial energy, mental or otherwise? Then again, Herakleion seemed to operate on baffling dream logic. Perhaps the relic's capacities were just another example of its preternatural laws.

Prince J lifted the relic to inspect its underside, exposing a tangle of broken cables. "So where do you place the book?"

"Waitaminute," Dixie said. "Since when did the tribes a Egypt pray on machines?"

"Hey, don't look at me just cause I'm black." Prince J brushed the cables aside to reveal a large metal clip like a hair pin. "Oh," he said to Nicandra. "We slip it in here?"

"Quickly," she said. "Then knot those ropes around it. For traveling, we can strap it to your back."

Dixie stepped forward, fixed on Joey. "I should be the one to take it. You're the sharpshooter a the bunch. Can't have you weighed down 'n' off-balance."

Nicandra put a gentle hand on his arm. "You must share the burden. Sustained contact will put you into a binding and continuous dream."

"Couldn't have that—less I get to pick the fantasy."

"Let me guess," Paul said. "The best of Plato's *Akademia*?"

"Good God, Shimmy, get your mind outta the libery."

Ignoring this exchange, Nicandra guided them around a stand of mangroves to an area of the pond where several changelings were fishing. They plied the rainbow-tinged shallows with woven dragnets and weir-baskets. The baboon-thing having the greatest success had a prehensile tail ending in large fingers arranged like the ribs on a folding fan. At a look from Nicandra, the changeling waded to shore and presented her with its netted catch—a smack of translucent jellies. The priestess plucked a specimen from the net by its clutch of thin dorsal antennae. "This is the second item you need for your task," she said. "A *quandyl*."

Dixie dismissed it with a gesture. "Sorry, ma'am. Still full from supper." He'd choked down the honorary meal of sour greens, tough, spit-roasted bullock and tasteless flat bread by washing it down with generous amounts of beer. Paul suspected he was a mite tipsy.

"*Quandyl* is not for eating." Nicandra motioned for the changeling to withdraw. "It will shroud you against the Duah-teh's *hequa*, rendering you invisible to their mind-sweeps."

"You mean like a, uh, good luck charm?" Dixie asked. "We jus slip one in our pocket or something?" Then, in an aside to Prince J, he muttered, "This would be a jolt for Kei, huh?"

Prince J inclined his head while lighting a cigarette.

The *quandyl* looked to Paul like an oversized salp or sea squirt. Its gelatinous body was about the size of a hat box. He could make out a single, free-floating eye and the outlines of a few organs, notably, a cleft brain and a slender nerve cord.

Nicandra waved Dixie closer. "Now, turn around."

He followed her instruction, shoulders twitching. "This ain't some kinda prank is it? I'm tellin you now: my trousers are tight belted."

"Do not panic, my upworld friend." Nicandra deposited the jelly on Dixie's head and the creature instantly ballooned to cover it, leaving his ears free but running over his eyes to the crest of his nose.

"Whoa, whoa, whoa." Dixie broke into a nervous jig, hands poised to rip the *quandyl* away. "I'm blind here, blind."

Some of the observing Nebwa pointed and jeered.

Paul gave a playful wave. "If it knew you better, it would've covered your mouth too."

"Capering around like he's got the jim-jams," Prince J said.

"Relax," Nicandra cooed. "Relax and the *quandyl* will find its center."

With an exasperated sigh, Dixie brought his agitations under control. The jelly swelled around his eyes, thinning its outer membrane into a series of irregular bulges. Dixie's breathing slowed. "Everything's a shadow more or less, but hey, least I can see now."

Nicandra said, "*Quandyl* are too weak to hide the psychic imprint of sorcerers like me and too strong for the changelings. But they should suit you upworlders."

"Uh," Dixie said, "I don't mean to throw cold water on this plan—I mean, I preciate havin a plan that ain't just rushin into some death-trap—but we can get these things off, right? Some of us have ladies to impress."

"Who knows?" Prince J said. "Maybe you'll be the head monkey in Paris who sets the fashion for the rest of us."

"It will revert to its former state on exposure to sacred crystal," Nicandra said.

"Parmatmar crystal? Like thee-uh living altar?" Paul surmised the Parmatmar crystal somehow destabilized the *quandyl*'s vital structure. He knew the crystal had disproportionate effects on entities with innate dreamtime powers, either constraining or intensifying their abilities, and hoped one day to discover how to manipulate the crystal to neutralize black magick. So far, his experiments had yielded only frustration and a few embarrassing time-space displacements. Most recently, he'd instantiated a two-second time loop. He was lucky the déjà vu effect had exhausted itself after three hours or so of real time.

"I have the crystal and the Duah-teh also. The *Ptahkit'b* rests on it and the priesthood's chief servant, Hema, has a healing-staff with an inset shard. She was the one who chased the spy-bird and prevented your friends from making reply. I encourage you to take the staff as a spoil of war." There was an uncharacteristic rancor in her voice. She crossed her arms and hitched herself up to her full height.

Dixie pointed to the *quandyl* nestled on his head. "This why you can't see our friends no more? They wearin these?"

"Possibly. But it is more likely they have been moved to an inner stronghold where my powers cannot reach. I have had only one mental impression since the bird returned …" Nicandra's solid, handsome face contracted in disgust. "The one you call Lan-cer. I failed to recognize him until that psychic flash. I know him as the Judge Foretold."

"I don't understand," Paul said. "How would you know him?"

"He was prophesied to become the daimon servitor of the Duah-teh. The energy required to reveal him stormed over Herakleion, giving me a dreadful glimpse. They will puppeteer him into battle against us and our own daimon—just as they once imposed themselves on every defiant spirit."

"They turned Lancer into a daimon?" The last word was almost a croak.

"No, there was no turning." Nicandra hugged her spare shoulders. "He is—and always was—a daimon. He merely wore the face of a man."

A dumb anguish laid hold of Paul. He squinted past Prince J, unseeing. His pulse marked the long seconds. How could it be true? He'd loved Nolin like a brother; more so, in fact, for being freely chosen. He'd trailed Nolin into war out of sheer fellow feeling. And in co-founding Integrand General, he'd pledged his strength and his life to Nolin, if need be, straight to the black end. In return, his 'brother' had deceived him, pretending to virtue, and gained early fame and public plaudits for it, all the while secretly introducing a grave evil to the team … The fact of Nolin's betrayal checked his compulsion to excuse and explain at every turn. God, blind me, Paul thought. How he abused my faith!

Prince J took a meditative drag on his cigarette, his face clouded by pain. Dixie chewed the inside of his cheek. They were waiting for Paul to say something, to provide relief or pronounce judgment. He faced the terraced stream and the wan, indifferent sky. In the full scope of Creation, this sting of life was nothing but ah, Christ in the here and now … He tightened his throat against a rising bitterness. He was at a complete and utter loss. He'd been made to confront the inconceivable. It was as if history itself was against him and yet, based on what little he knew and could guess, he had to decide: Would they try to rescue and recover Nolin or kill him as a mercy?

The Theater of Montu, Lord of Thebes

In the close quarters of the arena's second-story balcony, Hema smarted under the venerable Wer-Mauu's reproofs: *You are too much involved with these upworlders. Reserve your mercy for Herakleion and
the world beyond. Weighty is the word of Osiris. Not even the gods can
save everyone. Individual lives—they are as insignificant grains on the
scales. What matters is preserving the balance.* The Wer-Mauu angled
his head in the direction of the stage. The Lancer-daimon emerged
from the arched entry and lumbered across the sanded stone. He was
attired in a close-fitting battle crown and girdled loincloth. A coterie of
robed priests ringing the stage prepared to test their control over him.

Hema suffered in protective silence, afraid of accidentally betraying
the depth of her disaffection. She could barely bring herself to look on
the Judge Foretold. The figure from the mural had assumed a different
and horrific meaning. The creature before her was no willing savior. It
was a debased and abused soul, as much of an abomination as the *ian
bwt*. Even the epithet, the Judge Foretold, seemed a gross misnomer
now. The judge in this instance seemed the unthinking world, not the
man; no, the man was little more than an animal dumb enough to believe in the efficacy of his own will. She would gladly sacrifice herself
for an abiding and immutable Herakleion, but not others—not like
this—and especially not him . . .

The Wer-Mauu resumed his even-toned harangue: *Remember your
moral test in the Vault of Maahes. It showed you a decider on feeling
more than sense, therefore, this*—he tapped the crystal end of her staff
with a metal finger—*more of a healing tool than a weapon. Trust in our
superior wisdom. We are beholden to the cosmos and measure things
in their totality. Our lives—all lives—are dispensable. Persuade the upworlders to aid Horemakhet in safeguarding the book in my absence or
dispatch them.*

Five jackal-things bounded into the arena, howling and slavering.
They had been dogs, once, Hema knew, street-curs deformed by the
Ptahkit'b. Their corruptions ranged from spiked, multi-thonged tails

to sabre-toothed maws. The blood daimon set his feet and gave a cry of rage. The priests continuously repressed any inkling of human consciousness, leaving him the mind of a brute. Swollen with black-veined muscle, he thwacked his fists against his curved horns in anticipation.

Hema forced herself to radiate sincerity and obedience. "As always, Wer-Mauu, you are the master spirit in my body." She bowed, anxious to depart. The priest had already turned his attentions to the arena.

The first of the jackal-things to reach the Lancer-daimon leapt for his throat, claws scrabbling. The daimon snatched the creature in the air by a forward leaning bone plate and crushed its throat with an elbow strike. The remaining pack members snarled around him. Fangs and claws and mutated tails tore at his tough grayish hide. He twisted and parried to avoid the worst blows, catching a barbed tail before it caught on his back. The mutates thrashed his chest and forearms, drawing rivulets of blood. He wrenched a pug-nosed jackal-thing from its feet and slammed it against a quill-covered monstrosity, maiming both.

The spectacle sickened and shamed Hema. Her private qualms had amounted to nothing. In the end, she'd helped to corrupt Nolin's right-meaning heart. No matter the prophesied blessings, how could that be justified? The Wer-Mauu's calculating philosophy seemed to run counter to the very principle the Duah-teh professed to uphold. Ma'at meant more than observing a divine order with clear and direct mandates. It meant giving that divine order a human dimension. Perhaps the constant spectre of earthly misery had skewed her thinking. But she regarded authentic, self-aware feelings as the surest guide to rightness. If, as the Duah-teh insisted, Ma'at exceeded simple human understanding—even the capacities of language—then what else could she rely on? Not the words of priests.

Seshtah Weben, the Mysterious Overflow

The ground deformed and vented bursts of alabaster dust as Nicandra unearthed her daimon servitor, Ammit. The giant was enclosed in an ancient dream harness—a metal cocoon some thirty meters long. The segmented harness was filled with a viscous preserving fluid. Energizing studs supplied heat and bubbling oxygen to the daimon while it dreamed. Nicandra kept Ammit harnessed and buried between its assigned labors to prevent the creature's unique mental signature from alerting the Duah-teh to the location of her wasteland outpost. She also used the oblong tank to slave the daimon to her will. A capsule at the head of the artifact facilitated the transmission of thoughts via a helmet nested in cables and wires. With the aid of the helmet, she'd imprinted the daimon with a selfless love for her. This fabricated emotion ensured the daimon's obedience. She speculated that Osiris or one of his fellow gods had used the device in a similar fashion to convert unbelievers.

She rose from her lotus position in the dirt and made her way to the capsule, increasingly confident this would be the last time she'd have a need for it. Though the temporal stasis imposed by the Duah-teh made it impossible to know the date according to the old Sothic calendar, the confluence of events, starting with the arrival of the upworlders, suggested an imminent change of cycles. Releasing the *Ptahkit'b* would be the final catalyzing act.

The bulbous imprinting helmet awaited her. She pulled it over her head and eyes. An instant pinprick sensation along her scalp confirmed the helmet was in working order. Ammit was one of the few survivors of the divine war. She considered the daimon a natural product of the cycle of becoming and a potential model for life in the world-to-come. Reality, she thought, was becoming—a sometimes painful process of realizing the world-soul. To her mind, the *Ptahkit'b* was the world-soul made manifest. It was only to be expected that it should encounter resistance from common matter and, in overcoming that resistance, seek new forms to contain its essence. Hence, the rise of what the Duah-teh referred to derisively as the *ian bwt* or abominations. Once the book's creative energy was fully discharged, she believed it would express itself by peopling the world with new gods not unlike the daimon. Just as one of the primordial deities, Atum, later joined with Ra to become Atum-Ra. Or how Osiris was destroyed by Set then resurrected by his son, Horus, as lord of the underworld.

Nicandra faulted the Duah-teh for their myopic focus on the book's material effects. The focus on becoming as a material process locked them into trying to reconstitute the world-soul theoretically from observation, forcing it into inadequate and self-defeating categories. With their doctrinal outlook, the Duah-teh were simply incapable of grasping the continuity within the process of becoming. The priests were too busy breaking the process into a series of static and unchangeable states, reducing it to various material elements that, by their very nature, denied the possibility of the novel and unforeseen. She had no such limitations. She was a visionary blessed with cosmic scope and an artifact—the soulfire orb—integral to making it a reality.

The daimon's consciousness registered as a font of desire—for her and more so, for struggle and blood on her behalf. She punched the harness cover release. The preserving fluid began to drain automatically into the tank's tail-end reservoirs. She prepared to coax the creature out of its recycled dreams. Praise to Osiris, son of Nut for this day! The Nebwa's long-sought future was within sight. *Swadjet* or psychogenesis would reach its natural culmination. Becoming would give way to being. She'd light up the daimon's heart; the *Ptahkit'b* would light up the world; and the whole of Creation would burn—becoming an ash-heap cocoon—so the people could rise again, this time as gods themselves.

Chapter 9

Warbound

The Temple of Osiris, Lord of the Underworld

The severity of the spiral staircase prompted Katsuo to put a hand to the unfinished wall for balance. "You need crooked legs for this stair."

Babette glided down the steps without hesitation, crowding Hema then retreating at Gapti's disapproving squint. She was anxious for the uncertainties hanging over them to be resolved. "Down to the dungeon, eh?" Glancing back at Katsuo she asked, "Did the Egyptians have dungeons?"

"As I said, I am offering my help." Hema led them deep into the airy darkness under the sacred chamber. The attendant gleams from her staff disclosed a narrowing, rough-hewn passage. "War is on the horizon. The Judge Foretold will be in the vanguard. You must be properly armed to help him defend the *Ptahkit'b*."

"You're going to give us our guns back? My explosives?" Babette had vowed bloody revenge against the Wer-Mauu.

"My masters confiscated them. We go to the Vault of Maahes."

"And again, I have to ask: why should we trust you?" Babette's chin jutted forward, showing up her scars. "Sounds like you're just conscripting us into your army."

Hema spun around and thrust her gossamer light toward Babette. "Make no mistake: if the Nebwa capture the *Ptahkit'b*, Herakleion, the upworld, everything, will devolve to livid stone." A flustered lick of her lips marked a reflective turn. "We must defend it first then free Lancer."

The force of these words gave Babette pause. "So long as we get to that …" She'd refused to believe Hema's explanation for Lancer's metamorphosis, convinced the Duah-teh were wholly at fault. The alternative—the notion he harbored a secret wickedness—was too much for her to contemplate.

Katsuo, however, accepted Lancer's double nature as a symptom of the age. He chalked it up to spiritual impurities accumulated in the course of their missions and nothing more. The transformation was disturbing only because it seemed to prefigure misfortune for the team. Evil, he believed, was part of divine nature. Every era progressed from good to evil and back again. The corruption of the good—even stalwart examples like Lancer—was inescapable. What determined your character on earth and beyond was how you responded to it. Until he could discover the appropriate cleansing ritual, Katsuo thought fighting back in the pure, boyish spirit of adventure with which Lancer had founded Integrand General was the best response.

"Is it bad spirit, like disease?" he asked Hema. "Shinto—we believe *tsumi* pollution, sickness. Break link to spirit world. Is there ritual to, *etto*, clean—cleanse?"

"I do not know."

Babette reasserted herself: "But you can change him back, yes? Make him human again?"

"That much seems possible, divorced from the Duah-teh's influence." Hema slowed as she reached the bottommost step. Her staff cast soft, drifting shadows.

The stairway delivered them into a chamber walled in cryptic machinery. Various geometrical recesses and projections gave it the disorienting quality of a dusted-over kaleidoscope. Katsuo could make out distinctly mechanical shapes along the walls—couplings, cables, roller bearings, a possible herringbone gear.

Babette pointed out a shattered skeleton in a recessed portion of the vault. The fossilized bones were entangled in a vine-like wire. "Looks like a dungeon to me."

"No one has visited this place in … I do not know how long." Hema searched a series of alcoves. "The *Ptahkit'b*'s corruptions put an end to childbirth. That is why the Duah-teh expended precious energy to bring me from upworld. They hoped for a great spiritual warrior. But I am a disappointment …"

Gapti sprung onto a low-level projection then scaled from one alcove to another, pawing out the contents. He discarded a crystalline knife and a device reminiscent of a vice grip clamp.

"How many warrior you have?" Katsuo asked.

"People? Including you? Sixty and eight." Hema took a few tentative steps in his direction. "The rest are Duah-teh priests or baboon-soldiers. The Nebwa are even fewer in number. But they have Ammit, the Devourer."

A bark from Gapti drew their attention. He stood on the edge of a metal projection, eyes bright, a falcon-headed mace in his fist.

"Much thanks, old friend," Hema said.

"That the daimon you say Lancer fight—Ammit?" Katsuo thought it curious how Herakleion mirrored key aspects of the Egyptian underworld or Duat. From the back of the droner, the landscape even resembled a gnarled, chalk-desert version of it: a broad river valley bordered by opposing mountain ranges. The Duah-teh's principal god was Osiris, who arbitrated the heart weighing ceremony that determined the fates of the dead. Ammit, a.k.a., the Devourer, played a central role in the same ceremony. The crocodile-headed beast condemned the unworthy to non-existence by gobbling up their tainted hearts. Katsuo wondered if the Duah-teh or some other dreamtime-sensitive force had at one time exploited the *Ptahkit'b*'s energies to confer a kind of mythical symmetry on Herakleion. Perhaps the original purpose of the pocket dimension was to serve as a staging ground for some cataclysmic judgment—the heart weighing ceremony writ large.

Gapti dropped to the ground and presented Hema with his find. The one meter length of black metal ended in a pear-shaped head with five radiating flanges. On each flange, the winged sun symbol associated with royalty and power stood out in high relief. Hema worked three notched rings to remove the hollow head. "This is the start of a new weapon for Lancer. Though it requires I dismantle my own."

"Look," Babette said, eyes downcast in concentration, "I still don't know if we should trust you, but...*Eh bien.*" She gave Katsuo a hesitant look then clenched her teeth, decided. "We got a message from our friends among the Nebwa—carried by that honker bird. They may have been fooled into helping your foes. Is there some way we can communicate with them? I don't want to see them on the other end of my spear or whatever we're going to get here. And they need to know about Lancer."

Hema swallowed her irritation on learning of this secret contact. "I can try to contact them through the Unworldly River. Or, given your doubts about me, you can." She jerked her head toward the cut-granite stairway. "There is an ancient device. It was used in dream-sharing rituals by those without an inborn talent for the Unworldly River."

"Okay," Babette said as if trying to convince herself. The mystico-esoteric aspects of Integrand General's explorations had always unnerved her. Like Dixie, she was much more comfortable with straight out monster hunting. "Sure, I'll try it."

"First, however, we should see to your weapons." She deposited the mace parts in Gapti's hands and approached a dense hexagonal stele depending from the ceiling. The pyramidal mass hung about two meters above the stone flooring. Lion-headed busts ornamented each of its facets. Based on the metal pylons and ancillary cabling running through the core of the stele, Katsuo surmised it was a machine with a sculpted façade.

Hema bowed in prayer a short distance from the stele. The outward-facing panels flickered with decorative lights. "O Maahes, Lord of the Massacre, I have come to you pure of heart." The interlaced veins of light steadied. "Let these upworlders appear in your presence at the altar of self-truth and grant them arms in accordance with their natures."

Homage to you, servant of the Duah-teh. The disembodied voice was a sonic blur Katsuo struggled to parse. *Pleased I am for the god Osiris to unfasten the swathings that have been over my mouth these long ages. Now, may the creator-god Ptah grant me the power to bestow my gifts. Step forward, upworlder.*

Hema spoke to Katsuo and Babette in confidential tones. "There is nothing to fear if you are honest with yourself. It is only questions. Answer according to how you would act now—this moment—not how you would like to *think* you would act. Any gap between what you say and what is in your heart of hearts will mean ... punishment. Answer true and Maahes will determine the weapon most befitting your soul."

"Where do we go?" Katsuo agreed that self-knowledge was essential to the warrior; otherwise, you were a simple tool.

"Step under the relic. In the center, you will find a space—a pool of light. Put your head through it. That is the mouth of the lion-headed Maahes."

"Wait." Babette put a restraining hand on Katsuo. "What sort of punishment?"

Hema traced twin daggers in the air. "Are there no lions upworld?"

Katsuo returned Babette's touch with a soldierly squeeze that could mean either thanks or good-bye. He couldn't dream of valor but refuse to act when challenged. "I will go." He ducked under the block of machinery. Only a few meters of snaked together cables separated him from the shimmery base of the testing chute. His nostrils flared at the pungent aroma of ozone. He made his way to the particolored plasma field and crouched to inspect it before committing himself. The rippling of saturated color sparked and crackled. An active emptiness troubled his insides. This is the life I've chosen, he told himself. Daydreamed glories had drawn him away from the impoverished village of his youth and the graves of his ancestors and into this neo-Egyptian mindtrap. Holding his breath, he stood upright and immersed his upper body in the dappled void. A wrinkled warmth smarted his scalp.

Hail, upworlder.

"Katsuo," he exhaled. "My name is Katsuo, great kami." He used the Shinto term for any eminent spirit, good or evil. Floating bumblebee yellow accents stung his eyes.

Be truthful and live, rewarded, Katsuo.

"Yes, great kami." There was a slight catch in his voice as he found he could no longer feel his legs.

I put you to the question: You lead a small army consisting of warriors from two tribes—a hill tribe and a river tribe. The machine-god's mental rumblings shivered in Katsuo's throat like music. *You belong to neither, an outsider. A hill tribesman in your army is possessed by an evil spirit and kills a member of the river tribe. Freed of the evil spirit by this act, the murderer repents and wants to make amends. The river tribe refuses his apologies and will attack the hill tribe unless he is put to death. But the hill tribe refuses to kill one of its own. The only way for you to avoid absolute war is to kill the murderer yourself. What is your answer?*

The no-win scenario called into question Katsuo's romantic prejudices. He'd joined Lancer confident that they'd always be in the right. But circumstances had made determining what was right a problem in itself. "This about Lancer?"

I cannot say more. Be truthful and live, rewarded.

Katsuo struggled to blame the murderer in this case. Could he really be held accountable for his possession? No, Katsuo had to trust in the possibility of another, better solution—something unforeseen. "Sometimes, I have to believe luck. The key is: ignore odds." If, as Shinto suggested, everything tended toward evil as a natural consequence of living then luck was the only thing separating the innocent from the guilty. "I do not kill him, no. Talk out—hope—another way." The words had their own momentum.

Would your answer be the same even if the outcome was tribal warfare and your own death?

Confirmed in his argument, Katsuo addressed the void with a growing swagger. "Purity, even in small spirit like mine—it mean more than life. It go on to spirit world."

Then your choice is made.

The judgment rolled over Katsuo like a spent storm cloud. He tensed up, flattening his arms against his sides, tongue pressed to the roof of his mouth. Did he pass? Should he withdraw from the testing chute?

The color-flecked void churned into a majestic bleakness shot through with jagged, flickering zips. These irruptive flashes distilled into a small but recognizably human form. Katsuo opened his mouth as if to say something. Could it be...? Yes, unbelievably: *Issun-bōshi*, the One-Inch Boy, complete with magick hammer. *Shinji rarenai!* The mythical figure was outfitted in feudal samurai armor: a late-Heian Period cuirass or *dou*; a helm adorned with water buffalo horns; a faceplate and more—all cast in the same silvery metal. The manikin's name exaggerated his smallness; he was about 15 centimeters (six inches) tall. Suspended in the void, *Issun-bōshi* regarded Katsuo blankly. He lacked pupils and his mouth appeared fixed in a wry smile.

Little warrior, big spirit. Virtually invincible. I took this image from your mind. Is it not pleasing?

"No, I mean, yes, amaze." The manikin matched Katsuo's childhood idea of the legendary hero in exquisite detail. He was so absorbed in examining the cast-metal boy it took him a moment to register the helm on his own head. By touch, it seemed identical in design to *Issun-bōshi*'s.

The helm allows you to see through the little warrior's eyes and he, yours. He shall find you wherever you may be, quicker than a greyhound. Keep him in your thoughts and see...

With a mental twinge, Katsuo saw his looming self as if through a keyhole. The silvery helm gave his head an outsized silhouette. The reverse-perspective amused him. "Like sarsaparilla fizz in brain." He blinked back to his regular POV.

The manikin raised his hammer, pounded the void in mute excitement then jumped onto Katsuo's shoulder.

Katsuo reeled back and grinned. "Now we ready for bad luck."

The Tunnels of Amenthes

Bristling with warped and petrified bones, the tunnels beneath the devastated city struck Dixie as a calcified version of the trenches. He trooped under the weight of the Osiris fragment. The disc was strapped to his back crosswise over his chest. Though it didn't weigh much more than a standard field kit, he wearied under its influence. His limbs had assumed an unnatural heaviness and started to go numb. Periodically, he pressed his fingernails into the palms of his hands to revive the feeling in them.

The beam from Paul's electric torch flashed on a half-clothed arm poking from the sandstone. Dixie strained to keep his eyes on the uneven ground and its ossuarial hazards. Outside of the torch's direct glare, the gelatinous *quandyl* over his eyes only allowed for hints and shadows. Peripheral, floating figures loomed in and out of view—perhaps Duah-teh ghost-spies or searching mental pulses deflected by the *quandyl*. It was as if he were trudging through the phenomenal murk and slipperiness of things. Dixie looked to his boots for an assurance of forward motion and trusted to God for the rest.

A faint rumbling from the gloom ahead prompted Paul to drop his gear bag of guns and explosives. Dixie and Prince J formed on him. "That must be the changeable barrier," Paul said. "Means we're close to thee-uh the entrance."

"Should we wait on the honker?" Prince J asked. The bird, imprinted with their route, was on reconnaissance.

"It'll come back or we'll catch up." Paul made a show of examining Dixie. "We should switch now. You're listing to starboard."

"Nuthin doin." Paul had gone silent and inward since the revelation about Lancer. Dixie feared Paul's predisposition to overthink would make him more susceptible to the artifact. For once, his heedlessness seemed an advantage. "You know me—dumb as a stockfish. I ain't about to give this god-brain here anythin to work on."

"Well, you let me know soon as you start feeling blinkered."

"You…" Dixie lowered his voice, sensitive to Paul's internal plight. "You gonna let us in on your strategy for Lancer afore we storm the place?"

"Sorry." Paul's face slackened as he momentarily withdrew into himself. Then he broke from his self-absorption, shaking his head in answer to a different, unasked question. "I—I still don't know. I have to see him first. I have to know how deep his…sickness runs." His voice thinned from mental effort. "I want—I have to believe he's still the man I knew."

"Won't get no argument here. But this ain't no influenza…" An undulating shape along the wall diverted Dixie's attention for a moment. "I mean, there's gotta be a good reason he wasn't square with us."

Prince J raised his rifle for emphasis. "I think we should take a chance."

"Uh, not prayin reg'lar is takin a chance. This is like offerin the devil your neck." While Dixie loathed the idea of confronting Lancer, when it came to supernatural evil generally, he believed in the necessity of violence. I'm made of fight, he'd say and if push came to shove, he'd do Lancer the honor of his grief. He didn't know for certain if the world was destined for eternal war but he was prepared for the eventuality.

Prince J appealed to Paul: "How bad off can he be? He's still partly human. How does that even work?"

"I don't know," Paul admitted. "Genuine blood daimons—they're giants—four-five meters high. Powers are variable, depending on thee-uh type of conjuring spell. Incredible strength, debilitating auras, shapeshifting—that's common enough. On manifesting, they take on whatever shape thee-uh the spellcaster desires; then, on the hunt, thee-uh stronger ones mimic the victim's worst fears. Long story short, it's thee-uh the kind of bastard that would wear your skin for a scarf." He lapsed into thoughtfulness again then picked up the gear bag and resumed their march. "But as you say, Lancer's human at base..."

"So is that where his strength comes from?" Prince J asked, not looking at Paul but the mercurial barrier coming into view. "Not from all that training growing up, but this?"

Paul let the question expire against the crack and growl of mutating stone. The ropy ground-to-ceiling barrier retracted somewhat then blobbed into an impassable grid which, in turn, morphed into a serpentine tangle. Dixie struggled to turn away from its trancing effects. "'Splains why he's so hot for these supernatural artifacts. Prob'ly hopin for a cure."

"I have to say," Prince J remarked, "after everything we've gone through, I never imagined dying at the hands of a daimon-headed Lancer."

"Don't know if you're lacking readiness or imagination," Paul said.

The torchlight settled on the bloodied carcass of the honker. One mangled wing flapped uselessly against the stone.

"Saved me the trouble," Dixie said.

"Sure you don't want to bag it up?" Prince J secured the rifle across his chest for optimal maneuverability. "Prob'ly makes its own gravy."

"According to Nicandra," Paul said in a duty-voice, "there's a pitchy stretch here then the sentries, though none of her troops made it that far." He rummaged in the gear bag for explosives: five sticks of dynamite and a single grenade. "Needless to say, we should conserve the dynamite where we can, try to negotiate the changes..." This last word gave him pause. "Dixie, you go first and we'll bring you along."

"How do you want to do this?" Prince J asked. "We have just the one lighter."

"You light and throw. I'll hang onto one stick and the grenade." He shouldered the gear bag and looked to Dixie to start them off.

The southerner regarded the gauntlet of writhing stone with trepidation. His awareness pulsed in unison with its confusions, dilating and contracting. A cluster of hanging spheres or lobes filigreed into wild intestinal strands. He waited until the strands began to attenuate then dashed forward, twisting sideways to present the smallest possible profile. The artifact made for an awkward roll. He smashed an ankle on the harsh granite. The cabling burned taut across his chest and stung him under the arms. He sprung into a crouch, anticipating another disordering rupture. Migrant columns arced into his path, collapsed, and arced away to join the walls or ceiling.

The tunnel was a battering sea of stone and earthspray. His head swam with its liquid motions. Prince J shouted at him to move. A dislocating quake sent him backwards. He wobbled on his heels. Paul tackled him one-handed. The torch beam whisked across the turmoil. A pulverizing wave drilled the spot where Dixie had teetered a moment before. One, two piercing explosions shattered the darkness. Pebbled stone pelted the back of his head like hail.

"Up, up," Paul urged, a hand on his collar. But a sickening heave of earth sent him sprawling out of Paul's grasp. He smacked against the honeycombed wall, shielded by the disc, then toppled into an alcove. His hand brushed against something like shrivelled pump leather. Skin, a hand, bony fingers. He shoved away in fright and the fingers closed on his wrist. Slitted, milk-white eyes gleamed. A startled noise escaped him, bringing the torchlight. The sentry greeted the dazzle with a toothless smirk.

"Knife! Got your knife?" he heard Paul ask. Got my pants on, don't I? Dixie thought as if thinking alone were enough. Everything was clamor and frenzy and the arresting pull of an unbidden dream.

The ground at his feet torqued and surged. He flailed free from the withered sentry and a sputter of bullets rocked the skeletal figure on its perch. Was he tripping now or was it the stone beneath? The world seemed to be at a strange remove. Until a muster of rock smashed him on the ear, overturning him. Laying on his stomach, one knee under him, he closed his eyes and tried to will the pain to vanish. The damaged *quandyl* leaked a sticky ichor. His body seemed to shunt and flutter as if on a cruel ocean. He registered the subsequent spate of dynamiting and shooting as a distant furor.

Prince J reached him first. "Believe it...or not," Dixie mumbled, feeling his friend's hand on his, "I'm runnin out...a bad things...to say bout this place…I hate it 'n' I…jus want out." Though the consuming roar and crash of stone had ceased, its aching echo continued. He strained for the quiet fade out.

"Dixie shipshape?" Paul appeared as an indistinct boot.

"Prob'ly," Prince J said. "His head took the impact."

"We should've taken the artifact from him awhile ago." Paul tugged at the cabling.

"You know how he gets…Sometimes, he insists on playin the penny on the tracks."

Dixie had the distinct sense of sinking to his rest. He ground his teeth, inclined to prove he wasn't yet gone. "Ain't gonna…rank on me?"

"Not this time," Paul said, his voice nearly extinct.

"Mus be…in…really…bad shape." He couldn't be certain he'd done more than just move his lips. It felt as if he were subsiding into a watery dark. The hell, he thought. *Blather, burble—won't make a squinch a difference.* He gave in to the downward flow behind his eyes. He was going to get some distance from the world, end the shocks and hurts, to look back, safe, still, just breathing.

Outskirts of Duah-teh District

Attuned to the mental energies of their foes, the Duah-teh homed in on the Nebwa army crossing their district's collapsed southern ramparts. The flying armada constituted the greatest concentration of Duah-teh drafted into battle since the order's fundamental split. Dozens of warrior-priests barrelled toward the opposing scramble, some mounted on mind-controlled monsters, others seated in arcane machines. The Wer-Mauu himself led the offensive from the prow of an aerial trireme. Prophecy and desperation had begotten mad hopes. The priesthood would see its enemies obliterated or the end of Herakleion itself.

A magicked duststorm preceded the Nebwa—a last-ditch attempt to confuse their number and position. The white opaque gusted across the ravelled earth and into the sky. The Wer-Mauu directed his warrior-priests to maintain formation through the violent smother. They parted the torrent of dashed stone and chalk dust with a patient application of mental force. The Lancer-daimon, clutched to a winged worm-monster by ropy tendrils, shielded his eyes with crossed arms. The storm howled around him in a wedge and powdered him in the color of death.

Then the tempest abated and the settling haze delineated the sparse Nebwa troops in silhouette. The enemy formed an irregular front comprised mainly of baboon-things and other, larger and more fearsome abominations. To his left, the Lancer-daimon could make out a wheeled gun emplacement on a twisty avenue; and to his right, a series of smaller weapons spining out from a fallen bridge. The flattened span humped over several blasted structures to tumble out onto a steppe. There—coming up on a rubbled spire—he discerned the faint outline of the mutate servitor Ammit. The Wer-Mauu aimed the Judge Foretold at the Devourer to the exclusion of all else. It was as if the Lancer-daimon had stared into a nowhere like the sun. Everything was reduced to a bleary point around the demigod.

The worm-monster torpedoed in the direction of the Devourer, holding a shepherd's hook shape to keep its passenger upright. The wind filled the Lancer-daimon's eyes with tears. He was a half-blind berserker. Every reasoned impulse degenerated into barbarism. The Duah-teh had exorcised his humanity and supplanted it with the essence of his daimon blood—a desire for power unending. Or, in the absence of such power, annihilation. He was a heroic brute of will and wanton feeling. The rest of the world was a mere backdrop for his appetites and deserving of demolition, a pasteboard scrim on which to impose his will. Life was violent or nothing.

Ammit surged forward on all-fours to meet the attack, bearing neither armor nor weapons, and trailing a polluting mist from its pores. The creature was a mammoth chimera with the head of a crocodile, the upper body of a lion and the hindparts of a hippo. A shaggy mane framed a blunt, brimstone-eyed skull. The creature's fiery gaze worked to dispirit Nolin, forcing him to turn away. He hadn't faced a blood daimon since his fateful transfusion as a young boy. Those penetrating eyes surfaced long-suppressed memories, feelings of dismay and shame, his hated second shadow. No, he thought, not now, no, no ... He couldn't allow even a flicker of doubting self-awareness. In a growing panic, he sought the Wer-Mauu's psychic protection—the surest means of forgetting. His chest quickly swelled again in anger and malign intent.

As he hurtled toward Ammit, renewed in his purpose, the Lancer-daimon drew the copper fighting rod at his waist. The first Duah-teh to clash with the Nebwa strafed them with pineapple-shaped projectiles. Enemy adepts bent the landscape into defensive shields. The earth heaved up and turned back on itself. The projectiles surprised the Nebwa by erupting into blackening swarms of insects. Changelings scrabbled in vain for safety from the lethal, pustulating stings.

The spindly weapons along the bridge hummed to life, spewing electric arcs that combined to ray out like sheet lightning. The charged air prickled the Lancer-daimon's skin. Destructive bolts zigzagged from one Duah-teh to another, tumbling them from their courses. Most recovered mid-fall to resume their original trajectories or ease themselves to the ground; several, however, rendered unconscious, spattered the ruins with their watery blood. Baboon-things charged toward the bodies to loot and eviscerate them.

A barbed shadow whistled down at the Lancer-daimon. He jerked back to evade a deadly talon. The enemy bird shucked a cluster of bulbous eyes from the worm-monster's flanged head. The worm-monster shivered, dipped and lost its hold on the Lancer-daimon, membranous wings twitching only from reflex. A bomb-drop sensation seized him and sick-green blood sluiced over his shoulder as the worm-monster plummeted to earth. The enemy bird pulled out of its stoop and swung around for the coup de grâce. It closed on its flailing prey with razor claws and horned beak. The Lancer-daimon pushed from his dying mount and hammered his fighting rod into the bird's nape. Where, the Lancer-daimon wondered, was the Wer-Maau? Worm-monster, bird and daimon spiraled toward the ground in a confused mass.

Never before had war seemed more terrible, the means of it more deranged, the sky more grim and absolute. The wind screamed in the Lancer-daimon's ears then jolted to a dark stillness. He found himself in Ammit's unbreakable grip, unseeing, before he was cratered against the ground. The impact seemed to force his innards out through his teeth. Ammit towered over him through the cloud of stone dust, crocodilian jaws open in what might have been a smile. *Hail, upworld-brother.* The snarled syllables lingered in the Lancer-daimon's ringing head. *What manner of weak-blooded kin are you?*

"Defiant," the Lancer-daimon spit above the general din and tumult.

Out of mortal ignorance. Ammit hunched its back, indignant. *An avid longing gnaws at my heart—a longing to be the end and meaning of things. You share it in your way. Our common blood, our common instincts and secret knowledge assures me of that. Your priests offer what? A mere delay in the inevitable collapse. Time, however slowed, will undo your labors. So why not give your unreason its proper scope? Join me— your blood-sister—and return this universe to primordial silence.*

The telepathic appeal shook the Lancer-daimon to the nub. Mortal feelings beat about his heart. How often had he agonized over mankind's future-history? Railed in private against the limitations of reason and stoical understanding? But no, even if his doubts were merited, even if Ammit spoke true, he could never give up the possibility of redemption for the human animal; besides, his bestial pride refused the entreaty. Regardless of what vital anguish wracked his soul, he'd never admit weakness to this creature. He braved the demigod's hellish eyes. One way or another, human or daimon, deliverer or no, he would abide. "Your cause be damned."

You first then. With that, the Devourer snapped forward as swiftly as the rough-skinned lion it resembled and the battle was joined in earnest.

Chapter 10
Ecce Daemonium

Temple of Osiris, Lord of the Underworld

The dream sphere reminded Babette of Emmanuel Frémiet's armillary sculpture on the Luxembourg promenade in Paris. It was an oblong arrangement of sculpted metal suspended in air and ringed by fanciful organic shapes. Variously-sized conduits fed into a convoluted cauliflower-like structure at its crown. Hema waved her into the hovering sphere's central seat while Katsuo and Gapti watched. "Take your place there," Hema said, "and I will prepare the machine. We must hurry. The Duah-teh have engaged our foes."

Babette believed Hema's sense of urgency was compounded by personal concerns. She'd detected a secret light in Hema's eyes for Lancer. The attraction was understandable. Hema had grown up in ascetic thraldom; she knew nothing about the larger world and, more specifically, men, outside of myth. What notions she may have formed about the upworld, Babette figured, were likely romantic and absurd. All Hema knew of its inhabitants were a superhuman Irishman, a sanguine Japanese soldier and a French adventurer with a penchant for blowing things up—hardly a representative sample. Who could tell? In her naiveté, the first stirrings of affection might be tantamount to madness.

The dream sphere's seat rotated on its track to allow for easier access. Babette raised her gauntleted right hand before ducking under the outermost ring. The armorer god Maahes had gifted her a chased bronze claw beaded in Parmatmar crystal. "This won't interfere?" According to Maahes, the claw would not only multiply the impact of her punches but also suppress dreamtime magick to some as-yet untested extent. Babette was proud to wield this power and at once ashamed of Maahes' rationale for the weapon. She wondered if Hema had guessed at the god's reasoning.

"It seems unlikely." Hema operated a number of rods and levers at a free-standing console adjacent to the sphere. "Warrior-priests have received similar weapons in the past. They only affected *hequa* manipulated by the living, not machines. This device, ornamented in symbols of natural magick, works in the same fashion as your gauntlet. Instead of your bodily energy, however, it amplifies your dream energy, refracting, focusing or diffracting it according to your degree of mental control."

The machine's framework was warm to Babette's naked touch. She started in surprise then gave Katsuo a sheepish smile before climbing between the interior elements. Katsuo's overlarge helm made him look like a boy soldier. He nodded in encouragement. His newly-acquired sidekick sat on one shoulder, hammer across its lap, kicking its heels.

A piston-like apparatus along the backside of Babette's seat began to hum and a membranous air sac above her blonde bob inflated. The vibratory hum worried her insides. She exhaled slowly and licked her lips. Nolin's transformation, her missing teammates, Hema's sympathetic turn, Maahes and the gauntlet, the tribal war, her imminent foray into the dreamtime—the whirl of recent events was testing her edge control. Not that she'd ever admit this anxiety to anyone. She decried self-pitiers.

Hema put a hand on the mechanism topped by the air sac. "I am going to lower this now." She pulled the mechanism even with Babette's face. The main section was made up of a curved metal plate edged in sets of dials. Thin, iridescent etchings marked the inside of the black metal. "Close your eyes and place your forehead against the collecting shield."

With a last nervous exhalation, Babette followed Hema's instructions. Her bangs perked at the static electricity radiated by the plate. "What now?"

"Picture your friend and speak to him in your mind as you would in words. The clearer the picture, the better the connection." Hema cleared her throat. "I am sorry I cannot stay. I must join the battle. The Judge Foretold—Lancer—requires my aid. You can find your way back to the sacred chamber?"

"I can do that, sure." She swallowed hard, eyes closed. "Katsuo?"

"Yes."

"There's no reason for you to stay. You might as well go with Hema."

"You certain?" She heard his approaching heel-clicks.

"You know me. I'm not the sort of girl who shoots pinkie out. I'll be fine."

Katsuo pressed his silk fortune pouch into her hand. "For luck—you and Dixie."

Her gratitude caught in her throat and, by the time she recovered her composure, Katsuo and Hema were gone—disappeared up the stairs. She tried to relax her neck and shoulders, drift into the black behind her lids. Despite her casual attitude toward the Catholicism of her youth, she'd always believed in God as a universal and rational good. She feared the dreamtime would show her differently. She couldn't bear to know the real was wrong and irrational to the core. Nolin-as-daimon had magnified the possibility. His fundamental nobility had balanced the squad. He'd seemed to embody both the human and the humane; now, he threatened to induce a kind of psychosomatic illness.

Dixie, Dixie, she thought. She assayed to keep his face steady and foremost in her mind. But his visage, cheeks roughed by hard living and healed-over acne, wisped away as if ashen smoke. The isolating hum of the dream sphere encouraged wayward thoughts. It was easier for her to visualize a scene—nothing dramatic, just a moment of shared feeling. She recalled waking up next to him in her parent's house, the early morning light filtered through dirty windows, her entire body a remembrance. The hushed gold sun warms her as if she were a hatchling in its shell. She could've vanished in that moted haze. There's a trace of Young's 303 gun oil on his hands. Her ordinary need for control wanes. The moment imbues her with new reflexes. She curls her fingers over his and he stirs, blinks awake. The light over his bare shoulder intensifies, envelopes them, revealing rather than obscuring, giving them permission to be sweet, for him to indulge his goofy charm. She sloughs off her guarded and cosmetic self, her preconceptions, urges the light on ... *Love is an air that never leaves the lungs.* Dixie, répondre, s'il vous plaît. Her thoughts revolve like a gramophone record near to stopping, the needle scratching round and round its center ...

The sunbeam falters, flickers aquamarine. The earth tilts and her stomach lurches. The sky darkens, submerged, reappears bereft of clouds and vestigial stars, opaque. She stands on a hummock amid roiling waters. She peers downstream and there's Dixie—a mess of wet hair—speeding toward her, snagged and pushed by competing currents, choking, gasping. The world is made from this single drawn-out moment. She drops to her knees and calls to him. The shouts die in her throat. Where's the love in her lungs now? The Lalique-green river expands, swerves and yaws. Dixie plunges into a roller wave, bobs to the surface and careens away but seemingly no closer. It's as if the river is lengthening to match his progress. Anxiety cramps her up. She gives another silent cry then holds out a ghost ooze of a hand, desperate for him to see her, to pass and grab hold . . .

The stairway through the lofty emptiness dead ended in a floating stone resembling a musical note. Another wrong turn. A skim of muted blue spirited past. Prince J swore under his breath and about-faced to save Paul the effort of climbing farther. Paul, lagging under the mental weight of the Osiris fragment, managed a wobbly course. Prince J had been compelled to nudge him here and there to keep him on track. He hustled down the stairs, jumping the occasional gap between steps, two-handing the rifle. The gear bag smacked against his hip. Heady vistas of suspended stone receded into infinities on either side. The path unwound in fitful stretches, only showing what lay immediately ahead. He found Paul pallid and sweaty.

"Daydreaming again?" Prince J asked.

Paul reeled a bit as if caught out. "Galen's Hippocratic forerunners thought daydreaming was a boon to health."

"If that was true you'd be stronger than Lancer." Instantly regretting the reference, Prince J pivoted to the problem at hand. "No route forward that way. We have to go back to the intersection." He put a hand on the Osiris disc's chipped metal case to ease Paul around. "Guess there's only one path now we've taken the two false ones."

"Unless we're off on a tangent altogether." Paul shambled down a step.

"Fool honker bird. We should've made a backup map." From a strictly pragmatic standpoint, Prince J wished Paul had been left in the tunnel instead of Dixie. The Tennessean had an unerring sense of direction and the kind of naïve bravura that instilled confidence. The disc compounded Paul's tendency to drift into idle abstraction. He was practically in a trance already.

The path coiled in on itself in treads of uneven lengths and widths. Prince J kept one eye on Paul as they descended to a platform where four routes converged like the spokes of a wheel. When Paul stepped onto it, he pitched to his knees. Prince J bent to his drawn face. "You alright? Why don't you let me take the disc now?"

Paul brushed him off. "Just need a bit of a breather."

Prince J gazed at the sprawls of white stone against the dark. For some reason, the vista reminded him of the ice rink at Prospect Park. He'd lost the key to a pair of rented skates there once and been accused of stealing it. Though he couldn't have been more than eight years old, the sting of it persisted. He'd been a conscientious child. To have his word questioned like that—without basis—bittered him and at the same time, as the years passed, he'd become increasingly doubtful of his innocence. It was as if the mere accusation of wrongdoing were enough to make him guilty. Other, more serious incidents later in life had prompted him to question whether he'd ever get a fair shake in the States, regardless of his exceptional war record.

He was grateful to have landed a profession that took him far from home. The distance gave him a steadier perspective on things. Among Lancer and company, he was recognized for what he could do, who he was, not the color of his skin. Sure, it could be isolating sometimes in the bogs of Ireland or on the rocky coast of Egger Island. He missed the Berean Baptist Church, especially come Easter and Christmas, a certain easiness of manner he had only with his Brooklyn pals, genuine egg creams flavoured by Fox's U-Bet Chocolate Syrup, the prospect of a regular girl. But he was persuaded God had emptied his life in these respects to make room for a larger purpose. He considered himself a prayerful hunter and, like Shadrach and his fellows, trusted the Lord would see him through to a worthy end.

A faint, echoey scuttling set his heart to racing. He snapped the Winchester .30-30 to his shoulder and scoped the path to his immediate right: nothing but an empty downward curve. Still, the intermittent noise continued. He heard the scuff of Paul's service revolver against its holster. There was a bounding gleam—a sliver of skipped glass?—at the edge of the torchlight. Prince J zeroed on it, disbelieving. Through the translucent skin of the *quandyl*, the object looked like a figurine bearing a hammer.

"Fellas!" came a distant greeting. Prince J relaxed at the soft r's for l's and momentarily, Katsuo appeared above the lip of stone. "Haw! I find you." He removed the shiny helmet visoring his eyes, clapped his hands as if calling an errant dog to attention and said, "*Issun-bōshi.*" The manikin reversed direction and bounded onto his extended palm.

Prince J and Paul hastened to Katsuo's side and embraced him, careful of the mini-samurai settling on his shoulder.

"Did you break free?" Paul asked. "Where's Babette and—and Lancer?"

"And what's with the pipsqueak?" Prince J added.

"Oh, so much, *etto*, where to start?" Katsuo took a calming breath. "We no prisoner. Babette—she below, look for Dixie, use dream machine to speak, not know how close you are. Where is Dixie?"

Paul worked hard to keep the guilt out of his voice. "We entered from the tunnels under the temple and were forced to leave him just inside the stairway. He's asleep is all—locked in a dream. We can pick him up on the way out. There's a Nebwa witch who can help us revive him. She gave us these things." He poked his *quandyl*. "They might look funny, but they make us invisible to the Duah-teh's mental sweeps."

"I think—at first—maybe monster take over. Big time mind control in this place ..." He grinned at his toy-like warrior. "Hema, our guard—helper—take us god of war, Maahes. He give special weapons. This mine—boy from Japanese myth: *Issun-bōshi.* Follow my command, scout ahead in case ...Babette—she have glove, no, *etto*, gauntlet that cancel magick."

"What about Lancer?" Prince J asked. "We were told he, well, turned into some kinda blood daimon. That true?"

Katsuo screwed up his face as if to tell the story through pained expressions. "He made to fight priest enemy—now, outside."

Paul endured the news blackly. Prince J avoided his eyes. For his part, as much as he wanted to find Lancer, he dreaded what they might discover. "That where you're going?"

"No. The book—one you mention from note—I go there. Need defend from priest enemy."

"Defend?" Paul asked. "What for? The way we heard it, the Duah-teh's efforts to constrain thee-uh book's powers are responsible for despoiling this world." He shifted to give Katsuo a look at the Osiris fragment. "We're here to steal it."

Katsuo answered with a vigorous shake of his head. "Book ruin Earth next—upworld they say. Book cannot be free, no. Priest sacrifice themself for us."

"Sounds like Nicandra didn't tell us everything," Prince J said to Paul in a confidential tone. He'd been sorely disappointed in the Nebwa. As the first extradimensional Negro civilization they'd encountered, he'd hoped to find it intact and exceptional; instead, the Nebwa existed as a despairing huddle in a corrupt and increasingly diminished world. The alterations to the landscape had contributed to the decline in their store of knowledge. For generations, the largely oral culture had treated various features—hills, runnels, treelines, patches of desert et cetera—as spurs to mnemonic facts and truisms. The book's deleterious effects had not only rendered most of Herakleion fallow but also expunged much of its generalized wisdom.

Though the Nebwa's long decline had nothing whatsoever to do with Prince J, he took it as a personal failure in the same way as the Tower of Babel—a failure of human potential. He'd been brought up in a faith of self-reliance and brooked no excuses for failing to live into God's promise. In his opinion, difficulties and limitations helped people realize their true worth. When wishes were fulfilled without struggle, a self-defeating hubris developed. Prior to the Tower of Babel, he thought, science and religion were one and the same and it was only hubris that led to their crippling disunion. He assumed the book had its origins in a similar mortal failing.

"This is a rum do." Paul removed his spectacles and knuckled his eyelids. "There's no way for us to know the truth. But if we choose wrongly, we could put thee-uh the whole Earth at risk."

Prince J said, "And here I thought the war was guilt enough."

"How about we just secure it?" Paul asked. "Hold thee-uh priests hostage if we must but keep it safe until we can be confident one way or the other?" He looked to Katsuo for agreement.

"Hema say there is sph-inx monster on guard; at one time called Horemakhet by Egyptian. And the priest—they read your mind. You have more gun, maybe we have the luck." His voice was hardly reassuring.

Paul shrugged. "If it were a foolproof plan then it wouldn't be a plan at all but fate."

"Couple a real optimists," Prince J said, delving into the gear bag. He was certain, though, that after so much delay and frustrating weirdness, something crucial was at hand. The conviction gave him strength of purpose.

Outskirts of Duah-teh District

Swollen with bloodlust and atavistic joy, Ammit pounced on the Lancer-daimon, pinning him beneath a flexed paw. The Lancer-daimon thought his chest might cave under the pressure. A feral stench filled his nostrils. From paw to shoulder, the demigod was about five times his height. Ammit reared back in a fury and struck. The Lancer-daimon suffered the blows to his head in a crimson daze, feeling them, not feeling them, imagining the whop and smash vibrating out in a widening circle. Until a salvo of gummy meshwork trapped the demigod's bludgeoning arm against its chest. Ammit bellowed in rage and frustration at this interference.

The Lancer-daimon arched his throbbing back to see the Wer-Mauu press his offensive. The priest swooped down in the trireme, disgorging another barrage of stickiness from his large-barreled arm. Electric flourishes along a pair of coiled ligaments presaged each salvo. Gunky residue blasted one of Ammit's eyes and clogged its snout. The demigod writhed against these viscid restraints, pure will and ego. *Filthy priest! This short-lived irritant and your gabbled prayers cannot save you!*

While his rival thrashed to free itself, the Lancer-daimon rolled out from under its unsteadied paw and levered himself to his feet. The pains in his head and chest delivered sharp reminders of his mortality.

He was breathless with fear and confusion. Ear-shattering discharges geysered the ground somewhere behind him. A misshapen baboon stumbled out of the dust and abruptly sat down, one arm at a useless dangle, innards ballooning into its lap. To his right, several priests charged an unseen Nebwa foe, sending a continuous wave of earth before them. A large metal orb burst through the shield like cannon shot and, hovering overhead, bombarded the Duah-teh with spectral rays. The ghost-beams jolted the priests into incapacitating spasms. They clawed at their own slitted eyes and collapsed, frothing and frantic. The wave subsided in a pattering of stone on stone.

The Wer-Mauu refocused his fusillade on the orb, scoring a partial hit before it zigged out of range. A woman in a pleated robe emerged through the cascading grit and stepped over one of her convulsing victims. Though her eyes were whitespace blank, she appeared to see well enough. She pointed to the Wer-Mauu as if to fix him in place. "Great Seer! How does it feel to be on the brink of your final vision? To know the void-master has come?"

My life is of no consequence, the priest declared. *Our champion prevails. Of that, I am assured.*

The orb waggled first one way then the other, cracked against the ground, meandered back into the air. The Nebwa sorceress twitched annoyance. But her luminous gaze remained on the Wer-Mauu as they engaged in psychic war for control over the artifact.

Remnants of the Wer-Mauu's matting wafted down in feathery tufts. The demigod had succeeded in excavating its paw and was now ripping away the adhesive tangle around its snout. *Hold, little brother.* The Lancer-daimon darted to a toppled stone pillar and, crouching to bring his legs and back into play, swung it round. His chest strained with the wrestling effort. The column powdered against the creature's ribs and underbelly. Ammit keeled over, forelegs casting about. Loosed soil frayed out and over the Wer-Mauu. Down came the shortened column on Ammit's occluded eye. The demigod brayed in misery.

The Lancer-daimon discarded the leftover fragment and scrambled to retrieve his fighting rod. He planned to pry open the demigod's skull. The weapon lay on the ground between the psychics. He pulled up short when the orb banged the earth in front of him. The relic paused in the air, then, leaking ethereal energies, swifted past his head and straight through the Wer-Mauu's roll cage. The trireme dead-dropped about five long meters and shattered. Pieces scudded across the rubble. The Wer-Mauu expired in a shudder of splintered metal and riven flesh, one of the metal spindles in his head broken against the exo-suit. Embedded in the priest's middle, the soulfire orb sparked its last and darkened.

The image of the sorceress was etched in battle-glare against the sharded glass of the roll cage. "We know you for an unwilling savior." Her words sounded as if from a far remove. Clear of the priest's influence, the Lancer-daimon could feel his human side asserting itself, muddling his thoughts. "Desist and live awhile longer ..."

Or die facing your greatest fear.

The Lancer-daimon spun around on trembly legs. The recovered demigod wore a visage both familiar and strange: his own.

Temple of Osiris, Lord of the Underworld

The rushing water overtops Dixie, turning the sky to a far-flung slurry. He flounders, pumping his legs, clambering for purchase. It seems the knock-and-tumble might dissolve him altogether. He pictures his clothes frazzling, his skin coming away in weepy strips, his eyes bobbing out of distended sockets. He coughs, gasps, vision dimmed by the water beaded on his lashes. Where is he? Where is here?

Water, water, everywhere. A children's story? The roaring in his ears confuses his memory. The sound is no seashore lulling; more like a tectonic grind. Maybe he's swirling toward the planet's core, battered to and fro, down fathomless chasms and declivities.

The dank green water reminds him of the wartime enlistment poster inspired by the sinking of the *Lusitania*. The poster depicted a mother and child drowning in dreamlike stillness, the mother's gown reminiscent of grave clothes. In the moment, he believes that's what the Great War was about: a masculine defense of womanly values, motherhood, even (dare he think it?) virginity.

Managing a steady dog paddle, he raises his eyes above the churn. There's a shapeless mound of dirt and sedges on one side and another across from it. He's stranded between these twin heaps in whirlpool isolation. The hummocks rise against the dim horizon like the tops of primitive graves. Ah, the thinness of the barrier between him and the water—he must be a soul in wild transit, whither shall he go?

A figure takes shape on the mound to his right. Though it remains a bleary shadow, it assumes proportions he recognizes as Babette's— the kind that make for a lasting afterimage. She bends to the water in a pleading reach, mouthing his name. Feelings well up in him like a panic. To surrender to her understanding means he might never be understood again. He falters in his need and the eddy tugs him round. He dips and splashes and comes up even with the other hummock. Where the mound meets the water he discerns a bevy of female shapes—siren upon siren, untamed and willing, holding themselves. He can't tell how many or who's who in the headspin but what does it matter? What counts is the sense of limitless possibility, wonders to browse, pretty sport.

Yet and yet, what had that sense done but lead him astray? Prompted him to chase after phantoms, heads-over-tail? No, he thinks, no more. He likes the reflection of himself Babette returns. The time for finding himself in others is over. Even if his decision stands for a waning eternity. He gathers his strength and pushes against the revolving current to edge closer to Babette. This dream, he tells himself, is only the dream before the dream. He pushes again, more determined, and again, crossing in fitful kicks and flutters. The shudder and pull of waves exhausts him. The trilling currents urge surrender, forgetting. Obstinacy prevails. He throws his arms out in an awkward crawl. Nearly there, nearly all the way, there—the black earth, the future. Her silhouette becomes definite becomes flesh. The dream of Babette is Babette.

Dixie grasps her hand tight, tighter. Her touch is as unearned as spiritual grace and, despite his taxing labors, he's abashed and ashamed for the necessity of it. His remorse must be obvious because she says (without moving her lips): *I have every reason to wake you.* He puts a knee to the verge, weighted once more, shaking with a relief he knows he doesn't merit. The current still carries the low murmurings of the sirens. He must—he will—do better by her.

Good, he wheezes, affecting nonchalance, *cause you know I ain't no bard a the vale.*

The Japanese word *ma* can be translated loosely as vacancy, emptiness, an uncertain pause between two moments. The historic kanji or graphical version of *ma* combines the words for 'door' and 'moon,' as in a door open just enough to let the moonlight through. This term and its connotations of a suspenseful gap came to Katsuo as he surveyed the path ahead via the One-Inch Boy. The helm allowed for remote surveillance but not communication. Katsuo had stressed the importance of stealth before sending the mini-samurai up the final stretch of stairs, going so far as to demonstrate a light footed gait, heel-to-toe. He could only hope the manikin had understood.

The stairway ended in a small alcove on one side of the sacred chamber's central plinth. Katsuo could make out the cluster of priests enfolded in deep meditation. He narrated the scene for the benefit of Paul and Prince J sitting at his feet. "Duah-teh in trance...Who know if they wake? Ape soldier on far side—near arch?—archway—two, no, four."

"How far to the book?" Paul asked in a hushed tone. His face had taken on a pale, unfinished quality.

"Twenty, twenty-five meters." Katsuo shrugged. "He not look that direction anymore." The manikin had evidently targeted the baboon soldiers at a run. Their bronze greaves grew larger and larger in Katsuo's shaky field of vision.

"No other defenses? No guns or other weapons?" Prince J asked. "Seems odd is all, leaving this book almost wholly unprotected."

A lambent red beam cut across the manikin's path, sizzling into the stone floor. He rolled to avoid the threat, throwing Katsuo's sight into sea-sick confusion.

"*Are!*" Katsuo severed the link and jumped to his feet. A lashing out of forked energy sounded from above.

"What is it?" Prince J asked.

"*Issun-bōshi*—weapon in air?"

"Finally, time for a real punch-up." Prince J put a hand on Paul. "Follow as you're able, yeah?" He didn't wait for an answer before pounding up the stairs after Katsuo.

Due to an L-shaped screening wall, the alcove at the top provided a limited view of the sacred chamber. But from an interior corner on the right, the soldiers could see the lotus legged priests and beyond them, the manikin's assault on the simian guards. Dodging a sickle sword lunge, the tiny warrior crippled one guard with a hammer-strike then leapt chest-high toward the other. A saucer-shaped aerial craft flitted in and out of their line of sight. Conjoined sphinx heads rotated around the saucer's outer shell. The hollowed-out eyes suggested big-bore firearms. The undercarriage glowed a vibrant white. During the New Kingdom of Egypt, Katsuo knew, a solar cult venerated the sphinx as a representation of Horus in his role as sky god. This machine seemed a potent embodiment of the idea.

Prince J cycled the finger lever on his Winchester to load a cartridge from the magazine into the chamber and released the safety. "There's no cover to speak of out there. I'll try to get the flyer from here." He spread full length on the floor to aim properly.

Katsuo retreated behind a holding shrine to Osiris along the screening wall. From that vantage, he could see a section of Parmatmar crystal supporting the book and nothing else. He reconnected with the manikin as it hammered the last guard into unconsciousness and outfooted a beam that rendered the downed ape insubstantial. Then the manikin was on the run and the chamber stretched in perspective into vast lines and planes.

The Winchester barked once, twice, three times. Prince J alternately fired and ejected the spent cartridges in a calculated rhythm. "You know how good judgment comes from experience and experience comes from bad judgment? Well…" He resumed shooting, though without much enthusiasm. "I hope we live long enough to learn from this." He emptied the magazine and started reloading from the gear bag. "Cover me."

Katsuo disengaged from the manikin and peeked out from the border wall, handgun raised. The sphinx-machine was speeding toward the alcove, venting oily smoke, bas relief heads whirring. Several frontispieces bore pockmarked traces of Prince J's handiwork. Katsuo hunkered in the opening and popped five-six .32 caliber rounds into the craft's undercarriage without retarding its advance.

The sphinx-machine issued a gnomic directive in a metallic and eerily disaffected voice: "Judge by cause, not by effect." A head with small barrels protruding from the eyes rotated into the center position. Twin missiles darted out from the sockets, trailing glittery lights.

"Incoming!" Katsuo warned and dove for the corner shrine. The joint explosion razed the screening wall, dusting him with stone and setting off a continuous skirling in his head. Early in the Great War, he'd doubted the very possibility of death. He'd thought himself too young, too strong, too alive to lose everything at once. He was quickly disabused of that insensible confidence and ever since he'd kept up a dialogue with the *sai no kami* (deity of luck). Heaped under the rubble, he silently asked: Is it now? Now will I know whether death is real? He expected the answer to come in the form of a zip or a flash or nothing. This time, it was a whiffling spray of adhesive pellets. Whatever the pellets struck—the debris, the shrine, the gear bag—began to float gently upward.

The hovering sphinx-machine fixed its centermost head on Katsuo. Its mouth was an ominous hole instead of a philosophic smile. "For every joy there is a price to be paid." The sphinx seemed to have found its cruel serenity in the profounds of a higher existence. A slight rattling preceded the spew of anti-gravity pellets. Katsuo shielded his face with his forearm. Bounding from one fragment of drifting stone to another, the manikin deflected a scattering of pellets with its hammer. A few pellets cleaved to Katsuo's exposed torso and he felt himself lift up against his will. Prince J grabbed his wrist, preventing him from flying away. "Gotcha!"

"Look!" Katsuo jerked his head toward the manikin, now floating toward the sphinx-machine. If the little samurai was nigh-indestructible, why not …? "Can you shoot it up, *etto*, into—" He tossed Prince J his Remington 51 as the telltale rattling sounded from the sphinx again.

"Got it." Prince J tried to draw a bead on the gleaming figurine one-handed and missed. He yanked Katsuo down then let go to steady his aim and fired again. *On'yomi!* The impact volleyed the manikin up into the sphinx-machine's undercarriage. Prince J renewed his grip on Katsuo while he stoppered the pellet chute with the rest of the .32 caliber's magazine. Katsuo was amazed at his accuracy given the jellied *quandyl* around his eyes.

Issun-bōshi wasted no time in attacking the sphinx-machine's mechanical guts. The destruction progressed in short order from intermittent thuds to an insistent din. One head burst into a ragged husk. Circular gears, electromagnets, strands of cable, motor casings and other less identifiable parts cascaded to the ground. The discombobulated saucer veered here and there, screeching nonsense in meditative, albeit warped, tones: "Know the—world in yourself...Never look for yourself—in the the world...Th-that would be to to pr-project your illusion." The machine gave a high-pitched electronic gurgle then its undercarriage glow winked out and the whole affair smashed on the stone into a whirl of debris.

Katsuo and everything else suspended in air by the saucer's power abruptly crashed. Prince J covered his head against the falling rubble. "Can't stop king-hell with platitudes," he said through the dust. He started to go on but the words caught in his throat. Katsuo was stymied also in reaching for his dislodged helm, his arms paralyzed as in a nightmare. Even his thoughts seemed unnaturally slow and tidal. The priests, he realized at length. *Awake to us.* He breathed through the rush of dread.

Then out of the corner of his eye, he saw Paul crawling up the stairs, pushing the disc in front of him. He was glowering as if in silent argument. The disc topped the last step and scraped across chunks of stone. Paul flopped on its translucent face and put a handgun to the glass top. Not knowing what to expect, Katsuo braced for the shot.

The chamber was dashed with vivid blue-green lightnings and, in one voice, the Duah-teh sent up an excruciating psychic scream. Katsuo was like a knot of filament in an electrical storm.

Outskirts of Duah-teh District

When the priesthood's constraints on the *Ptahkit'b* fell away, the somber sky turned a bleed of white and the landscape shook and split in a great volcanic unfolding. Corrupting energies pent-up for ages surged from the outer wastes through the formerly protected Duah-teh district toward the sacred temple.

Observing the disaster from atop the droner, Hema wondered whether she should go back. She had no idea how much time was left before Herakleion's pinhole sun consumed everything or collapsed on itself. It's possible she could hold the book in check for a few moments on her own, but then what? She watched helplessly as the city below writhed and subsided into fissured stone. When the final darkness came, there would be no shelter.

The black plummets of battle appeared some distance ahead. Already, the newly-dead exerted a phantom pull on her attention. She felt their inceptive memory-forms coalescing. The few remaining combatants looked impossibly small against the naked wilderness. She saw the Devourer through the hot ash and smoke but no sign of the Judge Foretold. Her heart faltered at the possibilities. She reached across the saddle and put a hand over Gapti's. "We go on, yes? For the prophecy?"

An unexpected torrent of air and dirt and sharp grit like broken glass buffeted them. The droner lost an antenna and jolted, rollicking them side to side in their saddles. Then a flight of twisted scrap metal thudded into the creature, piercing the air sac in its throat and crushing one of its fragile forearms. Hema balled herself around the pommel of her saddle as they plunged into a terrifying freefall. She couldn't make herself small enough. There was no center to things. She gulped air in shuddering sighs. The convulsing earth spooled up at an alarming rate. The blood drained from her face. She gave Gapti one last imploring look then closed her eyes, thoughts flitting out of control. What would she leave behind? What memories of her own? What achievements? What loves? She waited for the unthinkable, angry for living and dying so uselessly.

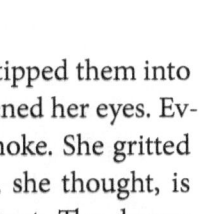

The damaged wing caught a fast-forming rise and tipped them into a repeated cartwheel. Hema bounced upright and opened her eyes. Everything was a blur of stone and animal and drift smoke. She gritted her teeth, still alive, anticipating, despairing. Death, she thought, is one of those things that's inevitable only in the instant. The droner wrecked against a rocky plateau and spilled her into emptiness. Her right leg caught in the stirrups and wrenched her round. She spindled to earth, landing hard on her upper back. Everything blurred to black-blind sensation. She rolled with the impact and cracked an ankle against the unforgiving stone before coming to rest facedown, a fractured arm trapped beneath her.

When she came to, Gapti had a moist hand on her forehead. She bolted upright as if awakened from a troubled sleep. The taste of blood was in her mouth. Not out for long then, she thought. Her healing staff and the mace lay on the ground nearby. She swallowed hard and pointed to the staff.

Gapti retrieved the prop and, with his help, she used it to maneuver herself up. Though largely numb to her various injuries due to shock, it was evident her left ankle was broken. Between that and the unstable landscape, she had no chance of delivering the mace to Lancer. She could heal her wounds with the aid of the Partmatmar crystal she'd transferred into the mace, but that would take precious time. She might as well have perished in the crash.

"I am sorry, my friend," she said, bending to meet the baboon's eyes. With the exception of a shallow slash across his chest, he seemed unharmed. She remembered how, as an infant, he'd worried her by frisking along the temple's balconies without a care. Ah, the number of far more dangerous feats they'd undertaken since . . . Even at his advanced age, a kind of immortality had been assumed. "I have to—" She lapsed into a stricken silence.

They regarded each other imploringly, willing themselves not to break down. She wanted to hold him and never let go. Neither of them were likely to make it unless their efforts were seconded by an unprecedented run of luck. "The mace," Hema choked out. "Can you get it to him?"

Gapti brushed her fingers with his own, fidgeting with the desire to be understood. He arched his skull against her palm. Hema ruffled his mane and kissed his furrowed brow. "There's no need for words." From her experiences with the dead, she saw history as a series of accidental felicities, false starts, dead ends and do-overs. She gave his hand a last squeeze, thinking everything should have been otherwise. "This is how love says goodbye: I am forever thankful. I am forever blessed."

The ape hesitated, eyes bleary with devotion. "Go on now," she said. "You will find him wherever you find Ammit." He loped over to the mace, tested its weight in his hand and smacked his lips in imitation of her farewell.

Hema gave him a tearful smile then watched him scamper down an embankment and disappear in a cloud of acrid smoke. It was unusual for her to smell anything on the open plains besides a dusty sterility. The *Ptahkit'b* had rendered the air a near-vacuum untainted by the business of creaturely life. She figured the atmosphere would be the last element to go bad.

The ground quaked and issued a snaky discharge that proceeded to spear the droner's mutilated corpse. Hema gimped toward a sheltering rise, wondering—and not for the first time—if chaos might be the natural state of things. Perhaps the eternal order and fitness of moral realities posited by the Duah-teh were mere wishful thinking. By doing their bidding, she might even be retarding some necessary cosmic process. The Unworldly River itself could be seen as an expression of chaos. As the ultimate nexus of space-time, it had no fixed boundaries, offering up the world before it was the world—inchoate, impersonal, a nascent whole. But her feelings—again—led her to believe that some fixed order was possible. There could be no rightness without it. The universe, she thought, couldn't be so askew at its base.

Then Nicandra stumbled out of the surrounding haze, casting doubt on even this meager consolation.

Chapter 11

Cosmosis

Outskirts of Duah-teh District

His fighting rod smashed to uselessness, the Lancer-daimon locked his fists and swung down on the Devourer's mocking rendition of his own skull. What vile god could that face be made in image of? Ammit flexed its jaws back into place, apparently unhurt, and bulled into him. Meat hook claws flashed, opening the flesh above his ribs. The wound radiated hot pain. This was his world now—brute violence and misery. All that shined for him were feelings, brief, vehement spasms, exciting his heart and quickening away. Bellowing at the faded sky, he rolled to his feet and flew at his rival. If despair was to be his fate then he would be a hero of it.

The demigod dispensed with its mimicry, rumpling out its jaws to snap at him. The Lancer-daimon dodged the attack and seized on the Devourer's snout, forcing it into the chalk-white dirt. The image of his hated shadow self persisted in his imagination. The image said to him: You thought you were human and alive but you were neither. This phantom sight added to his strength. His eyes filled with iron hate. He was multitudes of wrath. But still no match for a blood daimon on the boil. Ammit had no lingering compunctions about its nature. The creature urged hellfire to consume and become it.

The ground tremored at a walloping tail-strike that nearly pitched the Lancer-daimon to his knees. He stumbled and Ammit lunged, jaws agape. Twisting aside, he drove a knee into its pale underbelly. The creature buckled then hurled itself at him in a fury, a missile of unbreakable scales. They crashed against a fallen skyway support. The demigod whipped its tail around the stone column, encircling and binding the Lancer-daimon. *Why pursue this senseless struggle? Your cause is already lost!* the creature leered. *Look how the earth rebels and your priesthood flees in vain for safety.*

There was no denying it: all around them the battlefield heaved and ricocheted into the air to reassemble in new, higgledy patterns. Herakleion was born in chaos and chaos would take it back. Only a few combatants remained—mainly injured baboon-soldiers. At the first inkling of the *Ptahkit'b*'s release, the forces on both sides had raced for the Temple of Osiris to secure it, Nicandra among them. A pair of Duah-teh hovered just outside the range of Ammit's maddening secretions to maintain a hold on their champion. The level of concentration required to do that, however, prevented them from intervening directly.

At the silent urgings of his taskmasters, the Lancer-daimon roared and struggled against his sinewy bonds. His shoulders globed with the effort like a wind-filled sail, but he could feel himself deflating inside, the last ergs of the *ríastrad* dwindling in his veins. He would be crushed and his lifeblood would trickle into the fractured earth. Nothing human about him would outlast this end—no high emotion, no wisdom. He would die a stranger to himself. His vision blurred, fluoresced crimson. The bones in his chest and shoulders grated. The feeling in his limbs began to go. He had a matter of moments before he joined the wasteland's perfect mineral silence.

Then—what? There was a resonant *thok* of metal against resistant scale and Ammit's body jerked into a wretched shape, releasing him of a sudden. He dropped to his knees, extremities tingling with the charge of returning blood.

The Devourer's spinning action revealed a sickle-sword plunged to the hilt into its mid-section. The khopesh had been chinked between its scales. Ammit howled revenge on its surreptitious attacker: Gapti. The baboon-soldier clambered up its hide to avoid a murderous swipe. Either a mistake made in haste or purposeful suicide. Blood-red light speared out from the cracks in Ammit's natural armor, energizing its disorienting mists. Gapti shrieked at the virulent rays and tumbled to the pile of masonry near the Lancer-daimon. A melee weapon clattered out of his hands—a mace forged from black metal. Gapti raised his darkening eyes at the Judge Foretold then shuddered all over, baring his fangs, and stilled. A string of saliva driveled to the ground.

For lack of alternatives, the Lancer-daimon hobbled to the weapon. The Devourer succeeded in shaking the sword loose and turned back to its true rival. *This is the moment of unmaking—the death throes of Herakleion* it laughed. *What use do you expect to make of that puny hammer?*

Time seemed disordered to the Lancer-daimon—dream-slow for him, heart-attack fast for his foe. He staggered the last steps to the mace. Every footfall sent shooting pains through his legs while Ammit, delighting in his feebleness, thrashed its tail with supernatural alacrity. *You might as well bark poetry at me, mortal brother.* The demigod snorted and readied to pounce, a rolling mass of animal.

As soon as his fingers closed around the shaft, the Lancer-daimon knew the mace brimmed with reviving virtues. The weapon felt heavier than its proper weight. Intrinsic power coursed up and down his body. *Parmatmar crystal.* The metal must disguise it, he thought, else the Devourer would be on guard. Blood daimons have an instinct for detecting dreamtime energies, whether active or latent. The rings around the base of the falcon-shaped head jangled. The sound prompted an understanding in his Duah-teh overseers, which they relayed to him. Here was a chance to do more than simply shout in thwarted rage. He would churn the air. He would set an inferno loose across the land. He would bring cosmic destruction.

"I am that I am: a wide-awake beast," he declared, turning the rings as instructed. "Neither wholly mortal nor your brother." He pointed the mace, his bioelectric field its energy, his will its trigger, the crystal its focus. A god-blinding dazzle flashed out from the crown to harrow the Devourer. For a prolonged meantime, the creature kept upright, its parts in balance, unexploded, then its inner twistings blazed into certain oblivion.

The discharge flung the Lancer-daimon onto his back. His chest flared from something like a hard winter burn. His lungs hurt to inhale. He lay amid the rubble, the mace at his side, and stared at the smoldering sky. The spiral flaws around the sun now compassed the heavens. Annihilation was at hand and it was sublime—awful and sublime and freeing.

Temple of Osiris, Lord of the Underworld

The flurry of psychic energies from the Osiris disc abated, leaving the inner sanctum dimmed and the priests mere ashen husks. Paul gestured toward the friable corpses. "Well, isn't this a low party?"

"Feelin better?" Prince J asked, getting to his feet.

"Not quite myself yet," Paul said. The blood in his face felt thick and creeping. He sensed the *Ptahkit'b*'s influence filtering through the room like an unstable gas seeking to escape a high-pressure container.

Prince J returned the Remington 51 to Katsuo and took up his rifle. "What now? The disc is shot and Nicandra's prob'ly on her way." He resumed reloading from the gear bag. "Defend it in place?"

"Something like that, *absit omen*." Paul scuffed over the concrete debris, possessed of an oceanic longing. Already, he was visualizing the magick moment when he plucked the book from its display armature. It had always seemed his breakthrough ideas ought to come easier, faster, be more instinctive and innate. The *Ptahkit'b* promised to realize that yearned for felicity.

Katsuo let out a cheerful yelp. Tapping his silvery helm, he said, "*Issun-bōshi* survive. But, *etto*, need find hammer." He stepped out of the alcove to help the manikin comb the scattered remnants of the sphinx-machine.

"Let's not shirk safety now." Prince J followed, surveilling the shadowed chamber.

Paul approached the crystalline plinth with head bowed. The golden plate gave off a floating radiance. The projected starscape was gone and, in its absence, a stately darkness claimed the upper reaches. The plinth made an antenna of Paul, tickling his hindbrain with a soundless hum. There was a sensation of his skin listening for a noise that never came. His flesh pulsed in time to an alien vibration and, with a kind of mewling, his *quandyl* slipped to the ground, dried out in an instant. "Joey," he called, running a hand through his dewy hair. A simmering itch worried his scalp.

The process of removing the *quandyl* was repeated with Prince J. He toed the desiccated shuck of jelly. "Dead, you think?"

"Put them back under, they might resuscitate," Paul said. "Like brine shrimp."

"What about them?" Prince J pointed to the brittled Duah-teh.

"I'm a dab hand at machines, but ..."

"She didn't say it would kill them."

"Nothing more dangerous than an idealist with a gun, eh?" Paul glanced back at the *Ptahkit'b*. The book's *hequa*, the magick of the Unworldly River, pulsed in his temples. "You think these priests told Katsuo thee-uh solemn truth—that they're defending us, Earth?"

"Damnitall!" Dixie emerged from the alcove, leaning on Babette. "You went and had the big knockdown without me."

Prince J took a few steps in their direction. "Hey!"

"Don't tell me." Dixie let go of Babette and tottered a moment before finding his step. "In a act a true heroism, I said, 'Leave me behind, I'll only slow you down.'"

"That what those snores meant?" When Prince J got a closer look, his smirk became a concerned purse of the lips. Dixie's forehead was bruised and bloodied again and a streak of green ichor had dried along his jawline. "Yourself again?"

"Tip top. Jus workin on gettin my whinginess back." Dixie wobbled to a halt at Katsuo's approach, squinting at the winking light of the manikin. "Waitaminute. Am I still dreamin?"

Katsuo gripped his forearm. "Secret weapon." With a tinny creak of its joints, the One-Inch Boy raised its hammer in salute.

Dixie appealed to the rest of the squad. "Should I be sore this is my replacement?"

"Believe it or not," Prince J said, "he's got your crazy swagger."

"What happened to your jelly-cap?"

Paul motioned him over to the slab of Parmatmar crystal. "We can take care of that over here."

"Bout time," Dixie said, flashing Babette a drowsy smile. "Can't kiss my girl proper wearin this damn thing."

"Not until you bathe, *favori*." She kept pace with Dixie to lend a supporting hand. "*Je suis désolé* but you smell like years of dirt."

"How'd you find and wake him?" Paul asked her.

"This dream sphere device. It was fascinating. I'd show it to you but—"

"How bout talkin fool science later?" Dixie said, craning his neck forward.

Paul guided him close to the crystal. "Lean into it…"

With a wary eye, Dixie followed Paul's instruction, stopping just short of the plinth. The *quandyl* shriveled to a crisp shell and shook to the floor. "Gah!" Dixie mussed his hair in disgust.

"Here, let me help." Babette ministered to him, wiping residual gunk from the corners of his eyes.

"That your magick gauntlet?" Prince J asked in admiration.

Babette tucked an imaginary strand of hair behind her ear. "Look a picture in it, do I?"

Battle noises reverberated from the corridor: crashing stone, the *ffzzz* of plasmic bolts, ringing steel, cries desperate and damning. A scream ragged with hysteria died away in a bottomless fall.

"Hell 'n' hullabaloo," Dixie said. "We got a gun for Babette? Cause I'm bettin she'd like to face 'em with more'n a old boot in her hands."

Prince J accommodated her with a handgun and an extra magazine from the gear bag. "Check the ammo." Due to the gauntlet, she was forced to hold the gun in her left hand.

"Paul?" Katsuo's quiet voice got the rest of the squad's attention.

Perched on the bronze base, Paul was bouldering up the plinth. He had a knee in a rough depression and was stretching for a handhold on its topmost surface.

"You're not going to touch that bare-handed, are you?" Prince J asked.

Paul affected light-heartedness. "It's a book isn't it?" The *Ptahkit'b* insisted on direct contact. Finding a spur, he wriggled up and crested the plinth. The book's coruscating gold broke in on him. His temples seemed ready to burst. *One more easy reach…*

"You know it's goofered somethin terrible," Dixie said.

"Is that safe?" Babette added.

Their voices seemed fragile and remote. Paul's hands hovered above the plate, in limbo, postponing the moment. "Apparently," he said, clutching it to his chest. His heart gave a resounding thump—only one as if it had expired for good. Then the light boiled up in a whirl, enveloping him. His ears, mouth and eyes filled with its impossible energies. The book was stifling him helter-skelter *etiam potestas suprema* oh he must contain it, the inrushing light, cold with knowledge, God, the knowledge *omnia enta* across the chasm of unreason no inside no outside elemental kingdoms in and of themselves the threefold sight the body our outer world the soul our inner world the spirit our higher world and the poetically precise maths behind it all the infinite sphere curving on itself from one point to forever oh the mindbending *alephs* the vastness a terror an ecstasy vivid as a childhood nightmare up down wherever thought-lightning is waiting to be born there the starseed supraliminal the self both dreamer and dreamed struggling to remember being a man determined as much as revealed *ecce spiritus* God he could do nothing to stop the cascade of insights from penetrating him, submerging him, hence it hurted man may perchance nothing *nothing*—

He felt his center of gravity shift, his body tumble backward, grasping, sustaining arms closing around him, all the time thinking *Rejoice in the light always; again, I will say, Rejoice.* The light seethed out his eyes and his vision pulsed with unwonted dimness. Ah, cool stone against wanton thought. Self-perception came back in spasms of clarity. No longer the transcendental dreamer, if he moved his stung hands, he would know. *Rejoice in the light...* His heart panted after his mind. Voices reached him across a measureless distance.

"What do you think? He absorb the book?" *(Prince J)*

"It absorbed him more like." *(Dixie)*

The dimness took on dimension—the dome, the plinth and its auric rays, his mates. But the aftersurge of ideas kept him in a stupor, pulsing out porous formulae...Disrupted when the first of the returning Duah-teh announced their presence: *Hold, upworlders! Or die in a blood-frenzy at each other's hands!*

Outskirts of Duah-teh District

Eyeing Nicandra across the expanse of stone and shrouding smoke, Hema crutched out from the sheltering overhang as fast as her broken ankle allowed. A tilt of Nicandra's head gave credence to her immediate fear. The flat-topped rise shrugged into a pursuing landslide. She scrambled to outdistance it, revolving her staff in a quickening tempo. The ankle was an acute and exacting pain. She breathed through clenched teeth. The upheaval behind her closed at an alarming rate. She kicked her legs faster, faster, wanting to cry in frustration. It was almost over. Images of the end spurred her on, the rubble shifted to stillness, her body stretched full-length, mangled and covered over. A snatched-at moment, another, another at despair's own speed and—

There was a din like the knock of swords and shields under the earth. The ground somewhere close behind her collapsed and the debris chasing her down waterfalled into the sudden rift. Hema kept going, afraid the fissure would fan into a canyon and take her with it. She straggled over quaking rock, silently repeating her Sumerian mantra: *Ba-bee-lee A-noo-na-key.* Her ankle gave out altogether and she toppled amid an overpowering drift of dust and sand. She craned her head in the direction she'd last seen Nicandra. The churned-up vapor dirtied her vision. She collected her staff and got to her feet, eyes stinging.

Nicandra materialized from the haze a changed woman—older, more shrunken than Hema remembered. Her *atef* crown was gone, revealing a forehead crosshatched with wrinkles. Purplish rings enfolded her eyes. She approached slump-shouldered. Signs she'd exhausted her reserves of dream energy and was drawing down her body's élan vital. "I see the pity in your eyes, upworld slave," she spit. "Is this to be my final sufferance?"

"If you wish it." Hema hoisted her staff and worked the coupling at its center. Grimacing at the extra weight she was forced to put on her injured ankle, she split the staff in two equal sections and tossed one at Nicandra's feet. "I may be a servant, but I am not without honor."

"Why persist in fighting at all?" The imperious tone recalled the old

Nicandra. "The Duah-teh do not deserve your sacrifice."

"I fight to preserve Ma'at."

"Then you would consign us to damnation." Nicandra gestured toward the upheaved flatlands. They had the sea's singleness of purpose and a similar destructive power. It was clear Herakleion brinked on wrecking itself.

Hema twirled her halved weapon in warning. "Better us alone than the upworld and perhaps, worlds beyond."

"If the gods will it …" Nicandra picked up the metal baton. It was not unlike the weapons used in ceremonial stick fighting. "*Swadjet* is the catalyst for the next great pantheon," she said, citing psychogenesis in her defense. "You cannot overcome future-history."

"What you call *swadjet* we call *kekw wahhhw*—the chaos wave. Left unchecked, the dismemberment of Osiris would pale in comparison to the havoc it would cause."

"You expect your Judge Foretold to save you?"

Hema turned thoughtful and the bawling of the dead intensified to fill the mental quiet. The massing thought-forms disturbed and fatigued her. Like a chronic wind threatening to rattle self-awareness right out of her head. "I am beginning to think 'prophecy' has a meaning hitherto ignored. It is not fate so much as a caution—a chance for us to repent and change our ways."

"The earth shakes to its foundation. The sun recedes, leaving the sky a forgetting murk." Nicandra betrayed a haughty smile. No doubt she'd deduced Hema's key infirmities. "The time for atonement is long-passed." She charged in a fury.

Hema received her in a lateral stance intended to protect her damaged foot and facilitate a balanced retreat. In the arena before the Wer-Mauu, she'd worn a protective headdress and a wooden forearm guard and the contest was decided on points. There were no such protections this time. She dodged a pre-emptive swing at her head and blocked the follow-up to her ribs, spinning her baton to thwack Nicandra's weapon aside. Before she could strike on the pivot, however, the sorceress kicked her in the thigh. Hema's leg quivered with tension. Refusing to fall, Hema staved off another attempted blow to her torso and jerked back on her bad foot to gain some defensive space. The pain needled up her leg and around her hips. She exhaled a curse.

An advance lunge forced Hema to retreat, one, two, oblique steps. Perspiration sheened her upper lip. The crash had taken more out of her than she'd dared admit. Her limbs felt useless, disconnected. Her chest and sides flared with every parry or hasty riposte. She tried to lure Nicandra out with a false attack and, failing that, her own baton— psychically manipulated—smacked her on the temple. Dizzied, she missed a jab to her abdomen, stumbled, keeled over. The baton clattered away. There was so much pain she didn't know what to do. She just wanted to stop flailing. Her deep unconscious swelled with the heat and bother of the dead.

"That was hardly fair," Hema said without looking up.

"Me alive, you dead. What could be more just?"

"Maybe the dead can answer." Hema seized Nicandra's exposed shin and the black language of the dead spiked out through her palm. All the longing left over from their lives shuddered into the sorceress: the hurts and regrets, the loves unfulfilled, emotions still battlefield hot. These sensations were like a blood clot on its way to the brain. Nicandra folded up in shock, unsouled and fluttering. Hema crawled up her rival's body—from knee to hip, arm to shoulder and neck. The warm pulse there stymied her thumbs a breathy moment. This close, Nicandra looked husk-thin. *The 'I' in you fills and empties and fills again.* Could she…? No, she thought, shaking the tears from her eyes, this time there was no mercy in mercy.

Temple of Osiris, Lord of the Underworld

"Close on me!" Babette shouted, hugging Dixie to her side. Prince J and Katsuo hoisted Paul to his feet. Despite its enormity and grandeur, the chamber registered as strangely one-dimensional. A higher reality continued to penetrate him. He moved as if tripping down stairs, feeling indistinct, diffused, lost in threefold sight. Plato's idea about dreams in the *Theaetetus* struck him as indisputably true—they do give proof of ineffable 'first things,' he thought. *Enlightenment is waking to a dream, not from one.*

The squad formed on Babette, guns at the ready. She flourished her gauntlet and pointed a clawed finger at the huddle of priests. The embedded Parmatmar crystals caught the book's resurgent light. "See this? There's no perfume on the pulse of this wrist and I'm inclined to be careless."

"This how your glove work?" Katsuo asked in a low voice.

Babette squeezed the gifted fortune pouch tied to her belt. "Guess we'll find out together."

The forward-most priest crinkled his leathery cheeks in consternation. *This witchery will not stand.*

"Don't force us to shoot," Babette said, relieved and at once unnerved by their apparent defenselessness. The gauntlet radiated a faint red-gold aura.

Dixie gave her a grim look. "This might be our only chance."

"Cut them down like this?" Prince J shook his head at the prospect.

The urgency of the situation adrenalized Paul. He was the ranking authority here. It was imperative he take control and secure the book. The *Ptahkit'b* was like a resonating music only he could hear, prompting sympathetic vibrations in his head. He felt things shifting inside to accommodate the otherworldly signals. He aspired for his thoughts to flow into every last crack in the earth. Let it be mine, he thought. *Let it be mine, let this world be mine.*

The scene resolved into a living moment. Paul heard his own breathing again and his heart beat louder than ever. Shrugging free of his companions, he took a step toward the Duah-teh. "What if we take the book upworld?" He guessed that, despite the effects of Babette's gauntlet on their paranormal powers, the priests detected his vital connection to the artifact. Perhaps that would encourage a sense of trust.

And defeat our lifelong purpose?

"No," he said, feeling the word in his mouth. This was the day for a definitive Yes or No. The question was: could he live with the consequences? "I think I can neutralize its effects—at least long enough to hit on a more permanent solution." He was already working out how to replicate the time-displacement effect he'd generated by accident. If he trapped the *Ptahkit'b* in a stable time-loop..."Kei, can your wee man get it?"

"Easy." Katsuo whispered instructions in Japanese then, balancing the samurai on his palm, tossed it to the top of the plinth. The One-Inch Boy gave him a curt wave before disappearing from view.

"What happens to this place if we take it?" Babette asked.

It is too late for us. There are so few now. We lack the power to restrain the Ptahkit'b *for long. The cycle has come to its end. There will be no dawn to give absolution to the dead. Herakleion must perish and with it, our old enmities. If that is how the prophecy must be fulfilled then we go to Anubis satisfied with our place in the afterlife.*

"We have your word?" Paul asked.

The Ptahkit'b *is yours to master or destroy—if you can. The last of our strength will send you upworld.*

"Joey?" He squared his jaw. There was no choice: they had to leave now and not a second later. "Grab the disc, will you? We'll have to hope there's enough residual brain matter left to get the book safely to thee-uh surface."

"What about Lancer? We just gonna leave him?"

Paul struggled to square his emotions with the squad's inevitable circumstance. "We'll wait as long as the temple holds." What else could he say? The path he and Lancer had walked together since childhood had forked of a sudden, turning them in different directions. The *Ptahkit'b* was more important than either of them, or for that matter, anyone. It was like a magic lantern, throwing out new possibilities at every moment. With ready access to its secrets, there's no telling what he might accomplish.

Prince J grunted bitter assent then shouldered his rifle and raced for the disc.

The electric aura around Babette's gauntlet died out. "*Aïe! Vita fait.*" Her chest dropped from exhaustion. Dixie put a supporting arm around her.

A surge of trembling heads among the Duah-teh prompted Katsuo to level his gun at the priests. "Paul..."

"They fixin to swallow us up?" Dixie asked, raising his gun.

Paul motioned for them to hold their fire. "Steady..."

"Now that my gauntlet's out of juice." Babette turned it over and back as if looking for an 'on' button.

Prince J returned with the burned-out disc and set it at the base of the plinth, anxious to take up his rifle.

"Katsuo," Paul said, "work with Joey to get that book secured."

The mini-samurai stood on the edge of the Parmatmar crystal with the luminous plate hoisted above its head. Katsuo offered an outstretched hand while issuing more instructions in Japanese.

A series of rhythmic crashes from the corridor underscored the need to act swiftly.

The priests scattered at the rampaging entrance of the Lancer-daimon. Two additional Duah-teh floated into the chamber behind their charge. One of them carried an injured woman in his arms. The Lancer-daimon closed within ten meters of the squad and braked, cocking his head as if awaiting a final directive.

Nothing could have prepared Paul for the sight: the curved, cork-screwed horns; the deep-set eyes of crimson; the purplish lips and distended jaw; the lizard-rough skin; the outsized torso and thick, black-haired arms; the mace of black metal. There was no reconciling this monstrosity with Nolin. To do so would be to acknowledge reality as the mere spindrift of unreason. He wanted to shut his eyes, to shout blasphemies. G'd blind me, he thought over and over. But the vision persisted, terrible and demanding.

"We know him," he told himself as much as the others. "And knowing him, we have to believe in his essential goodness." He took several mindless steps forward, unarmed and unsure about what to say or do. There was no rational defense against this—this visceral horror. He'd failed to decide anything on the journey here. What did he intend now? Would he—could he—simply fold himself in the blood daimon's arms? Only had he even the breath to?

"You wanna save im, Shimmy, we gotta strafe the priests," Dixie said. "Should do it anyway for puttin him in that sleepin suit."

Paul continued his advance, determined to go on with his self-imposed test and if necessary, die under fist and footstomp. Ideas, emotion, arcane maths, memories, his head and heart, had been warped into unsettled abstractions. He tried to reason things out and ended up arguing with himself, pained by any violation of strict logic; he arrived at a clever solution then dismissed it, his thoughts expanding, narrowing, unbidden. What could he do in this doubtful state but rely on contingency and intuition?

As if lassoed by an invisible rope, a priest was hurtled into one of the painted coffins fixed to the wall and plummeted to the stone floor, broken. The rest divided into defensive clusters, blasting mental energies at each other. Whitespace misted out of their eyes. The injured woman limped away from the scrum in a hurry.

"Hema!" Babette pointed to Lancer. The half-daimon was convulsing in place, his will evidently split between rival masters. The mace fumbled to the ground. "Hema, can you help?"

"Forgive me pal," Dixie said to Prince J, "but these fellas—you gotta admit they all look alike. How do we know who to shoot?"

Joey shrugged as he held the disc on edge so the manikin could slip the book into the underside clip.

Paul came within the ambit of the quivering monster's reach. A raw animal musk assailed him. He wouldn't last a second if attacked. It would take only a single blow from the Lancer-daimon to knock his head from his shoulders. But he couldn't not try...He extended a hand. The mere holding onto existence fatigued him...Ah, wait, was it his imagination or had the horns started to recede? His breathing shallowed at the possibility. No, he was certain of it: the forehead was retreating, too and the eyes were clouding over. Loud nasal gasps punctuated the agonizing metamorphosis. The torso shook and sheared away to stressed and ruddy flesh. The pale and suffering figure of a man, his friend, emerged. Paul caught him by the shoulders and Lancer, shaking and ashamed, turned away.

A whole din of battle let loose as the priests sent debris from the sphinx-machine flying at each other. The woman Babette had greeted as Hema shouted above the tumult: "The gods have decreed this the last moment of unmaking. But this," she said, raising the mace high, "this can take you upworld." She motioned for the others to regroup around her. Prince J carried the disc on his back. The squad made welcoming noises in Nolin's direction, uncertain about what, exactly, to say. He brushed the halting words away with a palsied gesture, eyes downcast. Paul dreaded the conflicted feelings he'd have to face when the immediate danger passed.

Babette introduced Hema as a servant of the Duah-teh who had saved Nolin's life and helped her and Katsuo. For a servant, Paul thought, she held her head unusually high. She impressed him also with her rich brown eyes and a profile fit for coinage. She put a hand on Nolin's chin. "I am sorry, Lancer. You have already borne so much. But this tool—it is too powerful for me to hold—for any simple human."

"If you—" Nolin cleared his throat. His face was swelled up and bruised about the cheeks. "Will you ... come with us?"

Hema looked at him through wetted lashes and nodded.

Nolin accepted the mace from her and straightened his shoulders to address the squad. His eyes betrayed a disabling numbness. "Whatever happens—" An onslaught of arcing debris from the sphinx-machine cut him short. He hunched against its impacts. Hema pressed close, opposite him, and grasped the mace to modify its settings. Dixie and the others opened up on the makeshift missiles, deflecting or shattering them outright. The head of the mace emitted a preliminary glare.

Disordered mental commands screeched across Paul's thoughts: *cividualnotbackcarrestevenalltherwise*...He unholstered his gun and aimed in the direction of the priests. The air was diaphanous with a smoke like flash powder.

A weighty piece of junk barrelled toward Dixie. Babette crossed behind him to demolish it with a gauntleted punch. He flinched at the metal slivers that grazed his neck. "Thanks for that," he said. "No tellin what I owe you now."

"How about a decent vintage of champagne?" Babette battered away another whisk of scrap. "In a crystal flute. I am a lady, after all."

Dixie bestowed an air kiss. She returned it, her mouth a worn dash of lipstick.

"Close in and ready yourselves," Nolin said. "I'm not sure how much—" His voice degenerated into a hiss as the haft of the weapon sizzled with whitespace energy. Hema put her thin, scabbed hands over his and Paul, crowded between Katsuo and Babette, placed his over hers. Despite his anger at Nolin, Paul was jealous of the stranger's impulse. It should have been him. He met Nolin's startled glance. "Don't expect to be hauled back in a carry-chair." The energy resonated from the bones in his hands to the lining at the back of his brain. The growing brilliance was blankly ungraspable and stark. He set his teeth as a hot, sick pressure flooded his chest. Chaos was rampant and unstoppable. He ached with the knowledge of it, the power coursing through him, he and Nolin, together in humiliating retreat.

Nolin strained to hold the seething mace, direct its emanations. The cords in his neck went rigid. His vibrant groan could've been the last air from his superheated frame. The light bubbled out, subsumed them, barbing each at once to make a bursting sun. Energies from unguessed-at dimensions flooded in, buffeting Paul, routing his vital essence. Not to dissipate entirely—not to die—was all he could hope for. Breath was body and body breath and electric feel an atomized penumbra insignificant lost in the flux a dream a nothingness fear and ecstasy interfused in nightmare triggerings through freak blind terror ghosted bits of information to finally—how long?—contract into a body the mystery of himself a cold rippling murk the air salty and brisk the sky winter clear and the sun—his boyhood sun—a resurgent wonder above the coalescing waters of Abu Qir Bay, the book, Nolin and the others—everything—recovered in the tide as they'd been but different—illuminated...

Epilogue
An Isle of Their Own

18 January 1922
Egger Island, Greenland

The *Ptahkit'b* floated in a liminal space—there and not—in the windowless, lead-sealed chamber Paul had designed for conducting dangerous experiments. When shot through with two pulsing beams of light, the Parmatmar crystals enclosing the book generated a periodic stream of disruptive ions with entangled electron spins. One amplified beam created a magnetic field and the other partially flipped the spins of the atoms. The combination extended the natural asymmetrical ground state of the crystals, putting the book in a state of disequilibrium across time. Hema had warned him the *Ptahkit'b* would eventually adjust to the phase-shifting and reassert itself; for now, however, he'd managed to neutralize its effects.

The time-trap would've been impossible to build without the boost in intelligence conferred by the *Ptahkit'b*. The downside was the occasional lapse into delusional grogginess—a consequence, he suspected, of a turned-out unconscious. But he trusted these spells would pass once he got used to his supercharged mind. He was twitchy and effervescent with ideas. They arose in tenuous association like nesting bubbles, merging, dividing, bursting, pristine in their shimmery abstraction. The trick was to pluck these notions whole and intact from what he now called 'idea space' before they evanesced.

He knew something of the feeling and energy from which this mental space originated and also that he didn't know completely and probably couldn't. The book was like Georg Cantor's Absolute or V made manifest—a mathematical construct that contained every conceivable property of space-time. It was—in a word—infinite. *Energy is everything and information in its purest form is energy.* The scary thing is: one infinity implies another; in fact, based on the Reflection Principle, it implies an infinite variety of infinities. Paul worried he might have inadvertently introduced a threat to reality in all its forms by bringing the artifact home.

He exited the chamber to find Nolin sitting in the outer lab, waiting in the shadowlight. There was a pained awkwardness between them. With the exception of arranging security and other logistical matters, they'd largely avoided each other on the trip back from Egypt. Neither of them were given to bold displays of emotion. They tended to rigid quietude and stillness when disagreements arose. War, or even a stern, undemonstrative father, could do that to you. Besides, preserving squad unity had been more important than airing their personal concerns. But now…

"Stable, is it?" Nolin stood up. The natural clefts in his cheeks had begun to return to his swollen face.

"Wouldn't try to maypole around it, but…" Paul leaned against a steel frame table, daunted by his depth of feeling for Nolin.

"Alpha plus—as usual."

"Hema explained how thee-uh Duah-teh frustrated its effects for so long—before they resorted to direct mental control."

"Buffering it with mad people. Yes, it might do for awhile…"

"You thinking Vaucluse?" It was the asylum where Babette's mother and the rest of the French prisoners the squad liberated in 1917 were treated.

Nolin frisked his sandy beard. "For the time being, perhaps in combination with your time-displacement device."

"No, it's worth trying. I probably shouldn't—I mean, I'm still adjusting to what it's done to me. I go from visionary to addled at a snap." Paul thought it best to first confess a failing of his own before broaching his grievances. "Better off without daily exposure."

"The squad got banged on hard this time—you especially." Nolin shifted his focus to the shuttered chamber and adopted a serious tone. "Not only your—your heightened connection to the dreamtime—but…" He threw his hands up, frustrated with himself. "I'm sorry, mate. I truly am. I know I've let you down, that you feel an anger and betrayal your habitual good manners keep you from venting. I deserve it—whatever resentment you feel. I shouldn't have hidden my…condition." He caught Paul's studied glance then just as quickly bowed his head. "I put the squad at risk and worse, I broke trust with you. I understand if you think I can't lead any longer. I've had the same doubts, even considered retiring IG completely..." When he looked up, there was guilt in his dimmed eyes—guilt he'd never show anyone else. "But I can't stand the thought of losing you—your friendship."

The whites of Nolin's eyes were as white as a left-behind child's. Paul couldn't possibly hold onto his anger. "I have to say it: I was hurt. I *am* hurt..." His anger dissipated as he got the words out. The sadness of being mad at Nolin—the potential loss of their easy rapport, the sense of brotherhood—cut short his reaction. He made mincing movements with his lips. "To keep something like that a secret when I thought, well, it made me feel distrusted..."

"I—I won't dignify what I did with high-minded excuses. I was in a bad state and ashamed. And I thought I had it under wraps—I do..."

"Thee-uh daily force exercises..."

"You can't imagine the awfulness of it—the steady crash of blood in my ears. I'm everything we fight against."

"Not at core," Paul said.

Nolin had a look of twisted perplexity as if a string had gone taut in his chest.

"You mustn't think yourself a savage humped beast." Paul couldn't bear to watch his friend suffer. Self-judgments were the worst sort of verdicts.

"Humped you say?" A thin smile crossed Nolin's lips.

"How did it happen? Blood magick?"

"In a manner of speaking, yes, when I was a lad. Without it, I would've died." Nolin drew closer, watery blue eyes on the level. "One of my Latin primers was curiously preoccupied with the idiom *poenas dare*—to pay a penalty. Dido uses the term when she tells Aeneas to clear off, saying she hopes he and his companions drown." He grimaced. "*Poenas dare* might be the story of my life."

"None of us will be donning a black soutane," Paul said. "What made it all the more shocking was thee-uh contrast—between the Lancer we know—the idealistic leader—and that rough creature..." He dismissed the image and tried to think of Nolin as he was—human and fallible. Yet if the chief purpose of a man is right duty then Nolin had fulfilled it. When the Duah-teh wavered in their control of him, he'd mustered enough willpower to revert and get the squad back safely. Those were the telling facts in Paul's estimation and heroic on their face. It was the Nolin familiar to him from boyhood. It was the Nolin who'd saved him more than once at great risk.

"If you asked thee-uh team now who was true, who they'd trust with their lives," Paul continued with increasing difficulty, "in the upshot, your name would be first on their lips. They would do anything for you if it was in their way to do it." There was a constricting thickness in his throat. "You see: you're also—and for thee-uh the greater part—every-thing we fight for." He had to blink his eyes against the pressure of tears, his heart a ragged pulse. All too soon, the two of them—everyone—would be gone, irrelevant, forgotten. This existence was it.

He put his arms around Nolin as if to give him shelter, gently, gently, trusting his friend would know how much the gesture mattered, how it was a reflection of his worth and the beginning of forgiveness.

Babette reset the Victrola for the third movement of Debussy's *Suite Bergamasque* and climbed back into bed to have a second post-coital smoke. The gauntlet lay on the nightstand as symbol and promise. Herakleion in its stasis had seemed a nightmare version of one of her perpetual childhood summers. The floating melodies of *Clair de Lune* encouraged an indulgent nostalgia. *Comme c'est triste.* How she missed her 14 year old self: just coming into her womanhood; nerves fizzing with new emotions; family still a unifying force; her mother vibrant, always puttering in the garden; her father's alcoholism at bay; life a bucolic blur.

What would she tell that girl now? What words of wisdom that didn't have a sing-song falsity from overuse? The gauntlet came with unwanted self-knowledge. Socrates' admonition to 'know thyself' could be a curse. Preserve your generous feelings, your willingness to trust, she thought at her younger self. *War will shatter them soon enough,* à mon grand chagrin.

Dixie shouldered the door wide and entered dressed in long johns and combat boots, champagne in one hand, fluted glasses in the other. "Here ya go. Chilled 'n' everything." He back-kicked the cabin door shut and flashed her the bottle.

Her color deepened at his thoughtfulness. She'd expected a Kentucky whisky or even a flask of Tennessee moonshine. "Ah, Champagne Salon—made only from chardonnay grapes. Not a polished exotic like *Taittinger Comtes de Champagne* but well-known for its class and purity." She mashed her cigarette into the tin ashtray next to the gauntlet, letting the linen fall from her breasts. "Don't tell me you actually thought ahead on this?"

"That Brit captain helped me get a bottle afore we left." He kicked off an unlaced boot. "Gotta say, I'm a mite proud a myself."

"I suppose someone has to be." She gave a vulpine smirk as she received a wine flute. "Cut-glass?"

"Wasn't gonna search through all those movin boxes for the crystal dressed like this." He toed out of the second boot. "Coulda used something like Katsuo's li'l man. Guess I missed out on the toys. I'm like the kid got coal in his stockin."

"It wasn't as simple as that."

"Jus questions, right?" He thumbed the cork. It ricocheted from wall to ceiling and disappeared under the mahogany bedframe.

Babette extended her glass to catch the froth. Dixie poured, eyeing her nakedness. "God, you're a nother kind a beauty."

She lowered her lids, mock demure then raised them again along with her glass. "*Santé.*" She took a delicate sip. The vintage was light and rich and subtle on the tongue. "*Par excellence.*"

"Whatever Paul says, the wisdom a Neet-cha or whatever wouldn't make this taste any better." Dixie plopped onto the bed and kissed a thin scar on her neck. "Or me any happier."

She frowned in dismay. "There's a reason behind it—this toy." She grabbed the glove from the nightstand. "That machine-god fit the weapon to the soldier."

"That why Katsuo got the li'l man? Cause he's on the small side?"

"I'd say it was his boyish disposition and maybe his reverence for history. He's trying to measure up to deeds he heard as a child, to make himself honorable."

"And your story worries you? Gotta say, sometimes it's jus shell-shock. You know how it is—you don't always come back right away from some a these missions."

"No, this is something else. The dilemma I was given…I had to be honest with myself about the solution. If I weren't, who knows what would've happened…" Her lips thinned into a seam. "Maahes—the god—he said I saw myself fundamentally alone in the world, independent, almost, *enfin*, resigned to it. Like Guillaume d'Orange against the Spanish Muslims. He had his family but in the end, the struggle was his own." She turned the weighty glove over in her hand. Maahes had practically described it as distrustfulness personified. "Paul says the gauntlet draws its power from me—my bioelectric field. It means, I think, I depend overmuch on myself, apart from the squad."

"Or maybe you're jus resourceful. There's no shame in that."

"It made me wonder is all…" She recalled how she'd treated Dixie—testing him for sincerity—her attitude toward the squad and the sarcastic distance she'd maintained with the others. What was it Katsuo had told her about the Japanese kanji for 'person,' *ningen*? It was comprised of two images: *nin* (human being) and *gen* (in-between space). The word made it plain: no one is completely separate and atomistic; rather, we're defined by how we fit into the space around us.

"Is that why you came for me in that dreamy by-place? Feelin sorry for yourself…" He ticked and agitated, searching for something more to say.

"I'd planned to do that before, not knowing how the dream machine would work." He had to believe in her affection for him.

"Talk about embarrasin. There I was caught between love and desire—lust I guess you'd say—and I didn't know if I had what it took." Though Dixie cracked a mischievous smile she knew he was trying to spare her further self-recrimination. "Hearin my name from you, though, it was like a glassen word done broke over me. I was myself again, awake, head poundin somethin awful but awake." He ran a finger along the contour of her jaw. "Jus rest easy bout this. That Egyptian idol don't know you like I do." He set the gauntlet aside.

She was stirred and laughed and kissed him full on the lips, her mouth tingling with bubbles. In these moments, softened by kindness, she urged herself to remember—*remember this person here, this surge of warmth.* "If only we could live on champagne and frosting."

"That your idea of heaven?"

"Hema says heaven is the void at a squint." *L'appel du vide.*

"T'chaw. How's she know heaven?" He gulped the rest of his drink. "Looked to me like her people was worshippin daimons who done tricked em into it. That's why Christ came here—to choke them idols from their witchy pyramids."

Dixie tended to treat his faith as a call to arms in a forever war. She doubted he'd ever be able to say, Yes, all's fine and done with. But the knob-kneed rustic exuded a rare *jouissance* of life. She felt his pulse at the wrist. His heartbeat echoed in her palm, hardly any space between them and their feelings. She might end up with nothing more than a worn photo album but *quel amour!* she had to chance it. She breathed again with the whole of her body. They were still achingly young in truth. "So, arm-in-arm, we ballyhoo into every thunderhead?"

"No doubt." He brought her hand to his lips. "And even if we never see victory, the charge of it and bein at your side's enough for one life."

Nolin found Hema not far from the surface lift, framed by the beam from its safety lamp. She was wondering up at the soft iridescent green of the Northern Lights, a bundle of shaggy coat, swaying from side to side on her crutches as if partnered to the wavelike aurora. One pant leg had been split to the knee to allow for her plaster cast.

He crunched across the ice and snow in a fur-lined leather jacket like those worn by army messengers. The salted air invigorated him. The heave of the night-vanished sea was a blunted roar. He felt his own warm breath against his upper lip.

Chin aimed at the ethereal sky, Hema ignored his approach until he sidled close, saying, "Thought I'd find you out here."

"It looks like, up there, I could swim one ghostly universe to another." Having breathed an atmosphere filtered by the *Ptahkit'b* for so long, she'd apparently absorbed its powers of translation. She'd spoken perfect, if somewhat formal, English since bursting from the waters of Abu Qir Bay.

Her studied gaze reminded Nolin of his mother, an accomplished naturalist, who, on their walks together in the hills could be observed moving her lips silently, taking mental notes: *I see, I hear, I notice.* "The lights can be seen from my home country of Ireland too—the Inishowen Peninsula in Donegal and elsewhere along the Wild Atlantic Way." He followed her gaze. Silken twists of light shimmered up into a frieze of stars.

A winsome smile bloomed out of thoughtful beauty for him. What sufferings she'd endured: snatched to an alien land as a child; immersed in the ways of war and dreamtime weirdness; compelled to watch her adoptive city collapse altogether; then removed to this frozen outpost, again, an exile out of time, with only the dead for constancy. Out of respect for her disrupted life, Nolin had offered to set her up in Egypt or elsewhere in the Levant but she'd preferred to join him here, all hope and effort. "How're you settling in?"

"It is quieter here withal ..." She grazed her bottom lip with her teeth. "But the dead are still in my charge. I hear ghost tongues like wings against my ears." Her neat, sculptured profile caught the glow from the safety lamp like reflecting pins in the dark. "I could ask the same of you."

"I never meant to be a providence."

"Regardless, I fear the prophecy of Osiris may not be over." She examined him sharply. "What if it were not about Herakleion but this place—upworld, Earth?"

Nolin set his jaw, dismayed. "Is that a future you've previsioned?"

"It is hard to know." She nodded at something unspoken. "The Unworldly River is a realm where everything exists at once. Thoughts, ideas, lived histories, even delusions can have a tangible impact. Your Great War, for instance, sent shockwaves felt in Herakleion and elsewhere—energy that reverberated through dreams and back again. It is a fathomless confluence."

"I'm not sure I understand. What are you saying?"

"To be in a dream is not to be above nature but to see it for what it is.

Dreams try to translate natural secrets into the language of consciousness. I'd have to invent a language to tell you."

Nolin had experienced enough of the dreamtime at its most disorienting to understand. "I wish we could've done more for Herakleion."

"The land was suffering a curse trying to make itself out. There was no turning back the cycle..."

The notion of recurring historical cycles brought to mind Virgil's *Eclogue IV*, its fragmented prophecies, stoic beliefs about nonlinear time, myths about an age of gold...Nolin wondered if Hema had lived through its legends in one form or another. He had to remind himself sometimes she was nearly two thousand years old. Her liveliness and curiosity astounded him. At her age, he'd likely have outgrown meaning entirely.

She put a gloved hand on his arm and spoke from the well of those uncountable years. "You can stop questioning your conscience. You are a man with a good purpose and more importantly, you have brotherhood here. That makes you human at heart."

"What I see, what partly disappears in the mirror..." Nolin averted his eyes but there was no escaping what had passed between them. She knew him better than anyone outside of his mother—down to his deep unconscious. He'd been alone with his thoughts ever since the blood transfusion at age ten that saved his life and at once, made him a demigod and monster. From that time forward, he'd been split between 'me' and 'I': the Nolin standing outside himself, watchful and wary of his daimonic aspect, and the Nolin living in the moment. He'd perfected a kind of ventriloquism to get by, throwing his voice from the stoic persona he'd crafted from his philosophical studies.

This double consciousness had not only compelled him to question his own impulses but to close himself off from others for fear of discovery. Hema was the only one for whom no explanation and no repentance was necessary. When she'd resuscitated him, they'd hallucinated in sync, body and soul. She'd felt his lone-voiced intensities and accepted the two Nolins as only a master-dreamer could. In dreams, there are no simple divisions; rather, like a crystal, a multiplicity of facets, some hidden, others exposed. A tolerant, compound view of things came naturally to her.

"I can't let my fear and anger roam out again, Hema." Though his memories of his time in daimon form was a terrorizing muddle, the guilt and shame of it would shadow him to the end of his days. He'd entertained vast empires of bloody revenge.

"Suffering should be the measure of selfhood only in myth. Don't underestimate your spirit. You are a courage unheard of in Creation. You can remake yourself just as I must do." She raised her eyes to the low winter night and its hints of secret weather. "Hema—it is not a true name but a...title? No, role. *Hem-netjer* means 'god's servant.' Would you help me to pick another?"

"What would you like it to mean?" The words were out before Nolin considered the messy implications of naming her. He was careful not to betray too much emotion.

"The stars are like chains of thoughts. What is the word for the dark between them? Because there—in those spaces—lies true silence."

Every second Nolin paused deepened his nervousness. It wasn't the sort of nervousness he endured under fire but unrelenting and conscious. "There isn't a word, exactly—at least one you'd want people to call you. But there is an Irish Gaelic name I've always liked meaning 'dark' or 'dark-haired'—Ciara."

She tried the name on her tongue and laughed. "I suppose then," she said, reaching for his hand, "this is the first and longest moment I've been myself."

A fine radiance passed through Nolin as he regarded the faraway stars. Her words were a balm to him and her touch also. The flush of emotion felt painful but right.

TORVUS INDUSTRIES | REYNOLD B. TORVIS LIBRARY

Collection Reynold B. Torvis Library	**Publish Date** c. 1919
Object ID 2023.3.17	**Year Range** 1908 thru 1908
Object Name Book	**Catalog Date** 03.17.2023
Call# 097.42 Q18 1922	**Cataloged By** Terhune, Calvin
Other#	**Status Date** 08.07.2025
Old#	**Status By** Rajagopal, Anika
Accession# 2023.3 Lehman, Paz	**Status** Shelf
Home Loc. Library-Special Collections Room	

LIBRARY	☐ LIBRARY ☐ CUSTOM

Summary This volume contains a transcript of Pathe Freres Roneophone recordings made by Fianna I. Quigg that detail the last known sea voyage of her husband Liam T. Quigg and the first documented adventure of Nolin "Lancer" Quigg.

Subjects
1. Captain Nemo, aka, Prince Dakkar
2. La Société Voudon Gnostique
3. Mama Paris
4. Parmatmar crystals
5. Quigg, Fianna I.
6. Quigg, Liam T.
7. Quigg, Nolin "Lancer"
8. South Pacific Exploration

Author Quigg, Fianna I.	**LCCN**
Added Entry Quigg, Liam T.: Quigg, Nolin "Lancer"	**ISBN**
Title Forever the Star Finder: The Last Strange	**ISSN**
Added Entry Voyage of the Quigg Family	**Control#**
Series The History of Integrand (related frag-	**Physical Descript.** 10 v. 16 cm
ments; available by special permission in	**Language**
Added Entry the Rare Book Room)	
Event	**Copy#** 1
Site#	**Publisher** Not applicable
	Pub Place Not applicable
	Edition 1st (facsimile)

Notes This volume is a photocopy facsimile of the original transcript (c. 1919) which was presumably lost in the destruction of Integrand General's Egger Island compound (1968). Extant evidence suggests the transcript was made privately under the auspices of Fianna I. Quigg and collated with other materials by Nolin "Lancer" Quigg in preparation for a never-completed autobiography or official history of Integrand General.

The illustrations are also the work of Fianna I. Quigg, a naturalist by avocation. As noted in the text, she declined to draw any maps, either of the relevant South Pacific region or of "Arunachal Island" (so-called), in order to keep the locations associated with this account secret.

Technical note: the Roneophone machine on which the original recordings were made resembled the phonograph in design and use. It recorded on 7" discs rather than wax cylinders for greater durability.

Forever the Star Finder:
The Last Strange Voyage of the Quigg Family

Transcribed from the oral history
recorded by Fianna I. Quigg on Roneophone

"My son, as you grow into your manhood and begin to make your way in this uncertain world, I feel duty-bound to recount the loss of your da insofar as I know it and have the strength to put it into words. I say 'loss' instead of 'death' not out of misplaced hope or to spare your feelings, but because the circumstances prompt a humility of understanding. I, myself, prefer to think on him as a transcendental spirit released from worldly cares and constraints; in a word, free. Like a music outside the realm of the visible.

"As you know, he had an irrepressible urge to breathe the air of different worlds. He endeavoured to challenge nature's limits and to make place his purpose. In that way, he was a great hoarder of experience, your da. Whereas I would have been content with a common life. Give me a small patch of wilderness, wood, fen or heathland, chalk stream, the type of landscape matters not so long as I've the eyes to see things as they are in their essence. Ah, to have the penetrating vision of a god, inner and outer ... The spectacle of unfolding order, fully apprehended, would be enough to occupy me for a lifetime.

"But I digress into hope and fantasy from the start. I suppose this story, for I must consider these events somewhat in the abstract and fable-like if I'm to hold on to my thoughts, properly begins with the boarding of the family schooner. We were twenty-three days into our journey at that point, sailing eastward among the Remote Central Pacific Islands. Forgive me if I don't recite exact coordinates from the logs. I'd rather keep the details vague in the event that, through no fault of yours, this account falls into unsafe hands. Just imagine the havoc a shrewd privateer could wreak with the advanced magicks of Arunachal Island at his disposal! We came as close to that dire outcome as I dare consider ...

"The trip was meant to be a months-long educational jaunt and vacation. You were to learn sailing, astronomy and oceanic survival techniques, among other things, from your da whilst I taught scientific natural history. As you might recall, I'd begun surveying South Pacific avifauna years before with the intention of compiling a sort of regional bird atlas and thought to finish that work along the way.

"When I first spotted the great frigatebird in the rigging, I thought it sick or injured. Frigatebirds are known to follow fishing vessels in order to feed on the scraps and offal tossed overboard, but The Star Finder offered little of the kind. The other explanation would've been an approaching storm. According to Piddington's Guide for Sailors, seabirds have an instinct for storms—something to do with electrical charges in the atmosphere—and will use a ship as sanctuary. The frigatebird remained nested in the topsail, however, after several days of gentle weather, leaving its perch only to compass round for tuna, jellyfish or squid.

"In hindsight, I should've made the connection to Voudon based on the colloquial species name alone, which is iwa or 'thief' in Hawaiian, one trifling letter different from lwa, the name for the Haitian spirits venerated by the likes of Mama Paris. She must've thought herself fierce clever for adopting the frigatebird as her familiar and spy in this instance.

"You'd made a mascot of the bird by the time her French brigantine showed against the far horizon. As I understood from your da, the term 'brigantine' refers to the ship's rigging rather than its size or form. The rigging is two-masted, the foremast square-rigged and the main sail rigged with both aft-and-fore sails and square topsails. This configuration, combined with the lack of an identifying flag, worried your da on the instant. From his days as chief engineer on the Nautilus, he knew brigantine rigging was a favourite of pirates for the superior speed and manoeuvrability it imparts. Even our schooner, modified as she was with square sails to best accommodate the trade winds, couldn't hope to outrun her.

"Your da clambered the shrouds to the maintop whilst the first mate, Banon Molony—you remember him, yes? Large, bald-headed old sea dog—set about arming our small crew. Besides Banon, there was only the second mate, poor Cully, and the boatswain, Zhāng Jian. We had one magickal defence as well—a dazing whirligig your da called it. Some artefact Jian had acquired for him in the Orient.

"Your safety was our chief concern. Straightaway, your da insisted we ready the escape balloon. You were at my heels when I threw open the aft cabin hatch and opened up the hydrogen canisters. Only vaguely aware of our situation, you were more excited than scared to see the balloon trailing behind the boat, inflating. Your main worry was whether Pup-Pup would be allowed to come along. Pup-Pup, the clockwork dog ... How your da took pleasure in that bit of cleverness. If, due to his foremost and

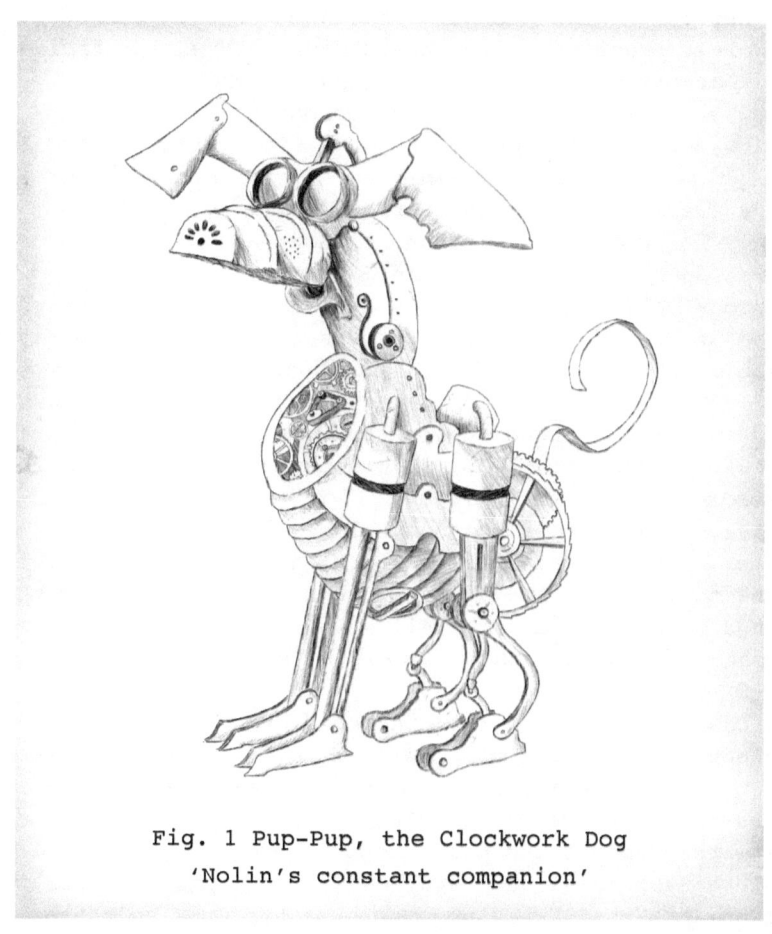

Fig. 1 Pup-Pup, the Clockwork Dog
'Nolin's constant companion'

necessarily remote role as mentor, he couldn't father you in the manner he wanted, he was glad to have at least cobbled up a suitable companion. He always spoke with barely-concealed pride of your attachment to Pup-Pup, the gleeful boyishness it brought out. Disporting like Childe Harold, he'd say. I don't know what you picture when you cast your mind back to those days, but I hope you understand how much your da couldn't do or say, how dearly he loved you, and curbed his feelings only for fear of weakening your resolve against the trials he put you through—trials that undoubtedly helped you survive this fearful episode.

"The balloon was near to fully inflated by the time we heard that first round of bar shot smash into the rigging. I don't know what would've been worse: facing the barrage straight-on, anticipating each blast, whether heated, chain shot or common, or suffering below-decks in the wan light of a slush lamp as we did, racked with uncertainty amid the din of battle. Your da answered with the ten-barrel Gatling gun. Janey Mac! The continuous peal and thunder above was like to shudder us into the ocean depths, I thought. Each riotous volley excited new and dire imaginings, though none as fanciful as what proved actual. I held you tight in the gondola, stomach clenched, running my fingers through your sandy hair to soothe us both. You protested my coddling, contending you could help, but stayed put, knowing better than to risk disobeying your da at such a juncture.

"Partly demasted, the boat slowed and steadied in the water. Your da and his men fought on in a vain effort to sink the iron-hulled brigantine, but Mama Paris had the range on us, and as you well know, the backing of a crew impossible to kill short of explosives or hellish gouts of fire.

"There was a brief lull in the fighting when your da released the dazing whirligig. It was a firework of sorts in the shape of a sparrow. Not much range, so he'd been forced to wait until the brigantine had closed on us with grapnels and boat hooks before using it. Tail ablaze, the balsa wood sparrow shot over the pirates to burst into what he assumed to be a hypnotizing pattern.

He and the other crew had turned their backs to it, of course, but its radiant dust played at the edge of his eyesight. In the smoky silence, he barked at us to be off already.

"I was standing to pull the release when a cannonball roared through the balloon, tumbling me heel over crown and whipping you out the hatch pell-mell. Pup-Pup clanged against the inside of the hull as you were flung into the open water. Based on your da's researches, the artefact should have put the brigands into a lasting trance, immobilizing them, if not turning them into suggestible drones. More proof that we faced an enemy armed with potent magicks.

"With my head ringing from the tumble, I lurched to the hatch to see where you'd gone. Though you were an expert in your strokes, I feared the sudden dunking might panic you, trifling as you were—as any mortal would be—in the plunk middle of the Pacific. It put me in mind of Pip from <u>Moby Dick</u>, the scene where he jumps out the boat and, abandoned to the elements, suffers that maddening vision of God as some indifferent dynamo.

"I heard Cully shout to your da, saying he was going for the dinghy to retrieve you. I made to reply, thinking I would dive out the hatch, when he was cut down with what your da first took to be an arrow. The missile transfixed Cully's throat, leaving him to choke on his own blood.

"At least that's how your da described it later—when we were Mama Paris's confirmed prisoners and on our way to Arunachal. The 'arrow' turned out to be a needle-like twig loosed from Loko's forearm with a twitch. The <u>lwa</u> spirit could be deadly that way, sprouting boughs of battering strength or twigs like poniards at will.

"Whether you heard my encouraging shouts or no, you started swimming for the boat. We'd come to a dead stop about fifty metres distant—an easy enough swim for you. I hurried from the cabin to drop the Jacobs ladder, Pup-Pup bounding after me. The pirates had just lowered the boarding plank when I arrived on deck. What a galling sight! The foremast had been sheared off a few metres above the deck and the severed mess tented one side of the deck. The main topsail had gone missing about where the gaff intersected it. Cannon shot also had exploded sections of the railing so the deck was littered with splintery debris. Your da and Banon had discarded their rifles and raised their hands in surrender. I'd never seen such a look of utter consternation on your da's face.

"Then I saw the cause of it—the privateers crowding the boarding plank, guns and cutlasses levelled. My heart skipped at the sight. Their eyes were misted white and their skeletons glowed a sick-green through their skin. Worse still, they were a damaged lot, bearing all manner of wounds—bloodless perforations and stumped limbs, ghastly pits around the mouth and nose, skin flaking off, grim parodies of men.

"They soon made way for that wizened mambo-witch, Mama Paris, and she sauntered across the plank in her black ruffled blouse and full-flared skirt as if she were the queen trooping the colour. Her headwrap, accented in dark purple like her skirt, was knotted at the crown, giving it the shape of a regal coronet. Every other step hit the plank with extra force because of that awkward hitch in her hip. When she reached the end of the plank, she extended a hand to be helped to the deck, squinting as she did with her left eye and ogling your da with the right. 'Bes' be kindly,' she said, 'ere you leave de boy fadda-less.'

"Banon took her arm, muttering, 'God rot you.' He was an excitable bruiser but loyal as a lion to its pride. Had a habit of making boxing gestures whilst he talked, rolling his shoulders, jabbing and feinting, occasionally smacking a fist into his palm for emphasis. I understand you have such steadfast men beside you in your adventuring and it eases my worries a tad to know it.

"Your da knew Mama Paris from his Nemo days. A high priestess in La Société Voudon Gnostique, she was a livelong pirate known for a hell or plunder attitude. He wasted no time in confronting her, saying, 'This is unforgivable—this deviltry and cold-blooded murder. I thought Voudon was about respecting the ancients, fostering the virtues.'"

"She got her back up, saying, 'Dat a lot a blaw-flum,

you tell me how practise my people faith. De virtues?
Hah, de word should mek you inside shrivel. You forget
I know what you done fo' dat saboteur Nemo? I know you
true self. You no pure Aristotle man.'

"'That may be. But if this is some misguided revenge
no one but me should suffer, agreed? Allow me to retrieve
the boy—'

"'Loko,' she called out. The Voudon spirit hove into
view on the brigantine's forecastle deck, now alongside
our rudder. 'This my <u>bon</u> <u>lwa</u> spirit elemental,' she
said. He was a stooped creature of prehensile, lichen-
spotted wood. A tangle of antler-like growths crowned
a broad face shaggy with moss. His eyes were small and
bright, his nose subtle divots and his mouth—a toothless
slit—was visible through his beard only when he spoke
(which was rarely). Because of his bent frame and
large, ungainly tail, he shuffled somewhat like an ape,
occasionally knuckling the ground. Without a glance in

Fig. 2 Loko, Voudon Elemental
'Living god or magicked human?'

our direction, he pushed up against the railing and spun
an arm into an ever-lengthening bramble.

"'Ah, sink me for a soundin' weight,' Banon remarked
above the prolonged wood-crack.

"The boatswain barked something in Chinese, raising
a shard of mirror he kept on a leather thong around
his neck. Jian later told me the mirror had a two-fold
function: to reflect the true appearance of daimons, thus
sapping them of spiritual force, and more generally, to
ensure heavenly happiness. His stern expression in the
moment suggested disappointment on both counts.

"I gave Mama Paris a hard look woman to woman before
starting aft. I got to the rail as the lwa hoisted you
out of the water. I shouted for you to relax in the
elemental's grasp, afraid you might shake loose in the
dangerous rolling gap between the two ships. The lwa
deposited you on the deck of the brigantine, leaving its
arm spiralled around you.

"'There's no need to take the boy hostage,' your da
said.

"Mama Paris put on a cunning smile but stayed silent
until I returned to your da's side. 'You fancy or
select?' she asked. 'A duchess, maybe? Dat would suit
Cap'n Liam la-de-da style.'

"Her appraising look made my skin hot. She figured me
for a Lady Bracknell on first meeting and never gave the
notion up. 'What do you want from my son?' I demanded.

"'Onè ak respè,' she said in Haitian Creole, meaning
honour and respect.

"'But why?' your da said, his face tight with anger.

"'Mama Paris found a crossroad twixt de world we see
and de one we doan,' she said. She had an aggravating
habit of referring to herself in the third-person. 'Mama
Paris sense in spirit-dream dis place. Island hereabout.
But Mama Paris need you help—you science—tuh find it
exact. Island protect wid much strong magick.'

"'Supposing I help you reach this crossroads, what
then?' your da asked. 'Would you conjure a blood daimon?
Absorb its otherworldly dream energies? Or in any way
cause ungodly harm? Because I won't be a party to that.'

"The frigatebird circling overhead fluttered down to
settle on the mambo-witch's shoulder. 'You white all

de same—dink Voudon some black magick,' she said. 'No,
Voudon 'bout create de harmony, balance, in service to
lwa. We seek de same—you, Mama Paris—possibility what
come wid knowledge. Freedom. This ol' world always sayin'
how loud and wrong I am. I jus' wan' say yes 'gainst a
world say no.'

"Your da flashed on Cully's remains. 'That why you
killed my second mate and now threaten my family?' he
said. 'For the sake of knowledge?'

"She laughed, hissing through her yellowed teeth. 'Ah,'
she said, 'Mama Paris first dink tuh show sad result a
ignorance. Mek knowledge mo' precious, wi?'

"The condition of The Star Finder forced us to
weigh anchor on the open water and to make shift on the
brigantine. Your da considered torching the schooner
outright. But in the end, he couldn't bear the prospect,
saying it would've been like setting fire to the family
album. I suppose its final disposition is another, albeit
subordinate, mystery never to be solved.

"Before departing, we gave Cully a makeshift burial
at sea. Your da wasn't a sentimental sort, driven more
by an irrepressible sense of duty than affection, but he
lingered over Cully's body and grudged Mama Paris for
his murder. Cully had been an aged bachelor devoted to
your da after years of shared perils. Your da had helped
him 'dry out,' and whilst Cully was given to goutish
wheezing and a too-mean cynicism, he was also clearly
grateful for the chance to be part of a mission larger
than himself. You likely remember him for blowing up
the kitchen boiler when, as a joke on the cook, he'd
filled the pepper castor with gunpowder. His humour
was volatile and twisted that way—the sign of a born
mischief-seeker. I only ever saw him laugh full-bellied
following a chancy prank or pratfall; still, he deserved
a better, more dignified end.

"The brigantine, furnished in gaudy opulence, had
plenty of open berths given that the dozen or so
zonbies—as Mama Paris pronounced the word—required no
sleep. On closer inspection, they seemed a cursèd weird
cross of flesh and plant. The texture of their skin was
not unlike the bark of the downy birch. Their hair was a
patchy, spray-stiffened moss and their eyes were veined

in subtle greens. They even gave off the dank odour of
basement-cool dirt and potato mould. Mama Paris remarked
on your easy acceptance of the creatures. We attributed
it to your da's nigh-mythical stories and your own
wanton imagination. I recall catching you a couple of
years before with that illustrated excerpt from the
bestiary chapter of the <u>Psalms</u> <u>of</u> <u>the</u> <u>Black</u> <u>Sun</u>, a
pamphlet strictly forbidden you. That mischievous smirk
of yours made it difficult to be stern. It dimpled your
cheeks just so ...

"Your da and his crew worked ship as hard as any
of the <u>zonbies</u> to expedite our journey. Banon treated
the creatures with undisguised contempt, calling them
'turnip heads' and 'sorry-arsed kindling' and Jian made
strange, avoiding them as he could as if their condition
were catching. The elemental, you'll recall, kept to the
hold for the duration. I suspect he went into a sort of
dormancy, removed as he was from any rooting soil.

"Though distressed by our situation, I enjoyed the
opportunity to study this alternate order of nature,
however surreptitiously. Mama Paris discouraged overt
observation, much less scientific study, and when asked
directly about the <u>zonbies</u>, gave vague, circuitous
answers. She wouldn't even admit their base humanity and,
if pressed, would threaten to blast my mind from my body
with a toss of juju powder.

"Before I met your da and became acquainted with the
supernatural, I misjudged the size and complexity of
Creation. I'd thought to keep my researches simple: the
dunnock creeping under the hedge, the song thrush in
its high perch, my notebook full of sketchy busts and
wing-shapes. Perhaps owing to my parents' Westminster
Calvinism and its dominion theology, I thought my
attentions gave nature meaning.

"The more I learned about the dreamtime, about faeries,
<u>daimons</u>, the entire panoply of otherworldly phenomena,
the more I understood that meaning existed without me,
and in fact, I barely existed in the order of things. I
learned to build up a sense of unity from particulars
rather than fit observations into some preconceived
whole. I let nature awaken my intuition of a universal
harmony—a harmony I still believe in, though I doubt its

dynamics will ever be captured in a single governing law. Because nature is a creative, ever-changing force, which makes knowledge provisional, or at least, relational. The highest we can probably aspire to isn't absolute knowledge à la G.W. Hegel, but sympathy with intelligence.

"My word, I seem to have gone off on a tangent there ... Recalling this episode tends to make me solemn and philosophical. I suppose that's another way for me to skirt or belay the worst of its emotional hurts. But maybe these digressions will take on a uniquely clarifying power on the second or third turn.

"To resume the tale, several days later we reached the island I'll refer to as 'Arunachal.' I assume Nemo named it after Arunachal Pradesh for nostalgic or perhaps symbolic reasons. Though the name means the Land of Dawn Lit Mountains, there was but one foothill on this small, remote isle.

"The dinghy we rowed to shore was crowded to the point of discomfort owing mainly to Loko's ungainly bulk and the four zonbies Mama Paris brought for added protection. Banon and Jian sculled us into a narrow inlet where we beached the craft and, taking our water, limited foodstuffs and a rucksack of scientific equipment, started for the steeply-sloped foothill. Mama Paris directed us one leg at a time, saying she sensed the path to this crossroads of hers only in periodic waves.

"We arrived on shore in the late-morning with the expectation of a short hike. Mama Paris had assured us the way would be straight and swift. She then proceeded to take us on a needlessly twisty and arduous route to no apparent end. We zigzagged up and down the rocky foothill as if sleepwalking in a body. The wind gusted warm then cool and sometimes strongly enough to compel us to squat against the rocks until it died down.

"I was attired in a sleeveless blouse and a rather impractical skirt. It wasn't the proper weight for the weather. Fortunately, I had my rustic hiking boots and my walking stick notched for measuring purposes. The stick was useful in negotiating the screes and spills of rock. I recall planting it in the dirt for you to use as handhold whenever our course took an especially

steep turn. You kept pace admirably, of course, not once
complaining. Apart from Mama Paris, who piggybacked
on one of the zonbies, Pup-Pup struggled the most. Its
hind legs weren't designed for continuous bounding on
an angle. The frantic twittering of its silvery whiskers
belied its mechanical calm.

"It was late-afternoon when we determined we were
lost and befuddled. Your da had periodically marked our
route with chalk. We crossed and re-crossed the markings
who knows how many times. Something had confounded Mama
Paris's recollection or dreamtime sight. And she wasn't
alone in her confusion. All of us suffered from headaches
behind our eyes and a stifling déjà vu that compromised
our sense of direction. I doubt I could have found the
way back to the inlet myself except by chance. Even the
compass was useless. The needle waggled at random in its
housing. Mama Paris then admitted Loko had returned her
to the brigantine on her first visit, but on making shore
this time she'd felt confident in her ability to locate
the crossroads. More of her imperious delirium.

"Your da and his men assembled the equipment in the
rucksack to attempt a fix on the crossroads. This machine
had been developed years ago by your da and Captain Nemo
to aid in the discovery of whitespace fields. In form
and function, it was similar to an electromagnetic wave
detector: a sizeable metal box topped by a rotating
array of field coils. A special sense antenna, which
conducted a precipitate of Parmatmar crystal, allowed
for gauging direction. In this instance, however, the
machine was so wracked by signals it couldn't give a
useful bearing. Your da was taken aback. He'd never seen
the detector give such a violent start. The strength of
it suggested the crossroads were directly beneath us,
that is, inside the island. 'That would also explain our
failing sense-impressions,' he said. 'Whitespace fields
often becloud the mind. We could be on the leaky edge of
its radiations.'

"Mama Paris immediately accused Loko of purposely
concealing the location of the crossroads. His intimate
connection with the earth, she reasoned, should have
yielded some inkling of its whereabouts. The vehemence
behind the accusation startled me. I'd thought the two

united in some nefarious scheme. But now it appeared
Loko might be just another victim of the mambo-witch.
Its straggly eyebrows furrowed up in consternation.

"At the conclusion of Mama Paris's bitter Creole
harangue, the lwa crossed its arms in what I took to
be a meditative state. Pale green shoots sprouted from
its hind limbs. These new growths quickly acquired
the thickness and strength necessary to penetrate
the granite. Loko's beady black eyes glassed over.
I apprehended the creature was in some high-level
communion with the island. Then its exploratory roots
reversed themselves, withdrawing from the alluvial soil
into its body, and its eyes resumed their typical hue.
'King Loko has open de gate for you tuh pass. Entrance
below tuh rock-temple,' the lwa announced. 'Thank you
de spirit in its graces.' The creature's voice was rough
and smoke-deep.

"Loko crabbed ahead to guide us down the promontory.
The zonbies followed, murmuring wordlessly but steady in
their course, dirtied trousers loose as sacks. It was
a goat-track of a ramble down to the rocky shore. To
remember it is to become a disembodied doom. I'm like
a ghoul now haunting lives tender and bold and already
over. It's hard to reconcile myself to the injustice of
circumstance, how we suffered these uncanny pains whilst
others, elsewhere, went about their day, oblivious,
enjoying their fried eggs and bubble or set dancing or
whatnot. Is it selfish to want things to have turned out
differently for us, even if that meant persons unknown
would have suffered in our place?

"There's nothing to be done for it, I suppose, but
either feel less generally or trust to the persistence
of life, of goodness and possibility. That's the sort of
consolation offered by Jules Michelet's The Sea. Though
it's a hodge-podge of personal reminiscence, speculative
science and rum philosophizing, I was quite taken with
its central conceit, that is, the ocean as an ageless
and indomitable life-giver: the 'tireless eternity that
will recapture us all.' The French title is even more
explicit about the connection: La Mer, 'The Sea,' and la
mère, 'the mother,' being homophones.

"Setting aside his antiquated account of life's

origin in 'sea mucus' and a 'fertile jelly' of the dead,
Michelet's idea of the ocean as a self-creating body
always struck me as poignant and right. It affirms not
only a real and continuous source of life endemic to
<u>this</u> world, but also a future long past our existence,
whether humanity rises from the depths again or no.
What's ineffable in the Abrahamic religions is rendered
solid in this view, or at least my version of it—
something we can see, breathe, immerse ourselves in ...
This assurance has served as a hurricane lantern in
the fog over the years. It's some comfort to think life
will continue after us, if only in the form of molluscs
and annelids. I mean 'us' in the collective sense. For
myself, of course, I have you, as fine a specimen of
manhood as ever graced this world ...

"We weren't much different than the earliest seafarers
in this situation: no compass to speak of, goosed by
ignorance and bluff-blind to the dangers. Your da was
alive to the moment in spite of himself. He thrived on
change, on movement. He even had a habit of kicking in
his sleep. Excess animal electricity, he called it. He
thought the greatest misfortune was stasis. Risking
death was preferable to monotony; in fact, do you recall
what he said when we reached the cleft down the shore?
He paraphrased the <u>Phaedra</u>, saying, 'The conscience
that looks death straight-on is the very definition of
freedom.' <u>Meléti</u> <u>thanátou</u> and all that.

"He paused only to retrieve his vest pocket torch
before leading us through the fissure. I never knew
whether Loko had somehow prised the rock apart or merely
sensed the cave entrance; regardless, the opening
was so narrow and jagged we wouldn't have recognized
it otherwise for what it was. The <u>lwa</u> had to contort
himself into a tangled yokemabob to get by. The air took
on a shadowed chill then we were engulfed in blackness.
I took your hand. You were reedy at that age but had a
firm grip. Your features dimmed to glints of teeth and
straining eyes. I confess to holding onto you more than
you held onto me. Though the path sloped gently downward,
my insides churned like I was in a frightful plummet. We
might have been negotiating a brink of earth.

"The cave mouth proper emerged from the gloom as if

bathed in a timid green dawn. An effect of phosphorescent
lichen, which varnished the cavern's pitted walls and
stalactite-pronged ceiling. The sound of our footfalls
made ominous, overlapping circuits. We settled into
a deliberate heel-toe gait to minimize the noise and
found ourselves on a thin strip of limestone bounded by
a calm lagoon. Light and shadow traded places as your
da's electric torch flickered over the circular chamber.
Everything else was steeped in a dusky haze. The black
water was an agreeable wonder, starry with eerie lights.
'The luminous algae of Pliny the Elder?' your da asked.

"I stayed you with a hand and approached the verge.
The phenomenon mystified me. The nearest lights winked
invitingly. 'Could be one of Ehrenberg's organisms,' I
said. In the 1830s, the German natural scientist had
discovered certain dinoflagellates glow when stimulated
with acid.

"Your da turned back toward the immediate cave wall
and gave a start at what his torch revealed: a towering
bas relief figure done in the Melanesian style. The
statue must've been between four and five metres high.
It had human hands and feet but the overlarge head of a
frigatebird. Eyeless sockets formed the blades of the
ceremonial dance paddles carved along its cheeks. The
torch beam evoked pinprick sparkles from the rock. A
series of glyph-like figures punctuated by circular
cavities ornamented the wall to one side. Though they
lacked wings, the human-bird figures were depicted in
various stages of flight. 'All I wanna know is: Where's
me pineapple-wedged grog?' Banon asked.

"We'd begun dilating on the origin of this surprising
find when Mama Paris hobbled into the chamber,
accompanied by Loko and the zonbies. The narrowness of
the entrance had compelled her to traverse it on her own
power. Without hardly catching her breath, she set about
giving orders: 'Stop a-gawkin' an' see tuh de confines a
this place. Do we hug de shore or cross de shallows?'

"Banon quickly determined the so-called 'shore'
extended only about fifty-sixty metres before dead-
ending. Your da's electric torch wasn't powerful enough
to disclose the far side of the lagoon. It might well
have led to the ocean. Nevertheless, Mama Paris demanded

Loko take her across on his back. The <u>lwa</u> waded into
the opaque water and wrenched itself into a sort of sewn
bark dugout. Its chest became the bow, its incurved back
the bottom and its limbs beavertail paddles. On command,
a pair of <u>zonbies</u> helped her into the makeshift craft
and Loko set off, shearing through a luminous algae bloom.
The organisms flashed out a lingering, convulsive light.
Mama Paris shrieked at the glare and pressed her palms
into the hollows of her eyes.

"Loko found bottom and scrambled for shore. Mama
Paris was shaking her head, blind and distraught,
tears speckling her cheeks. Your da grabbed your hand
and raced for the exit. A <u>zonbi</u> made to pursue. Jain
surprised it with a blow from his collapsible gùn or
fighting staff and I worsted another with my walking stick.
Banon joined the rumpus, fists upraised, threatening
to 'whittle 'em down to size.' He smashed into them
barehanded, unflinching and mad. The <u>zonbies</u> were
resilient but rather lumbering. He downed one and waited
for it to rise before banging it down again, proving
that the older, more desiccated <u>zonbies</u> didn't bleed. I
yanked on his sleeve. Banon's hot-headedness sometimes
got the better of him.

"The ruckus furthered Mama Paris' panic. She shouted
something in Haitian Creole and Loko loosed a dart from
its outstretched hand. I yelled to warn your da. The
blur of the moment was excruciating. Studies show time
passes more slowly at sea level than in the mountains
because the Earth's mass retards time around itself. The
difference must be slight. Everything seemed to happen
on the instant and at once: your collapse, the onrush of
recovered <u>zonbies</u>, Loko clambering forward, Mama Paris
jostling atop it, your da gathering you up in your swoon.
The jagged pain in my chest swelled into my throat.

"Your da let slip his solemn mask. If not for cradling
you, he would have doubtless bashed the elemental with
a rock to bring the mambo-witch down to his level. 'What
evil have you done?' he said, advancing on the <u>lwa</u>.

"Eyes still shut tight, Mama Paris tilted her head
in his direction. '<u>Kisa</u>?' she said. 'Dink you de pact
concluded? De <u>ti gason</u> recover you do you part.'

"'Recover from what?' I said, putting a hand to your

forehead. You were shivering with an incipient fever.

"'De <u>zonbi</u> poison,' she said. 'Take four, five hour afore it set permanent.'

"I put a hand on the dart in your shoulder and asked her if it were safe to remove it. She nodded in a distracted manner. The veins in your neck and temple stood out. I apologized for the pain I was about to cause and jerked the dart away. Such was your training you barely flinched. But I noted a greenish pallor to your face, especially around the eyes. 'The spreading green?' I asked.

"Mama Paris said, 'De brighter de worse it be. When it fix permanent, de <u>bway</u> will glow like de cat's eye in de night.'

"'Remember this, witch,' your da said. 'I am no one and nothing if I can't protect my family and crew. You've hurt me once on that score already. But I'll not suffer any more of your malignity without trying to even up accounts.'

"Her head bobbed as if she were tracking specks in her eyes or <u>muscae</u> <u>volitantes</u>. But she remained undaunted. 'So long as you find me way to de crossroad, you get de cure, de bottled tear of Saint Philomène,' she said.

"I tore the hem from my skirt to use as a bandage and patched up your shoulder. You looked at me with an unbounded trust and moaned. My heart almost buckled under my sense of inadequacy. Every possible action short of providing the antidote seemed mere gesture. Pup-Pup, disconsolate, flitted its whiskers in sympathy.

"Your da and his men focused their attentions on the figurative carvings adjacent to the birdman statue. Though the Melanasians had no written language prior to European contact, the closest being the rongorongo tablets of Easter Island, your da thought the inscriptions might constitute a pre-literate cipher that, once decoded, would explain how to safely ply the lagoon. They spent some time puzzling over it. Each wasted moment was an agony to your da, who kept shooting worried looks in our direction. Your face seemed to sink a little more with each troubled exhalation. The <u>zonbies</u> gawped and mewled about as if anticipating your induction to their ranks. Any trace amusement in their waywardness was gone. They were wholly dreadful now.

"Banon suggested trying Loko again with us blindfolded against the reactive algae. Stymied, your da was about to reluctantly agree when he noticed an unusual pattern. If the defining vertical lines of the centre- and side-most carvings were extended, they'd intersect at the first of the circular holes. He aimed the torch-beam into the socket for what must've been the third or fourth time, but spotted nothing new.

"Then Jian, braving the possibility of cave spiders and who knows what else, plunged his hand in up to his wrist and, much to our amazement, withdrew a hollow staff. It had escaped your da's notice as it was flush with the circumference of the cavity. Jian immediately pronounced it a ragdon trumpet, a horn allegedly used by Tibetan monks to achieve feats of acoustical levitation. You may recall he'd spent significant time in Tibet, in part, to fetch you a suitable tutor in Eastern philosophy.

"No sooner had Jian identified the horn when the lagoon was disturbed by the rise of eight or nine stone funnels; at that point, we could only speculate on the total given the limited range of your da's electric torch. The large top-heavy artefacts surged to the surface via unseen levers. The cavern reverberated with the underwater grinding. The noise shivered my molars. Removing the ragdon must have triggered the funnels' release. The stones settled at about a half-metre above the water, forming a ruler straight line into the darkness. 'Oh, Jerusha!' Banon cried. 'Is it too late to go back to me ol' hellship days?'

" 'Ah, de simple-footed help come trew,' Mama Paris said, blinking at the array of funnels. Her voice was gruff and haughty but I could see by the unsteadiness of her head and her irregular eye blinks she was still recovering from the shock of that algae light. 'What now, you dink?'

"Jian answered to your da rather than Mama Paris. He minimized his interactions with her as much as possible, considering the woman spiritually unclean; to his mind, every exchange put his own soul at risk. 'Sah,' he said, 'the Garuda Kagyu school of monk send prayer stone in air using ragdon of this kind.'

"The tapered horn was a good three metres of stone carved wood. The mouthpiece was shaped like an elongated bird head with a spindly beak which functioned as a thumb-hook. The fluted bell was scalloped to represent the head of a fish. Your da noted its resemblance to Melanesian war-horns used in headhunting raids.

"Jian instructed us in how to use it. 'Like saying letter 'm' with small tongue,' he said and gave the horn a short, experimental breath. The grating buzz surprised me with its force. The nearest funnel vibrated slightly at the sound. Jian aimed the trumpet in its direction and blew again, this time a sustained tone from deep down, not high in his throat. The funnel positively tremored. The reflected buzz tugged at his Chinese riding jacket and sailor's trousers and he rose to the tips of his leather shoes without any evident effort of his own. His heels returned to the limestone as the buzz faded. 'Zhēn méi xiǎng dào?' he said. Jian's fondness for that phrase—meaning 'Who would've thought?'—doubtless grew out of his experiences as your da's auxiliary.

"Our means of transport disclosed, your da and his men set about retrieving more ragdon horns and testing their effects from the safety of the shore. It took some doing to produce a coherent buzz. You had to bring the air up from your diaphragm and tighten your abdominal muscles to get a continuous sound. I worried aloud about running out of air. Your da thought we'd have a moment or two between funnels to catch our breath.

"As the most practised among us, Jian volunteered to make the crossing first. He approached it like—what was the field event John Breshnihan set the world record in?—the triple jump. Jian ran up on the lagoon like that, taking a few long, loping strides before launching himself over the verge. He blew the ragdon mid-leap and, at first, I thought he'd waited too long and would flop into the water amid a burst of angry light, but the reverberation caught him on the descent and suspended him in air, however precariously. The strange frequency of it worried my inner ear. You recoiled from it, too, clapping your hands around your head.

"Jian angled higher as he approached the initial funnel, peaking directly above it, then declining as he crossed the gap to the next one. As your da surmised, he'd time enough between to catch his breath and, in that way, bounded to the far shore. I followed the gleams from his silver-braided topknot as far as your da's electric torch allowed. Jian signaled us with a victory shout distorted by the weird acoustical properties of the cavern. A determined Banon went next, followed by the two of us. Sick as you were, you still had full use of your limbs and managed to hold on from behind without inadvertently strangling me. The only challenge was that initial spring over the water. But Loko solved that by inviting us onto its back and raising up into a three metre high platform. From that vantage, the lagoon was a dream-beautiful spray of stars and I have to admit, in hindsight, I found the experience exhilarating, like a weighted version of one of your da's astral meditations. We flitted through a seeming universe on vibratory waves, up, down, in giddy curves, you, the heart of my heart pressed against me, alive outside my body. It was a small god's view of night.

"Thinking on it now, I'm struck by how close the low frequency sound of the ragdon came to the perfect fifth. The musical system allegedly developed by Pythagoras revolved around this interval. It's said to bring your nervous system into perfect harmony. I hear it often on my walks through the estate: in the wind and woodlands, the fen under winter rains. No wonder those walks rejuvenate me. In any event, I was glad to reach the shore when we did as my air was about to give out.

"Apparently unaffected by the algae, Loko reformed itself into a dugout canoe and paddled Pup-Pup and the zonbies through a lightning-shot dark. Each silent discharge sent rugged shadows across the ceiling. That left your da to take Mama Paris, who, with her smoker's wheeze, lacked the proper lung strength. There were some anxious moments whilst we waited out this frog and scorpion situation. Only his concern for you prevented him from drowning her straightaway; still, such was her paranoia that the first thing she said when they made land was to accuse him of attempting it. 'You said you couldn't see more than fleeting brights and blurs,' he said.

"'Like raindrop set in de eye,' she said, reaching for the <u>lwa</u> to steady her. 'But don't need good eye tuh see bad thought.'

"With the aid of your da's electric torch, we found a corresponding array of cave wall sockets for our <u>ragdon</u>. The stowing of the last horn sent the funnels back under. This stele was different than the first in that it had a small tray towards the bottom—about on level with your eyes. So you were the first to notice when the 'marble' as you called it rolled into the tray from some interior channel. The marble wasn't of the milk glass variety, of course, but a small stone made round and smooth, I suspect, from long years of river action. It bore an inscription like a pair of chevrons. I was glad of its effects on you. Your eyes had begun to cloud over at this point. But the marble, a reminder perhaps of happier days, inspired a fascination that gave me hope. It meant your Lethean stupor wasn't yet total.

"The phosphorescent lichen revealed a cleft to the right of the stone slab. A quick survey with the electric torch confirmed it as the only viable tunnel, though, like the entrance, it narrowed at certain junctures, forcing us to edge sideways (and for Mama Paris to hold her breath) in order to pass. The air was stifling and mildly sulfurous from the flowstone above, putting me in mind of Hell, or more accurately, its antecedent in the Old Testament.

"There's only one word that approaches the concept of Hell in the Hebrew Bible: <u>Sheol</u>. Many scholars believe it was originally a reference to the Sumerian and Babylonian netherworld, <u>Irkalla</u> or 'the House of Dust and Darkness.' This is a universal underworld where all the dead, good, bad and in-between, are consigned to a gloom of ash. See, to the ancients, the worst possible fate wasn't to suffer the sundry tortures depicted by Bosch but to be shuttered from the joys of life and their vaunted source. That would certainly be punishment enough for an empirical scientist like me for whom nature at its best is a regular heaven. And there we were, the righteous, the unrighteous and the living dead, in caravan together, sequestered from the world by tons of solid rock.

"After about an hour of inching our way along, the
passage debauched onto a vaulted gallery devoid of
lichen but nonetheless lighted. Your da advanced
cautiously, prepared to wield the electric torch like
a club. Instead of emanating a greenish half-dark, the
chamber was split between spectral light and abyssal
darkness. The light source turned out to be a brass
ferry lantern fitted with Parmatmar crystals. It was
tucked in a high alcove in the limestone wall. The
slightly undulating beam, fixed on a cave shelf some
five or six metres up, blanked from view whatever it
encompassed. Your da advised us not to cross into it.
'How do you know it ain't lightin' our way to the pearly
gates?' Banon asked.

"'I suspect Charon's more likely than St. Peter to use
a ferry lantern,' your da said.

"Shows somebody civilized-like done been here, eh?'
Banon said.

"Your da probed the chamber with his electric torch in
search of a tunnel. 'That's what worries me,' he said,
assessing the perimeter. 'They either perished here
or had reason to keep it secret. None too comforting,
regardless.'

"I checked your condition in the residual light whilst
your da looked for a passage forward. You'd begun to
hunch over, drawing in your shoulders, and your face had
gone to dirtied sweat. I patted your cheeks and forehead
with my skirt. A troubling mist obscured the Arctic
blue of your eyes. So much depends on the eyes for human
connection. The power of a glance is atavistic. It goes
far beyond mere sight. It's what allows expressiveness
and understanding without words. We attune ourselves to
others by reading the subtle changes in their eyes as
changes in feeling.

"To be clear, I've come to make a distinction in
my studies between emotions and feelings that sets us
apart from the simplest animals. Emotions, I've come to
understand, are largely pre-set responses essential to
the internal regulation of the body (as first described
by the French physiologist Claude Bernard in the 1860s).
We emote in habitual-instinctual patterns, smile, frown,

give a quizzical tilt of the head and so on, and in
this way, emotions are actions as common to mayflies
as men. Feelings, in contrast, are available only to
creatures possessed of sufficient complexity of mind,
creatures capable of deep self-awareness and reflection.
The zonbies, I wagered, lacked that complexity. Their
minds were flattened to mere mechanisms and so, lacked
awareness of their own states of mind.

"At about this time I could sense your capacity for
higher feeling waning, and despaired of your falling
away from me and the rest of humanity. The eyes of a
dog—a live one, not to disregard Pup-Pup—the eyes of a
dog are more nuanced and affecting than those of a silver
gull with their stark black pupils and large whites. How
far down the chain of emotional connection would you go?
I wondered. The mature zonbies seemed as inscrutable as
any remote animal. I couldn't bear to think on you that
way; in fact, I've my hand over my heart as I recall the
moment.

"When your da announced he wasn't able to locate a
through-way, I tested the lantern's beam with my walking
stick, figuring the cave shelf might be our only option.
The light had no apparent effect. But as a further
precaution, I grabbed a zonbie by the elbow and thrust
its hand into the spectral ray. The portion of its hand
subsumed by the light withered to nothingness as if it
were a wad of paper in a sitting room fire then, much
to our amazement, appeared intact and suspended in air
above the cave shelf before falling out of sight. The
transfer was no illusion. The zonbi's hand had been
sheared clean away just above the wrist. I was glad
for once the creatures felt nothing, no pain at all.
The zonbi looked curiously at his new-made stump and
stumbled off, indifferent. More proof for my theory about
their mechanistic mind-state.

"Mama Paris, of course, wasn't so sanguine. Ignoring
her complaints, I said to your da, 'It seems the beam
can send us on our way. Provided, of course, we can
immerse ourselves in it fully. I'd rather not continue
as a disembodied head.'

"'There's no telling what sort of long-term effects it
might have,' he said. 'It's more time-consuming but less

risky for Loko to train the light elsewhere then form a
climbing ladder to the shelf.'

"Mama Paris directed Loko accordingly, impatient
as ever. We huddled behind a tapered stalagmite near
the shelf for safety and the zonbies gathered close-
by. Crouched directly under the lantern's beam, the lwa
elongated its arms in a broad pincer shape. The sound
of crackling wood resounded in the chamber like shots
fired by ranked infantry. Its extended fingers had just
about closed on the lantern when the Weaving Orb (as we
later referred to it) dropped below the light-beam on
glistening threads. The pale, viscous blob was about the
size of a medicine ball. Its ropy spew—vomited from its
surface in hurried pulses—enmeshed Loko immediately. The
webbing hit with definitive squelches. The lwa got in a
single useless lash before it crumpled into a gummed-
up mess. I pressed you closer to the flowstone. Your da
cursed Mama Paris for lifting his guns. He pined for a
harpoon pistol.

"The Weaving Orb wrenched Loko through the lantern's
beam, vivisecting the lwa and sending up a flurry
of bloodless traces. Mama Paris let out a shriek. A
glistening thread from the Orb promptly fixed her to
the cavern floor. That sent the zonbies into a frenzy.
They charged the amorphous beast pell-mell, though they
lacked a means of reaching it, suspended as it was above
the chamber floor. The peculiar odour of woodbine spice
permeated the air.

"Afraid we'd lose any chance of reviving you should
we lose Mama Paris, your da leapt to her defense. He
retrieved a spinal fragment from the lwa and, gripping
it like a suntetsu or Japanese spike weapon, hacked
at the tangle-webs around her feet. She was shrieking
nonsense in fright and confusion. Banon helped with
another wood scrap whilst the Orb concentrated its ire
on the zonbies. The undead auxiliaries flailed through
salvos of webbing to form a pyramid. Two dropped into
a crouch and another pushed off their shoulders to grab
a stray tendril and grapple within striking distance.
The Orb blasted the zonbie with elastic capture thread,
sending it tumbling backwards, its head completely
mummified.

Your da signaled Jian to take his place. He flipped the Chinaman the dorsal spike and returned to us, flush with a plan. 'This is it, soldier,' he told you. 'Time to put your training to use: a circus throw to the lantern, and then you swing the light on that creature and away from us. You're the only one who can fit in the alcove.' The idea seemed to cut through the mist in your eyes. You gave a slight nod and that was all your da needed to believe. He raced out from the base of the stalagmite, keeping the zonbies between him and the Weaving Orb, you following at speed. Your da was grim-faced but in control, resolute. He rarely showed it when his blood was racing. I knew him to feel keenly only in private. That two-sidedness threw some people. Nana Quigg used to say he was burnt on the outside and raw on the inside.

"The sound of his voice spurred you into unhesitating action. You bounded away at his heels without a glance at the Weaving Orb and its relentless barrage. Remnants of Loko spun into the upper darkness on viscous threads. Dry fear stoppered my throat. I don't know how you managed it. Perhaps the zonbi pox tamped down any panic, enhancing your focus. Whatever the cause, you dodged the Orb's attack, using the befouled zonbies as a screen. Your da made a stirrup of his hands, and you hopped into it for a somewhat off-kilter toss.

"I worried you might be hurled past the nook altogether, or worse, directly into the lantern's beam. You scrabbled against the rock on the ascent then jolted to a stop, pinned to the limestone just below the knee. The webbing accumulated from there: thwup-thwup-thwup. But stretching full-length, you got a one-handed clinch on the lip of the alcove, saving you from tipping into the transporting beam.

"With you and your da completely exposed, I could hardly keep countenance. I grabbed up my walking stick, reversed my usual hold, and charged the Orb to deliver a powerful overhead blow. God knows if the featureless thing actually felt it, though. The stick lodged in the monster as if it were clotted cream. I might've caught a shadow-glimpse of writhing insides. I can't be sure. A deluge of icy threads confused my sight and next I knew, I was in the air, tilting, spinning, struggling to free myself.

"My legs swung outward and towards the lantern light. I tried to alter my trajectory by pushing against the Orb with the stick. No odds, as Banon would've said. The stick only plunged farther into its gelatinous guts. I surged to meet the beam certain I'd lose a foot up to the ankle before I was carried into some blacker horror. Such are the pains of contingency and chance, I thought, gritting my teeth ...

"Then the ghost-light veered across my vision, blinding me. I heard an angry hiss, and in the space of an eyeblink or two, the Weaving Orb was reduced to a few gluey strands. The beam had come to rest at a distant point somewhere on the ceiling. Presumably, the creature was coiled up there, fuming or relieved. But I wasn't free yet. The high-tension threads around my hips contracted, yanking me towards the ceiling. Stalactites awaited me like the spikes of an iron maiden.

"If not for Banon I would've been amputated then impaled. Using a downed zonbi as a stepping stone, he seized the filaments as if hauling line aboard ship. His efforts returned me close to ground, and in the moment before the strands went taut again, your da sliced through them with a splintery stump from Loko. I tumbled less than a meter to the cavern floor. Banon, however, was ineluctably fused to the webbing and shot away before your da could reach him. Banon gave a wry smile before a volley of catching threads jerked him into the vaulted darkness. Then he was gone, silenced, buried and alive at once.

"As you well know, the adventuring life compels you to face your mortality at every turn. Even now, thinking about Banon, your da, the other dead, seems a preparation for my own passing. They exist only in my memory, my longing, my ability to recreate the past. The stories I tell myself about them are little different in substance from the stories you'll tell yourself about me. Perhaps that's my secret motive for giving this account—to fix this episode in time insofar as words allow. It's a privilege the likes of Banon and Cully were denied. They left behind only scattered impressions, memories of varying force, and, with the exception of us, their charges, and some artefacts of note, ephemeral testaments to their goodly characters. In an argument once, your da asked Banon to stop being so damn adamant. Banon said, 'Leave me religion out of it.' He was righteous-stubborn, the old salt. I can only hope there was some Emersonian compensation for his sacrifice.

"Though numb from shock and loss, we hastened to free ourselves, fearing the Weaving Orb's reappearance. The threads were saturate with adhesive dew. Jian and Mama Paris worked to release the zonbies, which had been shrouded in place. I stood on your da's shoulders and cut the webbing from around your legs.

"With the danger passed, the last natural light in your eyes faded. You seemed rather impassive, gripping the edge of the alcove. There was no tension in your arms or neck. Odd how frailty gives credence to our humanity. Your disposition set me to pondering which of your senses were failing or dead. Did your hands feel gloved? Or as removed from touch as the end of a walking stick? And more, how soon would you lose your precious self-awareness?

"Consciousness, I suspect, is more instinct than anything else. Your behaviour during this period and directly after suggested the idea. You responded to my voice or, occasionally, to a playful bump from Pup-Pup, but were otherwise inert and withdrawn. Your manner put me in mind of a child in the bath, soap bubbles in his hair. I could imagine those bubbles as your highest level thoughts and feelings popping into emptiness, wafting away, each vanishing a hurt; and deeper inside, the source of those bubbles—your forebrain and, on down the line, your midbrain—slowing, perhaps fossilizing, until even your lizard-like hindbrain was barely excitable. I could imagine you diminished to the most primitive impulses. I could imagine you without feelings, an intimate stranger. And the thought frightened me more than the prospect of the Orb's return. You were—you are— my only child and I loved you as if no other life were possible.

"When you'd been extricated from the webbing, your da urged you into the alcove behind the averted lantern and, acting on his instructions, you disappeared one of the

zonbies to the cave shelf. The ethereal beam vaporized
the zonbi with nary a change in brightness then restored
the creature as soon as it was removed away. It was a
science of a kind unheard of. The lantern was surely the
quickest means of escaping the Orb.

"The experiment satisfied your da enough to risk Jian
next, followed by Mama Paris, Pup-Pup and me, then the
rest of the straggling zonbies. Jian, meanwhile, had
uncoiled a climbing rope from our supplies to help you
and your da up the slick limestone face. He affixed the
rope around his waist and I helped brace him against
your summative weight, eyes on the ceiling. There was no
sign of the Weaving Orb besides a few vestigial threads.
But who knew what other threats that night-black cope
might conceal? When you dropped from your da's back,
safe, I pressed you to my side, taking the flat of
one hand in mine as if to warm you back to normalcy.
Worriment was in my every breath.

"Your da's electric torch confirmed there was, indeed,
a forward path. It was narrow and notched. Like a slot
canyon. The trailhead was marked with a stone slab akin
to the previous. You broke away to examine its tray. The
inscriptions were of a piece with the others in terms
of style, some in low relief, others incised. Instead of
bird people, however, these glyphs seemed to represent
farmers or woodsmen. The figures carried square-sided
axes in contrast to the usual rounded or elliptical
Melanesian axe. I don't know what possessed you to do
this, but you put a thumb to the knob end of the axe
above the tray. The bas relief glyph sunk even with
the wall and a stone marble near-identical to the first
rolled out. I was examining the symbol on it when Mama
Paris cried out, distraught.

"Your da shushed her, fearing her hiccupping sobs
might attract the Weaving Orb. She crouched over a
sizeable hunk of the lwa, stringy vegetal matter and
what looked like the bones of a small animal. 'Is
it ...? Is it him?' she managed between breaths.
'Everting change shape I blink.' Cool command had given
way to nervous head bobbing.

"'Didn't you see?' your da asked. It was only then
that we began to grasp the full extent of her impairment.

She was not only flash blind. She was subject to
continual hallucination. 'Dat my son,' she said.

"'No,' your da said. 'I have a son, a true child, one
born of flesh and blood. That was a monster, a conjured
servitor.'

"Mama Paris shook her head, eyes watering. 'Ah, you
dink me off my head? I give uh de flesh to bring him
live. My own sinless baby ...' She blubbered into her
bosom. But she'd already said enough. We knew the mambo-
witch had sacrificed her infant son in some unthinkable
ritual. She went on to describe her heartsickness in
broken phrases: ' ...lay de fine feader uh my soul on de
chile-god ... Now, what good my konesans? Only time Mama
Paris breathe life ... Pour much love, much imagination
into 'im ... Hah! And what a stubborn, prideful thing
dat chile become ... Ann alé! Who left tuh love ol' Mama
Paris on her las' day? Ah, de hollow inside, de wan' ...'

"Your da denied her pity or remorse. She'd cost him
our schooner, two devoted friends, endangered you—
and for what? A chance at power without purpose. He
grabbed her by the forearm and demanded the antidote
straightaway, swearing to abandon her otherwise.
Anticipating a reaction from the zonbies, Jian extended
his fighting staff. In Loko's absence, however, the
creatures tended towards a passive shimmying, like dogs
diverted by sounds on a higher order of perception. They
just foostered about making dry chittering noises.

"There was a twinge of weakness in Mama Paris' face.
'De tears of Saint Philomène, de healin' sap,' she said,
'it come from de chile Loko.'

"I could see the bad temper rising in your da. You
know his juddering jaw when he grew agitated? That
trembling along the jawline, likely from clamping down
so tight. He was always so determined to confront danger
with a steadying silence. Not that I fault him for it,
mind you. My own pulses were jumping at the solidifying
prospect of losing you.

"You'll come to realise when you approach my age how
these involuntary memories and their associated feelings
constitute a world more permanent than the material
one. I can pluck any moment from this misadventure as
if from an ever-present invisible world whilst I can

barely recall my breakfast the day before yesterday.
The material world is a blur of deadening routine, of
blanked time passing. The invisible one, in contrast,
is a fixity in the air and always available in its
particulars. To describe an hour in the detail I recall
would take an hour. I've abbreviated for your sake,
Nolin. But trust that I remember every aimless step,
every sweat-matted curl of hair against your forehead,
every ragged breath, much of it against my will, and
further, the older I get, the more these images and the
feelings they call up constitute what's real.

"Mama Paris shook like a willow leaf in your da's
menacing grip. He said, 'You'd best tell me there's
another way.'

"'De <u>carrefour</u>—de crossroad—is de only answer,' she
said in a theatrical undertone. 'It give Mama Paris de
right kinda healin' power. Touch de afterlife world, I
see, I know what de spirit know. I cure him from de soul
out.'

"Though he shook his head at her claim, your da
relented because, emm, we needed to believe her. His
own knowledge of the dreamtime and its effects was
largely theoretical. He'd studied the lore to discover
heretofore unknown scientific principles and, if
necessary, to protect us, our home, with various wards,
not to become a full-fledged adept. He could work a few
basic spells and was practised at astral projection,
mainly as a survival technique. But by no means could he
match her practical skills in the mystic arts.

"She was well aware of this advantage, of course, and
turned away, exultant. Oh, I got pure thick with her at
that moment. I kept picturing her smug profile against
one of Banon's glory-o songs, 'Song of the Battle Eve'
or somesuch. That's the only thing I ever saw him get
sentimental over—the old fighting spirit. Had a habit
of it when he was deep in his cups ... But I kept my
frustrations to myself. There was no getting around it:
we were trapped with her and our own dire thoughts until
we completed our appointed labour.

"Your da resumed the lead, with Jian right behind. I
gripped you under the arm, prepared to haul you upright
if you should slump into the disordered gait of a <u>zonbi</u>.

I'm not sure to what extent you registered the pressure
of my hand. You'd quieted well into yourself at this
point. Even Pup-Pup had given up trying to nudge you
into sportiveness. Every time I glanced at you, I held
my breath as if to preclude the moment passing into
the future, into a greater state of entropy and decay.
I remembered folding your hand in mine when you were
younger, the pulse of you so damn simple and shocking at
once. I wanted to carry you safe inside me again. But
time pressed on, and before I knew it, your skin had
accrued a tinge of green.

"The seriousness of your condition made Mama Paris
all the more insufferable. Her behaviour, her veiled
remarks, the core of her miscreant philosophy ... Though
one of the <u>zonbies</u> carried her like a bride, head
cradled between arm and chest, she wheezed in showy
exhaustion. She was in desperate want of a sedan chair
in the style of Queen Charlotte's. That was all she
valued of the modern world—mere luxuries. She derided
civilized governments and common morality as the makings
of poor, unimaginative minds. Laws existed only for
dupes. Ordinary life was nothing but deceit and damp
sentimentality. Success in crime, in magick, bestowed a
kind of predatory clout. What was hers was hers and what
was her neighbour's was also hers. She saw herself as
a jaeger or frigatebird, one of those hostile seabirds
that thieves from other breeds, harassing them until
they disgorge their latest catch. This crossroad, she
was convinced, would be her greatest spoil. She deserved
it because she was clever and alive and superior to
cultured falsities. Following the incident with the
Weaving Orb, she took to keeping a sachet of juju powder
close at hand.

"After about a half-hour of tramping through this new
passage, we emerged into an arched chamber of shadowy
dimensions. The high walls of a labyrinth prevented us
from accurately gauging its size and shape. The first
junction occurred only a few metres past the entrance.
We paused at this strange and unexpected obstacle. The
walls were a mass of large entwined roots topped by
broccoli-like florets, albeit colorless.

"Jian slipped off the rucksack and stepped towards the

mouth of the labyrinth at caution, fighting staff extended.
Bunches of oblong fruits protruded from the ends of the
wall or leads. Their leavings dotted the ground. Jian
stepped around the fallen fruit. The florets radiated
a hazy, pollen-flecked light on his approach. He froze,
eyes fixed on the gloaming ahead, then tested a thick
supporting root with his gùn. No reaction. 'Zhēn méi
xiǎng dào?' he said. Your da asked him to retrieve a
dropped fruit for my inspection.

"I rotated it in my palm. Lacquered over in a dense
translucence, the fruit was the same smoky hue as the
labyrinth and in no ways pliable.

"'Is it, indeed, a fruit?' your da asked. 'Can you
tell?'

"I shrugged. 'Looks like a drift fruit kindred to the
mango or hog plum. Whatever it is, it's rock solid,' I
said. 'Perhaps it's a seed or fossilized.' I closed my
fingers around the fruit and received a distinctive jolt
of warmth. 'There's something to it, though,' I added.
'A vibratory heat.' I held the fruit to my ear to better
discern the vibration's pitch and, much to my dismay,
made out a sibilant warning: 'Desissst, ssstrangersss ...
we ssstand againssst you ... imprisssonment and
sssuffering awaitsss ...' I repeated the words as much
to settle them in my own mind as to inform the others.
I could scarce believe the labyrinth was alive as some
compound intelligence.

"Mama Paris insisted on hearing the threat for herself.
I pressed the fruit into her hands. She listened for
a few moments then shouted in a language I recognized
as the ceremonial tongue of Haitian Voudon, Langay. I
caught mentions of Legba, guardian of doorways and
barriers, and Saint Peter, his Catholic counterpart, but
couldn't follow the substance of her tirade.

"'What did you say?' I asked.

"She put the fruit to her ear for the expected reply.
'What else, mwen renmen anpil? Mama Paris promise set
dem afire.' The colloquy between her and the labyrinth
went on for several minutes. There was a German-made
matchless lighter in the rucksack. But we gathered
she meant fire of the magickal or conjured sort, which
would've been a near-miracle. Only the greatest adepts

can manipulate the material world. I dismissed it as
a careless boast. She was a practised liar, what your
Nana Quigg would've called a 'good for nothing sleveen,'
though in this case, her cunning seemed to work to our
advantage. The negotiations concluded with the Kobiari
(as the collective was apparently known) agreeing to
light our way through the maze.

"Beaming florets proceeded to guide us through a
bewildering series of twists and turns. We doubled
back on our initial course almost immediately. I
remember that much. I was clenched with worry about your
condition. I lived one heart-pause at a time, dreading
the loss of you. I followed the subdued lights without
much thought beyond the need to keep on. There was a
nauseating sameness to the labyrinth, its grey, tangled-
root walls, the stone-lined path. It was easy to fall
into a miserable trance-like state, striking out with
one foot then the next, unthinking. I might've been
one of the young Athenians sacrificed to the Minotaur,
trudging to my doom.

"I didn't realise how weary I was until we reached the
stairs. My thigh muscles protested. I leaned heavily on
the walking stick, pausing to glance at you, stooped,
staring fixedly, your bones too close to your skin. It
staggered me to see your face so slack and waxen. And
your eyes ... sunken, glazed, the blue gone horribly
white ... I gave a hoarse little gasp. You were becoming
or had already become something I couldn't understand.
I was afraid to call to you, to have my worst fears
confirmed. Seeing you prematurely aged by that Voudon
sickness ... I recalled the fallacious advice I received
when pregnant with you, that I should avoid thinking of
ugly people, the deformed or diseased, lest I mark you
in the womb. I couldn't help feeling responsible, judged
by supernatural forces beyond our purview.

"For the first time in years, I prayed to the God of my
childhood. The prayer was in my head but no less sincere
for being silent. My Catholic faith had withered to
nothing on exposure to your da's supernatural travails.
Who could keep the Biblical peace of heaven in their
heads after knowing the terrors he'd faced? But the
acuteness of my pain humbled me, brought me round to

girlhood comforts. I flattered God with the Shorter
Catechism, to what end, I don't know ...

"Then the stairs under Pup-Pup collapsed in a whirl-
blast of dust and we scrambled away, chasms opening
around us, <u>zonbies</u> tumbling. I latched onto your forearm
and leapt to the closest wall, clambering over its base
roots. Pup-Pup was nowhere to be seen, though you were
scarcely in a state to notice overmuch. Jian dangled
from his extensible fighting staff, the ends of which
bridged the rift between loosened stairs. The staff bowed
under his weight, encumbered as he was by the bundle of
supplies and sensing equipment. His topknot slipped from
view. Your da, pressed against the gnarled wall like
us, shouted for him to release the rucksack. There was
a distant crash of metal. Jian reappeared and pulled
his eyes even with the ragged edge of the stairs. One
arm-length swing was all he needed ... Then a grabbling
<u>zonbi</u> pitched into the breach, jerking him askew. The
staff skidded free and he plunged after the creature into
the cavernous dark.

"I redoubled my grip on you, helpless, and angry at
my helplessness. Your da called after Jian through the
settling dust but received no reply. The stairs gapped
here and there with infernal grave plots, preventing
us from investigating straightaway. Those hidden depths
reproached us. I looked on them wondering what went
through Jian's head at the first inkling of freefall,
what plea, what curse or final blankness. There it was
again, unavoidable: the awful decree of circumstance. I
was a natural scientist, unaccustomed to these sorts of
shocks. I'd accompanied your da on a few expeditions,
of course, but none so harrowing. In many ways, my
model was the American naturalist Henry David Thoreau,
thoughtful and exact, besotted with nature in its
myriads. Oh, for his staid life! As per <u>Walden</u>, his
worst fear was a burgeoning railroad unchecked by human
interests.

"Mama Paris had been hauled to safety by one of the
two surviving <u>zonbies</u>. It was perched on a serpentine
root and she sat on its lap, clutching the maze-fruit
to her chest. 'Dese heah Kobiari,' she said. 'Dey doan
unnerstan who dey tryin' tuh boss.' Her mouth pinched

into a scowl. 'But doan you worry, duchess. I gots de black magick tuh learn 'em right.'

"She crossed her legs, preparing to meditate on the dreamtime, when Carantok, shed of Pup-Pup's metal husk, soared from out the fissured earth with Jian in tow. The Heroic Faerie appeared in his natural guise: about a decimetre from toe to spike-haired crown; naked apart from a leathern kilt; eyebright and pale of skin; wings a shimmery grey. The shining youth of him startled as much as any other aspect; however powerful, Carantok was still a child, not unlike one of Raphael's heavenly cherubs. Fortunately, he was eager to prove his worthiness to us who had provided him home and family in his lostness outside Faerieland or Mag Mell. He deposited the unconscious Chinaman next to your da then alighted on your shoulder, hopeful of an approving word. I believe he considered himself a younger sibling, always looking to your affections, whether in knight-play as Pup-Pup or in the library at his grimoires. His pudgy little chin doubled in worry at your abstracted visage.

"Of course, Mama Paris claimed to have never been fooled, saying she'd detected the tell-tale glamour of the Aes Sidh from the first. She wondered, however, why we'd never directed Carantok to use his 'Faerie stroke' to make her sick or otherwise incapacitate her. She couldn't have known of his condition when we'd found him, the severity of his war wounds or how they'd diminished his powers apart from levitation, occasional invisibility and some elementary shapeshifting. His impaired state was a considerable source of anxiety. That's why he preferred the pretence of Pup-Pup to his genuine self. It gave him purpose, albeit mostly frivolous by our standards, and at once imbued him with talents unlike any other Aes Sidh. The facade restored his confidence somewhat, though not enough for him to feel comfortable returning to Mag Mell. Among the martial Heroic Faeries, he would've been considered a liability.

"I asked Carantok to retrieve the rucksack and Jian's fighting staff. He tended to be more responsive to me than your da, perhaps due to my diffident attempts at his native language of whistles and Scottish-style glottal

stops, or to the sensual proclivities of the <u>Aes</u> <u>Sidhe</u>.
Regardless, he carried out these tasks with his usual
alacrity and returned to my side.

"Your da delved into the rucksack for the case of
smelling salts. He tapped a dose into his handkerchief
and, cradling Jian's head, waved it under the Chinaman's
nose. Jian shuddered into consciousness, gasping at the
pungent aroma. 'Story horse?' your da asked. 'How far
did you fall?'

"Jian pushed himself into a delicate sitting position.
A bruise purpled through his hair above one ear. He
brushed rock dust from his riding jacket as if he'd
suffered only a minor pratfall. 'Not so far, sah, I can't
get up,' he said.

"'Emm, let's not try for heaven in single bound, eh,
<u>péngyǒu</u>?' your da said, helping Jian to his feet.

"Jian balanced atop the mangrove-like roots with the
aid of his staff. Mama Paris shot him a skeptical look.
He felt for the fragment of mirror under his shirt.

"We deliberated about what to do next. Mama Paris was
wont to put some Voudon curse on the Kobiari. But given
your condition, your da and I were anxious to push on
if a torch alone could ensure our safety through the
labyrinth. He constructed one in short order from a
swath of torn skirt, my walking stick, and the matchless
lighter's spare methanol. The torch would burn quickly.
Flourishing it in the direction of the sensitive florets
atop the wall, however, produced the desired effect. The
maze-fruit buzzed in agitation against Mama Paris. 'Are
they letting us pass?' I asked.

"She was about to reply when a rhythmic quaking
overtook us. The disturbance seemed to originate below
the stone-set path. It surged in intensity, building to
a crescendo under our feet. Carantok bore you aloft just
as a massive humped carapace burst from the fissure. The
creature thrashed to gain purchase. Its crustacean-like
front legs churned up the stones whilst it rolled from
side to side in an effort to impale us with the spines
that protruded from either side of its head. Your da
gripped my forearm and steadied me over the roots and
away. You and Jian spirited ahead, following the lighted
florets. Despite all the excitement, you hung slack and

disinterested from Carantok's arms. Your listlessness goaded me on. I didn't give a second thought to the possibility of slipping on the throes of exposed root. My sole concern was keeping you safe, human or no.

"Mama Paris and the <u>zonbies</u> were lost to view behind the monster. There was nothing to be done for them. We lacked even the most rudimentary weapons and that creature was at least the size of an African elephant. Its chuffing and braying pursued us a while down the convoluted passage. Then there was only the thwack of our boots against the filigreed wood, my open-mouthed breathing, the pulse inside my head counting down the time ...

"When we made that last curve before the precipice, your skin glowed against the yawning dark like a Paschal candle on Maundy Thursday. How long had it been since the infection? I could guess based only on my uncharacteristic weariness. Your face was drawn, expressionless, your cheek cold to the touch. No reaction, not even a twitch. Your eyes were clouded over entirely. My chest clenched in a black panic. I feared I'd lost you forever. You seemed a body made of nothing save its greenish-bright skeleton. I filled the cavern with my grief, startling Carantok into a nervous arc.

"Your da gave a sigh of distress but refused to accept things as they were. That was his way, wasn't it? Everything except fated death was changeable as if by will alone. Perhaps that's what made him such an exceptional leader of men: not his poise or strategic intelligence so much as his resolute stand against appearances. This habit could be calming in situations unprecedented and awful; at other times, however, it was infuriating. I felt seen-through. I was, after all, a trained observer and hardly given to gross misapprehensions. You remember how he loved to quote Aeschylus from <u>Works</u> <u>and</u> <u>Days</u>, the words of Prometheus: 'In those days, men saw, but saw badly; they listened, but failed to understand ... They took action, but never realised what they were doing.' Thinking on it now, I don't know if he quoted those lines as a humbling reminder or damning judgment.

"It occurred to us the Kobiari might've led us

into another trap. The labyrinth dead-ended at this
chasm crowded with floating rocks. Your da surmised
the distorted gravity was due to the concentration of
Parmatmar crystals detected earlier. The crystals were
known to corrupt time, space, any of the fundamental
forces, singly or in combination. The electric torch
suggested a receiving ledge some seventy meters or
so across the fantastic drift of rock. Jian was of a
mind to climb the maze wall to determine if there were
another, better route. But your da showed with the toss
of a halfpenny coin that the same power supporting
the rocks might also support us. The weighted rucksack
seemed to confirm the idea. Jian heaved the baggage
into the breach and, instead of plummeting into the
precipitous depths, it hovered on level with the
rocks as if cast into space beyond our atmosphere. The
experiment didn't mean there weren't other dangers, say,
another hostile creature of some sort.

"So to minimize the risk, I asked Carantok to ferry
Jian. The faerie was fierce irritated at this point,
knackered, hungry and worried after you. With his
child's understanding, it was hard for him to fathom
your remoteness. He'd known you since your infancy. He
knew as well as I that your body had formed as much
around your heart as your brain. Your lack of emotion no
doubt seemed a callous snubbing. Like the unforgiving
hollowness of a poured wax doll.

"Carantok hoisted Jian into the air, tight-lipped
and grudging, and of a sudden, the rocks tumbled into
motion, confusing his path. Intelligence, or more
accurately, mental energy, appeared to be the catalyst.
The rocks circulated in slow, roughly elliptical
patterns. Carantok fluttered up, down, varying his speed
as necessary to avoid collision. Jian tucked his legs
in order to make himself as small as possible. The
swirl of rock and dust soon obscured them, and it was
some time before Carantok returned, successful in his
task, announcing he'd collected the rucksack as well. He
was in no shape to haul the three of us in succession,
however, so shortly after he set out with you in tow,
your da and I decided to navigate the scudding rocks on
our own. The pressure of saving you was everything.

"I targeted a passing boulder and lunged into the
breach, landing on all fours with a clawed grip. The
impact set the rock to spinning. My walking stick
spiralled away. I revolved head-over-heels in a lopsided
wobble, slowing as I approached the top of its arc
before rolling underneath. There was no breath in it as
in the earth topside. It was a mere object in collision,
cold, a quirk of nature.

"I pushed out into the emptiness and through pricks
of orbiting dust and pebbled rock. Your da had adopted
a similar strategy and, rather than capering from rock
to rock, we swam in the transmuted air, windmilling our
arms as necessary to miss the larger objects. The chief
danger here was losing our way in the creeping maelstrom.
The combination of electric torch and our refined sense
of direction, however, saw us through. Under other
circumstances, I might've enjoyed the experience,
fluttering, cutting, diving like a storm petrel without
so much as a feather in hand, but I couldn't think past
your affliction, whether we were already too late.

"When we alighted on the opposite side, we found you
next to Jian examining a third stone marble in the
now-familiar phosphorus glow of the cave-lichen. The
dispensing tray was part of wall-length stele similar to
the others. The carved hieroglyphs depicted a newly dead
man before what I took to be a powerful ancestor god.
The dead man was identifiable as such by the frigatebird
symbol cut into the palm of his hand. In some Melanesian
cultures, only those bearing the mark of the sacred bird
are allowed to pass into the spirit world proper; the
others are cast into a fathomless gulf to perish in a
second death.

"The continued allure of these marbles assured
me somewhat that your inner self hadn't been fully
extinguished. I simply couldn't fathom the origin of the
connection. I didn't recall you ever playing marbles or
'taws' or whatever you lads called it then. The closest
object in form I could recall was your da's small brass
orrery, which displayed the six ancient planets, Ceres
and Halley's Comet. Though you were well aware the
clockwork mechanism was past all fixing, you couldn't
resist ribbing your da on occasion by asking to wind

it up. There was no malice in it. But your meaning was plain enough: 'So much for Nemo's vaunted engineer.' I know, I know, given your arduous training, how he seemed to regard you first as a soldier-scientist and a son second, you couldn't help but think on him sometimes as an intellectual rival.

"The symbol on this third marble consisted of two opposing curves (not unlike parentheses) above a wavy groove. It was reminiscent of the rongorongo hieroglyph for the new moon. Across much of Oceania, the moon with its changing phases represents mortality and the human side of divinity. The moon serves as a symbol of continual dying or suffering, though with the promise of periodic brightness or re-birth. In Melanesian culture, every symbol has a spiritual power or mana which connects the tribe to the living reality beyond this earth. All things, plants, animals, objects, possess some degree of 'mana,' and the Melanesians thought success in life was the consequence of manipulating it through magick. I figured the marbles were 'votive stones' used in one or more mana-enhancing rituals practised by whatever long-vanished tribe had lived there. Whilst that may have been the case, the marbles turned out to have a much more practical purpose for us.

"A short connecting passage, illumined like the others by the ubiquitous lichen, led us to a sizable cavern Jian immediately termed the 'graveyard.' (Though unswerving in his duties, he had a habit of putting a dark cast on things.) The term was prompted by a flat expanse of petroglyphs, dozens of them like primitive headstones. The statuary varied in size and shape. The tallest, adorned with a glyph akin to a gaping mouth, must've been close to three metres. We wended our way among the carvings, alert to the possibility of danger. Who could say what eerie menaces this expanse might harbour? I sent the faerie to scout out possible trouble.

"Your da and Jian made up the van some four or five metres ahead. I kept pace beside you, forlorn in my grief. You responded to our directives on the quick but without expression. Like a living mummia. Each glance at you pricked my conscience afresh. I yearned for something to do, for some prayer or cursèd labour to relieve your suffering. Even if we found the crossroads, without the aid of Mama Paris, we didn't know how, if it all, we could use it to reverse your illness. Dread uncertainty threatened to jitter me straight out of my skin. The knots in my stomach might've been the only thing holding me together.

"Carantok returned and informed us of a massive door on the far side of the graveyard. He described it as a portcullis: a metal gate set within grooved jambs. The design sounded anachronistic compared to the steles and statuary we'd encountered so far. We hurried to it, aching and cautious in the collective hope we'd find remedies for all our pains. Beyond it, I imagined a vault brimming with Parmatmar crystals, big, transfixing heaps of ethereal glitter, a magickal cure for you, and my own mother-sickness.

"The gate was, indeed, immense: about three metres long and about four high, with no discernible pulley mechanism. It appeared to be wood plated in iron rather than solid metal; still, it was too heavy to raise under our own power and too sound to crumple even if we somehow managed to fashion a battering ram. Apparently unconcerned, or perhaps altogether oblivious to our dilemma, you began to roll the marbles in the palm of your hand, idly, without bothering to look at them. Jian suggested sending Carantok back to the labyrinth to lure the subterranean monster into the graveyard. Then, he hazarded, we could kill the creature using a sharpened leg of the whitespace detector and harvest its armoured shell for a battering tool, or alternately, Carantok could deceive it into smashing the gate for us. Those options seemed sensible enough in the moment, and Jian had already started grinding the end of a joining rod when you dropped a marble. It followed a limestone gully to rest against your da's boot. The glyph chiselled into its surface caught his eye. He held it up for examination. 'How many of these did the lad gather up?' he asked.

"'Three,' I said. 'One after each obstacle ...'

"' ...almost as reward,' he said, motioning for me to bring him the other marbles. I mentioned my 'votive stone' theory.

"You scarce registered my touch as I relieved you
of the stones. Your da made a quick study of each then
ambled into the graveyard, eyeing the statuary. 'There,'
he said, pointing out a fern-like petroglyph matching
the one incised on the second marble. 'I thought I
remembered seeing it.' He raced to the petroglyph
and, with a searching look at its base, wrenched the
statue counter-clockwise. 'The South Pacific gyre moves
counter-clockwise due to the southeast trade winds,'
he explained. 'That's the Melanesians idea of the open
ocean and by extension, the direction of all open things.
Help me find the others.'

"Here was a purpose your da, the inveterate puzzle-
seeker, could understand apart from physical courage. He
found the petroglyph bearing the chevron-like symbol,
and I discovered the last one, the statue with the glyph
for 'moon,' or so I'd assumed. It was about ten-twelve
metres from the gate. Unsure of what would happen, your
da shouted for Jian to ready himself before he swivelled
it round. As soon as the petroglyph locked in place
there was a synchronous rumbling from behind the door as
of weights and pulleys thrown into motion.

"The gate began to retract and a rift of blue-tinged
light spilled out from underneath. Sidling up to you,
Jian shaded his eyes with a bent arm. The door receded
out of view. I leaned towards the exposed chamber, weak
in the knees. It was unlike anything we'd seen in the
course of our strange journey. I looked to your da for
comment, but he also was in a mild state of shock. The
chamber was entirely smooth and glassy, not unlike
obsidian, which develops when lava cools so fast there's
no time for crystals to form; and suspended in the
centre, hovering some three metres from the reflective
floor, was the mysterious light-source, the object and
unwanted gift that could be said to have wrecked our
family.

"Little about the enormous object suggested its true
function. In its essential shape, it resembled the Early
Cyrillic letter Ze, which, as you may recall from your
Russian studies, looks similar to the Greek or Latin 'z'
with a wavy tail on the bottom. The top arm of the 'z'
extended past the off-centred stem and bottom arm, the

latter of which was fanged in Parmatmar crystals. The surface was a mix of crustaceous shell and a brighter, more virulent form of the phosphorus lichen evinced elsewhere. The sculpted surface, pitted here and there by lacy varices, reminded me of a fossilized mollusc shell. It was a tangled skein of textures and hollows and crystalline radiance. Several sailing ropes depended from various parts of the object. Perhaps only the portlights in the arched segments of the top arm gave any real hint as to its use.

"As we approached the glowing object, our shadows writhed far behind us, so that every gesture was mirrored and elaborated. Your da remarked on the similarity of the object's segmented design to the outer plating of the _Nautilus_. In hindsight, this observation should've been proof enough as to the island's master and taken as the sternest of warnings. This is where my ghostly self, the tale-teller of the present, is tempted to prise time out of time, reverse events, truncate things to their end, or otherwise intervene lest I dispirit myself all over again.

"Some speculate the past is an actual place rather than mere abstraction, but impossible to reach for reasons mathematical and philosophical. We know, however, the dreamtime offers a potential, though unpredictable, means to revisit it. Aristotle, your da once noted, was the first philosopher, or perhaps the first _Greek_ philosopher, to describe the subjectivity of time as grounded in the soul. Theravada Buddhism has made much of this notion, acknowledging this dependence of time on consciousness, suggesting that time has no existence insofar as it's relative to the observer. The dreamtime or astral realm theoretically allows consciousness to treat the past as place. In dreams, after all, time, the full range of fundamental forces, are subject to passing whim. The fault is mine and mine alone for failing to realise this potential. It's my lot in life to lack the necessary constitution. Lord knows I've tried, with and without intermediaries.

"But the past as a liveable island remains closed to me, irrecoverable. It would be better had I never learned of the alternative. Then, perhaps, I'd be

content to struggle with the limitations of simple
observation. My avifauna project ... As ambitious in
scope as it was, it still fell short of plan. There's
nothing so comprehensive apart from the mind of
God Himself that can explain even the most mundane
phenomenon in its entirety. Hence, my general ease
strolling the estate, loitering in the garden, taking
comfort in a world shrunk to the size of my comforts.

"We walked the eighty-ninety metre length of the
object, noting the curiousness of its asymmetric
design, the ridged undercarriage. I couldn't shake
the impression it was something grown rather than
constructed, like a _murex_ _spinicosta_ or any other
molluscan shell that forms through calcified accretions.
Where it was devoid of rough covering, the bottom arm
of the 'z,' attached as a kind of outrigger, and again,
delineated in crystals, gleamed pearlescent in the
same way as an inner layer of nacre. One of the ropes
dangling from this part of the object seemed an open
invitation. Your da, of course, was bulling to go. Some
quick reconnaissance by Carantok confirmed the rope was
fixed just outside a glass-less portlight.

"Out of concern for _my_ safety, your da tried to
persuade me to stay with you and Jian, but out of
concern for _his_, I refused. He shortly resigned himself
to the idea of me coming along, though showed his
displeasure by dismissing Carantok and, tucking the
sharpened metal rod into his belt, tackling the Manilla
rope hand-over-hand without benefit of his legs. I
followed under the faerie's power. It was a shame we
appeared to have exhausted our opportunities to resist
the urge of gravity. We could've done with a lighter
attitude about then.

"I glanced down at you as I ascended in Carantok's
childish grip. You were fidgety and distracted,
your eyelids raw, busy in your head or altogether
unthinking, I couldn't say, but working on another
frequency, regardless. I recalled how, on discovering
I was pregnant, you were a feeling of almost violent
wonder. Whenever I despaired of you, in the midst of
some especially arduous training, under the influence
of this _zonbi_ poison, I came back to that feeling of

us, together, and its promise of abiding closeness. I
regarded it sometimes as Anixamander regarded humanity's
origin in the <u>galeoi</u> or dog-fish, the so-called 'smooth
shark' whose young are attached to their mothers by a
navel-like string. We were connected, I thought, by
a similar, albeit invisible and imperishable, string.
Yesterday, however, was already long ago. Your details
swiftly decayed into a soft green contour. If nothing
else, your corrupted silhouette made it clearer than
ever that you weren't mine any longer, but separate and
apart.

"I'd just slid through the portlight when the gate
clanged shut. Your da assured me he and Jian could
muscle it open, but what about whilst we were exploring
the object? If something should attack, say, another
Weaving Orb, there'd be no escape for you and no
defensive shelter. We needed to work swiftly, find the
source or chief repository of Parmatmar energies, and
assess how we might use it to restore your health.

"The object's interior left us beggared of words. We
could've been standing in a dream. The walls and ceiling
were made of shimmery gelatinous matter. Irregular
oblongs like slipper animalcules, complete with
aqueous vitals, crisscrossed the chamber. They tensed
periodically under the influence of sharp electrical
pulses. A pervasive odour akin to a dirty-wet penny
followed each electrical burst. Though these ectoplasmic
strands appeared well-insulated, your da used the iron
rod to lever a path rather than risk touching them bare-
handed.

"The strange exigence of the situation demanded calm.
I swallowed my fears and picked my way forward. Our
boots scuffed against the coral-like flooring. It was a
level stretch of stalks and polyps apparently moulded
to its purpose, pearly clean until we came to a site of
some earlier violence. There, the gelatinous walls were
shrivelled as if diseased and their colour was of smoky
glass. Electrical charges arced intermittently from the
stumps of torn strands. Your da tossed the iron rod to
one side of the corridor to draw the voltages safely
away. A russet of dried blood stained the floor. The
smeary trail ended several metres ahead in a honeycomb-

like chamber. An eerie white light venting from the floor
exposed a shadowed figure, a man, propped against the
wall, bowed in sleep or death. My breathing was suddenly
loud in my ears. Oh, how I've wished since it would've
been death, mors tua, vita mea.

"Your da recognized him before I could make out little
more than his emaciated silhouette. With a staying
hand on my arm, your da said, 'Nemo.' He always used
the East Indian prince's Latin alias. Though Nemo had
lavished precious coins, jewels and other treasures
on your da, providing the foundation of our wealth,
they'd parted on quite bitter terms. According to your
da, Nemo, increasingly enamoured of his own genius,
had adopted a bloody, calculating terrorism designed
to quote 'close history.' Nemo thought the nature and
trajectory of mankind obscene and the Christian duty
to love your neighbour absurd; no one who's plumbed
his own blackest depths can honestly love himself and,
by extension, anyone else; democracy was a farce that
elevated mediocrity; its supposed freedoms, especially
among the colonized, were negligible, and tolerance,
when it existed at all, was simply the result of a lack
of energy rather than popular wisdom. Your da told me
Nemo once said of himself: 'I have a shark's soul. I am
preternaturally conditioned to consume the weakest and
worst.' The Nautilus was not only a research vessel and
weapon; it was an alternate, self-contained world under
his control.

"The man slumped before us stirred and straightened
at the first dry whisper of his name. He put a hand to
his grey, unshorn beard then to the khanda or Sikh coat
of arms pinned to his turban as if to make certain his
head still rested on his shoulders. The dark blue of
his loose warrior's robe and matching trousers obscured
the full extent of his wounds until we stood at the
edge of the light. His innards had spilled into his
panelled skirt, crusting his legs in blood to the knee.
He compassed the vermicelli of guts with a stiffened arm.
'Naturally,' he said in his genteel Oxfordshire English,
'as in Dante's ninth circle, the righteous, or at least,
self-righteous, come to gloat over the frozen sinners.'

"'Is that what this is? The inferno tipped upside-down,

with Satan throned at its apex?' your da said.

"'There are, as I'm certain you've seen, devils aplenty here,' he said. 'But I am not among them.' His wry, good-humoured smile practically obliged agreement. Charisma is perhaps the most difficult characteristic to get across second-hand. No glut of adjectives could capture Nemo's singular allure. Suffice it to say that when he set his gaze on you it was like winning the attentions of some natural force thought to be wholly impersonal. Like the air or gravity itself.

"'And you're frozen how?' your da asked.

"'A fortunate accident,' Nemo said.

"Your da recited the old Roman proverb about luck and the sea: '<u>Qui non cessit, non navigare</u>,' and then added, 'You've always had an unmistakable talent for hanging tight to life.'

"Nemo cleared his throat and summoned a new strength into his voice. 'Ah, my manners have deteriorated along with the rest of me. I apologize. Who is this lovely and adventuresome sylph?'

"'His wife, Fianna,' I said, bowing in greeting and bringing a hand across the bright division between us.

"'Hold there, good lady,' Nemo said. 'Unless you want to join me in an immediate and endless cycle of moments. This whitespace leakage preserves me, yes, but after a decidedly Promethean fashion. I'm trapped in a juddering time-slip, made to suffer these wounds once and again. My bowels recede and empty out in an endless cycle. Linger long enough and you're sure to witness one. The first few dozen times it's fascinating enough.' Part of his unmistakable aura of command was due to a peculiar quality of voice. His gentlest words struck you as someone chatting at top volume. You felt them resonate in your chest.

"'At first,' Nemo went on, 'I thought this stasis a trick of the mind. I'd come to the conclusion à la Kant that consciousness persisted beyond death and here I was, here I am, doomed to inhabit a hell of my own making. Neither ideas nor discipline matter. Inexorable stillness. Truly the worst of all possible outcomes, wouldn't you say? I recall you as a peripatetic sort, Liam, ever on to the next thing and the next ...'

"Your da indicated the man's cradled guts. 'When did this happen?'

"Nemo gave the date as March 1891, which was about twenty years after he'd scuttled the <u>Nautilus</u> in a South Pacific grotto and about seventeen before we discovered him. You know better, of course, than to pay Verne's dates any mind. The '<u>menteur professionnel</u>' as your da referred to him purposely confused the timelines in his fictions to obscure Nemo's true identity and objectives. Curiously, those stories served to enlarge Nemo's charisma, the multiplicity of fictions both disguising and mythologizing him. Your da informed Nemo how much time had passed.

"The Sikh closed his liquid black eyes to internalize the news, and when he opened them again he looked noticeably older, more broken, as if the checked years had come into his face all at once. 'I suppose then I'll learn the extent of my prophetic intelligence. Has the globe fallen yet into plutocratic chaos?' he asked then held up a hand. 'No, don't answer. It matters not. I've always been treated as a Laocoön, scorned as mad or otherwise incomprehensible, ignored in any event. Perhaps my death, too, will come as a trick of the gods. This place teems with giant serpents enough.' He indicated his extruded intestines with a jerk of his beard, saying, 'A damnable mutate did this—dished out a bit of rough handling, you might say. I don't know why, but it went on a berserker tear, ravaging the deck, damaging the engine, such as it is on this dream-vessel ... Had you figured it? This is no mere artefact. It's a ship ... a ship powered by the fully-enlightened mind and capable of traversing realms beyond the dark of our riven earth.' His apparitional look belied a dismaying self-assurance. To hear him was to eavesdrop on a higher form of speech. 'I use the term 'mere' in reference to this vessel,' he said, 'as Shakespeare would have done, meaning 'pure.''

"'These 'mutates' as you call them, the ones we encountered, came from this ship?' your da asked. 'The luminous algae, the orb-creature, the Kobiari ...' As he recounted these menaces, the symbolic or, daresay, allegorical, dimension of our journey to this point

occurred to me. We could be said to have passed through
the four vital stages of life: birth, represented by
the lagoon and its hidden intelligence; consumption, as
embodied in the acquisitive form of the Weaving Orb;
then the monotony and confusion of middle age suggested
by the maze; and finally, death, the abyss, to fly at
liberty or fall forever ...

"Remember what I said earlier about the distinction
between emotions and feelings? Our emotions about life
and death, relaxation and alertness, defence, they're
integral to how we maintain normalcy in the face of
wrenching events. It was then I first had the notion
that the entire underground, from lagoon to cathedral-
like docking bay, was intended as a spiritual trial, the
purpose of which was to trigger a higher sort of steady
state. In this way, perhaps these challenges helped
prepare your da for what came next.

"Nemo said, 'As best I could determine before my
untimely injury, the missing crew of this vessel traded
bodies as easily as we choose garments from a wardrobe.
Most of the mutates, I suspect, came from the storage
chamber above us. Some, however, could've once been part
of the ship's strange biological defences ... There's
merit to you escaping the Kobiari,' he noted. 'The
collective's stone fruit is no simple communication
device. It's a means of psychic rapport. The Kobiari
direct pilgrims through the maze according to the
travellers' unique spiritual needs. Their name for the
stone fruit translates as something akin to 'fruit
with a head that yearns for the gods.' The history of
this underground suggests most pilgrims were deemed
spiritually bereft and summarily dashed into one chasm
or another. This vessel is a visceral sub-b-lime ...' A
tormenting spasm forced him to break off. His innards
began to slither of their own accord into his perforated
gut. The strain on Nemo's face presented the slightest
crack in his statuesque composure. I pitied him,
unsuspecting.

"Nemo's stomach wound reversed itself up to a fair
dab of bloodletting, and then his bowels re-emerged at
grim intervals as if shaken from him. He spoke through
the visible pain: 'If you,' meaning your da 'would allow

me, I can guide you in my astral form through the body-swap procedure. As Mama Paris can attest, I've become quite adept at projecting myself. I'll take one of those monstrous forms from the storage chamber over this tortuous cycle. Bodies, in the end, are simply husk and waste. The conscious mind is the one true phenomenon.'

"The request put your da instantly on guard. His expression hardened. 'What would you do afterwards?' he asked.

"'Resume my explorations,' Nemo said. 'Utilizing the full power of this ship, all and sundry latitudes of existence will open to me. The Nautilus was only a poor approximation of this vessel. I lacked the courage on first discovery to do more than model select parts of my submersible on it. I daren't then risk its secrets ... Technologies of this magnitude are not simple means but rather, a way of revealing. The operating principles of this ship entail a vast re-ordering of nature. I wasn't prepared for it, then or now, as subsequent events proved ...'

"'And you'll never come back here, to this world?' your da asked.

"'Never? I can hardly agree to that,' Nemo said. 'Who knows what redeeming wisdom I might glean elsewhere? I'll be equipped, after all, to pass from heaven to heaven. Whatever happened to your youthful sense of high social purpose?'

"Your da said matter-of-factly, 'You know; you happened. What began with legitimate grievances dating back to the Sepoy Mutiny ended with knowing cruelties: unprovoked attacks on the Royal Navy, the murder of defenceless merchants—'

"'All complicit in slavery most cruel, malign sorcery or dangerously ignorant scientific pursuits,' Nemo said, measuring his words. 'Take the Royal Navy, governed by a Home Office whose pasteboard morality masks evils of every stripe and feather ... Freedom, equality, aid for the suffering, bah, even if realised, these purported ideals would smother the infant genius in his cot. Discipline in the face of hardship is the sole means to advancing the race. Despite the evidence, you refuse to acknowledge the possibility: what if democratic

morality is an impediment to human excellence? I say,
then so much for democratic morality. Think, man, had
we permitted the British government to retain those
Parmatmar crystals, who knows what Biblical end-storm
would've engulfed this world?'

"'Yes,' your da said, 'those were the early days, the
days before you sounded a tyrant, declaring 'There's no
saving this world without ruling it.' The days before
violence became self-justifying, the second strike
validating the first, the third strike the second and so
on in a sad, self-defeating progression.' I could see
your da's jaw muscles working. The decision lay hard on
him. 'With your Olympian attitude,' he said, 'perhaps
it's fitting you pine and die this way.' This reproach
amounted to quite a diatribe from your da. Except for
periods of direct instruction, when he cited vast
ranges of knowledge with ease, he was prone to a brevity
verging on silence.

"'You've confirmed for me,' Nemo spat, 'why the Roman
Emperor Titus Flavius Domitian insisted on lining the
walls of the colonnades with polished phengite stone
so he could see what went on behind his back.' Nemo cut
his shrewd eyes at me and asked: 'What of you, Fianna?
Are you prepared to countersign this verbal lettre de
cachet?'

"Your da turned to me, his eyes dark and full. 'You
understand he means to inveigle his way into my head.
I'd be compelled to share his consciousness during the
procedure,' he said. Then, facing Nemo again, he added:
'Did you seriously expect me to say, 'Hookum hai!' and
have done with it?' That was the customary phrase of
assent aboard the Nautilus.

"There are times when we scarce know why we do what we
do, and others when our active purpose is like a wire
drawn taut from our chest. We were beset on all sides,
by ancient traps, by witches and otherworldly creatures,
by the undead, grudging adventurers, and worst of all,
by fell conjunctions. I was weary and despondent. You'd
already suffered so much, and to what end? We'd set out
on a routine family outing, and bungled it, putting you
at risk. You were like a lad who's been hatched and then
immediately forced out of the nest, exhausted and nearly

bald-naked, to fend for himself. I had to ensure your
recovery, your future. The wire in my chest tugged and
tugged. The only way forward was through Nemo.

"After appraising the tyrant-prince of our situation,
I proposed a bargain: your da's help in securing him a
new body in exchange for mending you, whether by some
alien mechanism or otherwise. I avoided meeting your
da's eyes directly as I laid out the terms, but I could
see him shake his head, jaw tensed, at the periphery
of my vision. How he ached for a different answer. He
expected more from himself, I know. He wanted so much to
be Homeric, that is, to embody the ancient Greek ideal
of wholeness, to be cunning and wise, a witty speaker,
strong in body and soul, good as any carpenter with his
hands, an exceptional all-rounder like Odysseus. It was
a rebuke to his character to ask for Nemo's aid.

"It's your curse, I suppose, to have inherited this
ideal. I remember your da, early in your schooling,
teaching you the Greek word, <u>hamartia</u>. It's often
translated as 'error,' 'fault' or 'crime,' but taken
more literally, it means 'missing the mark.' The word
signifies the ancient Greek belief that a mental lapse
is as blameworthy, and perhaps as dangerous, as a moral
one. It's a lifetime hazard, conflating failure with
sin or its ancient equivalent. I trust you've learned
to be more forgiving than the Greeks, of yourself and
others ... I apologize, son. If I ever listen back on
these recordings, I fear they'll be rife with tangents
and disordered thoughts.

"Needless to say, it was heavy call on me to arrange
for your survival. We agreed, Nemo and I, to place
you in the whitespace field next to his crippled form,
keeping you in stasis until a lasting solution could be
devised. He mentioned the possibility of manipulating
the whitespace energy to reverse time, or mounting a
dreamtime resuscitation of your original consciousness.
We discussed other ideas, too: immersing you in the
fluid conserving the alien bodies in the ship's storage
chamber, flushing the <u>zonbi</u> poison from your system
through a transfusion of saline or animal plasma,
enacting some ritual magick ... But my immediate concern
was arresting your condition. The engine room leakage

that had heretofore sustained Nemo was the obvious fix. With his eyes hard-set and a furrow across his brow, your da told him, 'I'd only countenance freeing you for the sake of my son.'

"Then we left Nemo to retrieve you and carry out this arrangement. It makes me sick at heart to confess your da and I argued over this course of action. We did so in our usual, stifled manner. We were always measured with each other, which sometimes made our disagreements worse. In the main, though, our relationship was as complementary as could be imagined. He was worldly, philosophic, restless with ideas and the urge to discover. I was a seeker also, though decidedly more provincial, a country lass at heart, and seventeen years his junior. At the risk of overstating my case, I'd say I was his earth-fast rock. He was free to go adventuring because he felt secure at home, secure he had a home. And he, in turn, broadened my views and understandings beyond the natural world. He led me to places I'd not seen or heard before. We wrestled with how best to

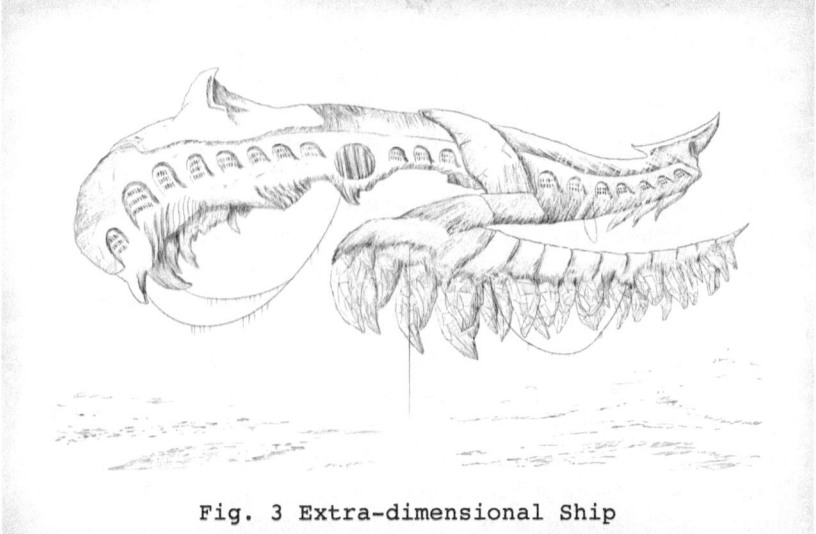

Fig. 3 Extra-dimensional Ship
'Psychic-powered vessel of unknown origin'

raise you, it's true, with the particular rigors of
your unusual training. We concurred, however, that such
training was necessary, and thank God in this instance.

"There was no disagreement, however, about whether to
risk ourselves on your behalf. That was a given between
us from the day you were born. But I regret those were
among the last words I ever spoke to Liam. I regret more
I didn't bury my face in his shoulder out of fear for
us all. I should've liked to have held him close, alone,
my cheek against the rough of his short-haired beard,
my hands on his bare forearms. But he was too solid,
too squared up and tightly held. There was no getting
in, it seemed. To your da, the ancient Greek notion of
excellence, or more precisely, <u>arête</u>, implied perfect
autonomy.

"Shouting from the portlight, we informed Jian of
our plans and Carantok hoisted you into the ship.
You had a stoic expression and a persistent middle-
distance stare. I resisted the notion to test the
extent of your detachment by giving you a peck on your
cheek or forehead. When you were a nursery child I'd
occasionally kiss you whilst you were sleeping. I always
wondered if you felt the imprint of my lips, if only
in dreams. Regardless, though nonplussed by the ship's
alien interior, you were cognizant enough to obey our
instructions, ducking and sidling and shying away from
potential dangers as directed. We kept you in front
of us, holding out a hand now and again to steady you,
which you ignored.

"Your degeneration worked its way into my smallest
thoughts. There you were: so young and tender,
vulnerable despite your training, a promise already
ruined. Everything I'd done struck me as a betrayal.
I tried to console myself with the notion you might
somehow be freer in your thoughts, like an animal in the
wild, immersed in immediate experience, participating in
the world's mysteries without any interfering ego. As if
you could decay into a state of primal transcendence ...

"Nemo had the good grace to say nothing about your
condition. Perhaps holding us to ransom had satisfied
him for the nonce. 'Come,' he said, ushering you into
the ethereal light. 'You'll be as safe as in a tented

garden.'

"You looked to us for confirmation and your da put a
hand on your shoulder, saying, 'Go on, man dear, and
stay until we come for you.' It was the first and only
time I heard him use that expression. It was his way,
albeit subtle, of acknowledging you were no longer a
lad or even a soldier in training, but a man, pure and
simple.

"The whitespace energy shifted your greenish glow
to tallow-white. You settled on the floor next to Nemo,
heedless of the blood, unblinking.

"Nemo assured us of your eventual recovery. 'I'm
confident of this,' he said, 'because in my time here
I've learned the fundamental principles of matter and
its arrangement. Everything in existence has a distinct
energy field, which I've given to calling 'life fields.'
To use a crude analogy, these life fields act like the
'lines of force' radiated by a magnet. As you know, iron
filings scattered on a card held over a magnet will
arrange themselves according to these lines of force. If
you replace the original filings with a new scattering,
the same pattern will manifest, as each magnet has a
signature shape to its life field. This phenomenon occurs
in us as well, in the process of losing and regenerating
cells. Our distinct energy fields ensure new cells
always take on the shape and function of the old.' He
patted you on the arm and said, 'We need only restore
his original life field and his body will repair itself
in short order. The storage chamber should have the
necessary mechanism.'

"He then described the sequence of steps to affect
the body-swap. First, he'd go into a trance state
and send his consciousness into the dreamtime. From
there, he'd enter your da's head and guide him to the
storage chamber. The chamber consisted of two central
platforms. One supported a glass-like capsule brimming
in breathable plasma but otherwise empty. The other
was a bare dais, awaiting the user's selection of an
alien form. The monster-shapes were arrayed along the
walls in identical capsules. A hand-operated switch
controlled their position. With Nemo's guidance, your da
was to rotate the selected host creature onto the second

platform, and then climb into the adjacent capsule.
The last step was for me to initiate the transfer from
another set of controls. Nemo detailed their operation
and I confirmed my understanding by repeating his
instructions verbatim.

"The apparent simplicity of the process belied its
dangers. To Nemo's knowledge, no human had attempted
this feat and there was no way to anticipate the
intensity of the psychic forces involved. 'The mental
pressures might reduce you to a lizard-like state,' he
warned, 'either because you lack the strength of mind,
or because your life field proves incompatible with the
host body. I've surmised that the creature tasked with
powering this ship had an energy signature uniquely
designed to complement that of this vessel, alive
in its own fashion. Unfortunately for me, the giant
crustacean's fled and dug itself a refuge under the
Kobiari. I hope to find a suitable replacement, so the
host's psychic capacity must of necessity be formidable.'

"It's impossible to know if this were ever Nemo's
scheme or if it collapsed under duress. I can say the
initial projection into your da's head went off without
a hitch. They sat across from each other on the deck,
cross-legged, eyes closed, divided by the sharply-edged
field of whitespace energy. Your da hummed a tuneless
mantra to help bring his consciousness into sympathetic
alignment. Gradually, Nemo's head lolled against his
chest and his shoulders slumped, signalling the flight of
his astral self. Liam perked to life and, waving away my
inquiry after his state of mind, retrieved Nemo's kirpan
or ceremonial dagger, sash, scabbard and all. 'For luck,'
he explained. His voice was recognizably his own but
abstracted, as if spoken over gently rippled water.

"I looked into his china blue eyes and found nothing
changed about them. But your da blinked, distracted,
when I asked about Nemo, describing him as 'a whispering
out of his hindbrain.' Then he belted the dagger, and
without a second glance at you, led me to the corridor
that connected the vessel's outrigger to its main
compartment.

"The corridor was segmented like a vertebral column
and set at such an angle I had to grip the joints for

balance. It opened onto what I took to be the ship's
control room. I made this observation on the basis of
a device resembling a gyrocompass. The device, or more
accurately, the projection, as it seemed made of pure
light rather than any solid substance, was a starry,
multi-levelled construct. The model described therein
included more dimensions than seemed right. I had only
a moment to look it over, however, before I was ushered
through an adjacent hatch and into the storage chamber.

"The menagerie on display in that chamber was of
an unprecedented character. I expect Herbert Spencer
himself would've been hard-pressed to construe the
evolutionary urge behind those unearthly anatomies.
Under other, more sanguine circumstances, I would've
spent days sketching them; instead, in the aftermath, I
managed to draw only a handful from memory, and of those,
none in its entirety apart from one. I'll endeavour to
include these illustrations with the eventual transcript
of this recording so you've some better notion of what
we encountered. I'm afraid words alone will conjure up
hopelessly confused impressions. There were creatures
with finned throats and withers bristling in serrated
fur; heads like sucking pump organs; torsos ending in a
burst of tentacles; pincers fringed in antennae; great
horned beaks and pouched jaws; eyes in the shape of a
lazy 'w,' which presumably operated on the principle of
acute polarization ... Janey Mac! Assuming the creatures
weren't wholly manufactured, the assemblage was the
ultimate proof of nature's infinite variety.

"There was a distinctly Victorian instrument bracketed
to the open platform. It was comprised of an elevated
funnel out of which ran a pair of tubes. The smaller of
the tubes ended in a cannula. The equipment could mean
only one thing: 'You've tried transfusion before?' I
asked your da as if addressing Nemo directly. He had his
back to me, hunched over the console for positioning the
host bodies. The main 'switch' was actually a ball-and-
socket device. He rolled the protruding ball to the left
and the softly illumined capsules clanked along their
designated channel in that direction.

"'A failed attempt to save my manservant,' he
said, fixed on the revolving display of monsters. 'We

manufactured a funnel from scrap à la Blundell's
Gravitator. But it was too late. One of King Louis
XIV's physicians, Jean-Baptiste Denys, demonstrated the
viability of transfusing lamb's blood. Failing to find
another solution, the potent fluids of these creatures,
however foreign, should serve your—our—son better.' He
stilled the rollerball, halting the alien procession.
The capsule that came to a stop adjacent to the open
platform was a right shaggy <u>daimon</u>, like something
from the picture Bible your grandad kept on a chain in
the loo. Its elongated, skeletal head was crowned with
prodigious horns. Its arms were akin to those of the
three-toed sloth, thicker at the wrist and paw—palm?—
than at the elbow, and its hooves were overlarge to
accommodate its bulk, notably its distended belly. A
large prehensile tail would doubtless have helped to
balance it upright if roused to life.

"With no idea of how this atavism would come to shadow

Fig. 4 Blood Daimon 'Mutate'
'Nolin's balm and bane'

over our lives, I'm grieved to say the creature's
fearsome aspect cooled the blood in my veins. It was,
however, a purely visceral response. I'd remind you that
the most pertinent lore uses the ancient Greek 'daimon'
rather than the Middle English 'demon' precisely because
it doesn't imply malevolence. In Plato's Symposium,
the female philosopher Diotima tells Socrates that
'Everything daimonic is between mortal and divine.' She
goes on to characterize daimons as demi-gods imbued
with divine might, existing between earth and heaven,
'interpreting and transporting human things to the gods
and divine things to men ...' Contrary to its appearance,
this husk, I'm convinced, was intended by its unknown
masters to be an intermediary between men and the
Celestial Pantheon, and in your own distinctive way,
you've begun to realise that ambition.

"Your da manipulated the controls to deposit
the daimonic host on the empty platform. The clatter
resonated in my chest. Your da got to his feet for a
better look. The condensation inside the capsule left
the creature wet smears of black and brown. It was
shrouded from horn tips to hooves in a heavy fringe. An
open eye gave off a ghostly reflection. Leaning over the
capsule, I could look directly into its bell-shaped
nasal cavity and fanged maw. The front two incisors
extending below its lower lip were like the chiselled
blades of an adze.

"'In your Christian Bible,' your da said, the word
choice indicating he spoke for Nemo, 'the disobedience
of Adam and Eve is regarded as the sin of all mankind.
Your priests say they turned away from divine nature
to nothingness. But what if that was the wisdom God
granted? What if nothingness is divine nature?' And
here he flinched, pained but determined to complete
this thought: 'We—we are ... the receivers of
consciousness ... not the source ...' He trembled on the
edge of saying more, eyes watering, then convulsed, arms
wild, lashing out, and fast upon that, drew the kirpan.

"I jumped back to avoid the crazy arc of the dagger.
A tinnitus of alarm overwhelmed me. I scanned the
chamber for a shield or better yet, a means to disarm
him. He waved me away, straining to speak but managing

only punctuated gasps. I retreated towards the hatch, thinking there might be something of use in the forward room. That's when he spun the blade around and attacked the ball-and-socket control with the pommel, smashing and smashing it, each blow reverberating in my chest. He was relentless in his single-pointed effort. Furious. The ancient Greeks would've recognized it as thumos, the anger of the honour-lover. He pounded on the mechanism until the skin on his hand began to tear away.

"But it was his face, his red contorted face that was the real mortal agony. I'd never seen him so heated and terrible. Sweat glistened at his temples. His jaw worked against invisible pressures. He half-shut his eyes, narrowing his vision to the violence. The inverted blade rose and fell in deliberate rage. Past his furrowed determination, however, I perceived a growing struggle within. There was a forced grimness that ran counter to his character.

"The control fractured, chipped, and at last, broke apart like marble. An oily wisp issued from the exposed workings. Your da seized up and stutter-stepped towards me, and I thought, or hoped rather, the berserker spasm was over. His colour deepened, his breathing came in arpeggiated bursts ... and as I dared draw nearer, he jerked towards the daimon capsule and, with one great whacking blow, shattered the casing, suffering divers cuts on hand and wrist, splashing plasma everywhere ... On the instant, the chamber was steeped in a sharp chemical reek. Your da scruffed the daimon to the surface by its neck-mane, recoiling, turning back, dagger blade down now. A variety of lunacies played across his face: greed, desire, bloodlust ... He was divided against himself, alternately vitalised and resigned.

"A spate of dagger-strikes settled the issue. Swift. Vicious. Bloody. The monster's chest was pilloried into butcher block waste. Your da let go the creature and dropped the weapon, twitching, spent. The daimon's blood muddled the tank. I could hardly breathe from fright. 'Liam?' I asked. It was awful to hear my faltering voice. He slumped to the floor, back against the wrecked console. 'Nemo?' I tried, dreading the answer. The kirpan was within reach. He could be anyone or anything, I thought.

I grabbed the dagger up and assumed a defensive crouch.
The acuteness of my fear humbled me. 'Are you ...?' I
said.

"He twisted in my direction. There was a faint hurt
around his wavering eyes. 'It's me,' he announced
hoarsely. '<u>Void</u> <u>ab</u> <u>intio</u>.' It was one of your da's
favourite Latin phrases. It encapsulated his notion that
death wasn't an imposition but an innate urge like the
compulsory ripening of a honey dew. Ripening is what the
honey dew does in its very being. He declared Nemo gone.
'Disappeared into the never-never' were his actual words.

"I gave a high cracked laugh and, discarding the
blade, embraced him, heedless of the wounds and blood-
spatters. He was a rare man, your da, my husband, a man
in whom courage was an instinct. His survival was one of
the few simple facts capable of squaring my thoughts. I
hugged him close to confirm his living spirit. He smelled
familiar, like a dry cedar gone pithy. He gave me an
awkward squeeze and made light of his injuries, saying
he'd managed better than Viscount Horatio Nelson as he
still had use of his 'right side.' Though most of his
wounds were superficial, they demanded attention lest
they become infected. I found the railroad surgeon's
kit Nemo had partly cannibalized to construct the
transfusion device, and treated him with antiseptic
sponges and gauze.

"Whilst I bandaged him, your da described a terrific
psychic skirmish with Nemo: runny watercolour explosions
and paralyzing music; defences constructed of wavy
energies (like Achilles' shield in Pope's translation);
skeins of obscuring mist; energies pearling into one
another; all the while his head cracking from the
inside. Nemo was by far the stronger astral presence,
having had little to do these past seventeen years but
practise. Your da held on through sheer unpredictability.
He reminded me that 'dreaming' in archaic terms meant
some sort of chaos—noise, jubilation or music. He'd
conjured up one distraction after another, like a vast
night-time flower peeling its petals back and back under
the moonshine, never to disclose its centre, emm, at
least long enough for him to destroy the console and
the <u>daimonic</u> vessel. Lacking a ready host, Nemo had

no recourse but to return to his crippled form or seek
another, say, the Weaving Orb, provided he could rout
its native consciousness.

"I'm compelled here to note another theory of mine as
it bears on this episode, more specifically, how brain
might be distinguished from mind. Though the discrete
mechanisms of the brain are as yet undiscovered, the
whole surely operates on a principle of layers, with the
lower allowing ever-higher grades of thought. I suspect
mind isn't synonymous with brain but rather an emanant
consequence of chemical lightnings across these various
layers in much the same way that particles of hydrogen
and oxygen are not liquid in and of themselves but when
combined as $H2O$, and through interactions with millions?
trillions? of other such molecules, attain the property
of water.

"Perhaps Michelet was more right than he knew in
giving the sea the qualities of an organism: the heating
action of its volcanoes; the electrified sea mucus
thickening into gelatine; the lacunar circulation of
the currents; salt water becoming fresh water becoming
water vapor; the ocean's self-organizing purposes aided
by God's own weather ... Yes, I think it probable the
objects of this world manifest some species of thought.
Consciousness conceived in this fashion might seem
superstition, but if everything were subject only to
nature's laws then what, pray tell, would separate
us from witless brutes, acting and reacting according
to cause-effect? Ah, that's my relation to nature in
the space of moments. I go from fanciful abstraction
to rock-bound science and back again. Each position
inspires its opposite in a dizzying cycle.

"But enough natural philosophy. You're likely quite
impatient with me now that I'm on the cusp of your
rebirth. This part I'll try to relate as I experienced
it, naïve, expectant, rather than in retrospect. If I
don't adopt this attitude I'm afraid I'll get so caught
up in hindsight I'll lose track of events in a rush
to explain them. Sometimes in the still of a beautiful
evening, the sky shot through with elegy, I have to
remind myself: life is this way and not the other. These
might-have-beens are thick with me this weather ... Did

you know Charles Darwin wished for beasts that wept so
we'd have companions in our misery? Proves even the
greatest of minds can fall prey to moony sentimentalism.

"At all events, your da and I arranged the Gravitator
as Nemo called it, to dispense the daimon-imbrued plasma,
and then set out to retrieve you. I sashed the dagger to
my hip, and on approaching the spill of whitespace again,
led with it, wary. Even crippled or dead, I didn't trust
Nemo. How could I? Imagine the superhuman patience his
survival had necessitated. It spoke to a wicked, self-
regarding greed on level with Tantalus. If anyone could
crack on after so much time and laid up willpower ...

"The body, however, gave no sign of independent action,
not even an eyelash flutter. Excepting the whitespace
field's reverse-time effects, it was a lifeless clay
as crude as any other. I was almost moved to place a
finger on its forehead and give a benediction, perhaps
First Timothy 1:17: 'To the King of Ages, immortal,
invisible ...'

"Your da disregarded the remains, almost contemptuous,
and helped you to your feet. You lumbered up in a
monster's shape, glowing like a half-lit ember. Worse,
the zonbi poison had apparently seeped into your
personality. You accompanied us to the storage chamber
like a servile child, mute and withdrawn. Under the
circumstances, though, I could've been the child, still,
watchful from my corner, waiting for recognition from a
long-absent parent. Your varnished stare was a grievous
reproof. I wanted so much for you to look deep into me
and know everything I felt, to know how much I suffered
for you and longed for a cure. There was no getting
around it: I'd failed you. Irrevocably. That blow to my
mother's pride has never healed entirely. My heart is
rawer for it yet.

"The plasma in your designated capsule was slimy and
cool to the touch. (As an aside, I've always referred
to this fluid as plasma but I don't rightly know what it
was. The term seems a natural fit, however, given its
viscidity and milky-yellow colour. It was an American
doctor, by the by, who suggested in the 1870s that
plasma might be used for transfusions. I know this
because I prepared a ration of dried plasmas for your

da's South African expedition in 1901. Cape Town was
lousy then with bubonic plague and I thought it might
be a necessary counter-measure if his situation got
desperate.)

"With a hand on your elbow, your da guided you into
the capsule. You arranged yourself to fall backwards
and, perfectly trusting, sunk into the semi-translucent
liquid. Your skeletal light diffused through the tank.
I could just make out the white opaque of your eyes
in the murk. I wondered what you saw, whether of this
world or the next, perhaps both, one superimposed on
the other. You calmed immediately. Small bubbles issued
periodically from your mouth, a slight assurance of your
humanity. We adjusted the transfusing instruments. Your
da drew your arm to the surface and inserted the cannula.
You took it without a flinch. Thank God for that funnel
and its accoutrements. I don't know what we would've
done without it.

"I was about to ask your da how long the transfusion
should go when the chamber was rocked by a walloping
bang. The whole of the ship swayed on its theoretical
keel. I caught the smashed control panel for balance.
Your da cursed under his breath and held out his hand
for the dagger; instead of giving it over, however,
I gestured for him to lead on. The ship pitched to
starboard, the stressed hull screeching. I braced myself
against the hatchway walls until the rolling eased,
and then continued after your da. He took us down an
unfamiliar corridor at a martial pace, pausing only to
weather the recurrent jolts. The top of his spine bulged
in anticipation of what we'd discover. I suppose that
was the moment my earlier, quashed suspicions appeared
to be more than mere jitters. My palms went slick. How
could he have known the route to the cargo hold, much
less how to activate the release mechanism?

"The cargo bay opened on a most unexpected sight: Mama
Paris seated atop the labyrinth monster as if she were
a Persian mahout. She braced herself against one of two
upright spines framing its head. The six-legged creature
had been ramming the outrigger with its armoured
hump. 'G'wan and git from 'im, duchess,' she said in
her cornhusk voice. 'Dat dere's not your betrothed. Dis

is.' She gestured at the monster's large blunt head, its pupil-less eyes less a colour than oily gleams. The monster underscored her claim with a dissonant bleating like something from a warped conch shell. When it comes to animal noises, feeling is a matter of pitch, and though I couldn't discern its subtleties, the sound was plainly one of grave distress.

"The wail continued in my ears long after its echoes faded. I opened my mouth to say something, to scream or curse, but sickened by fear, it just filled with rushing air. Your da—Nemo—extended a comforting hand. The awful pantomime nauseated me. I slapped his hand away, and then went very still. I wanted to recede from the moment. My overtaxed heart, however, insisted on it, thudding in my chest no matter what I felt or wanted. Despite your da's habitual risk-taking, I'd expected to live in his warmth forever; now, I saw him, not-him, as a cold and indifferent shuck, Nemo's phantom brain hovering above, its tentacled ganglia passing through his body like puppeteering strings.

"Nemo (as I had to regard him) gave up pretending and broke into an arch smile. 'Your husband,' he said, 'has ever been like a child in lamenting this world's disinterest in his good intentions. Perhaps now, a choice beast but a beast nonetheless, he'll finally resign himself to the notion that this world, this life, is one of tragic limitations. We live a fragment of time without coherence, not understanding its origins or its end. I, for one, could hardly have foreseen this rebirth.' He thumped his chest with the sharp of his palm.

"I sidled closer to the edge of the open door, flicking the dagger in Nemo's direction, pondering whether to leap on the monster's back. Jian stood in its shadow, staff in one hand and mirror talisman in the other. He acknowledged me with a nod. Carantok flitted about at shoulder-height, agitated. Past them, across the obsidian-like floor, the portcullis was a wreck of splintered wood and misshapen metal. I looked from the monster to Nemo and back. I'd been a thin, big-eyed girl and I pictured myself that way trying to grasp the situation, weak-kneed and staring, gobsmacked.

"Mama Paris clucked the monster forward a step or two
and said to Nemo, 'You wan' dis ship in whole piece?
You wan' crew? Liam be your helmsman you delivah de
duchess and de <u>bway</u> safe to home. He got de <u>daimon</u>
body fo' it now, <u>wi</u>? De one dat fit de engine.' She
gestured towards the outrigger. Yes, I could picture
it, the helmsmonster's head and back snugging into the
outrigger's underside, powering the vessel with its
psychic energies. 'Mama Paris come also,' she said. 'Dis
world offer nutting but slow sad falling off. Dis vessel
mean new world, dozen, new chance at mystery. To have
a sense a many world is tuh have a sense a de mystery a
dis one as it is. Dat Mama Paris' girlhood wish: to know
de mystery fo' certain.'

"Nemo accepted the bargain with appalling gusto:
'<u>Hookum hai</u> then o' mistress of the void! Prepare to cast
off! Yare!' The stun of misfortune practically blinded me.
Liam trapped in a monster's shape and slaved to Nemo? It
was all I could do to keep my head. I kept thinking <u>anam</u>
<u>cara</u>, <u>anam cara</u> ... You know it? From the <u>Martyrology</u> of
Óengus? 'Soul friend,' it means. Because some eyes are
windows and others mirrors, and his, emm, they always
hinted at a little more universe, and whatever I gleaned
from them I wanted to believe in.

"I was in such shock at this sudden development that
Carantok's winged sortie against Nemo didn't register
until the faerie was nearly at his throat, shrieking,
cherub hands glamoured into dragon claws. It was his
faerie sight, I'm sure, that induced the attack. The
mismatch of soul and form must've been an indelible
foulness. I scolded him, angry, aghast, flourishing
the short sword. What else could I do? Nemo wore your
da's aspect. I couldn't let it come to harm lest he
lack a body to return to, as I thought—think—he might,
eventually ...

"Carantok broke off the assault, loosing a high-pitched
stutter of doubt. It's no wonder he was confused. He'd
never come in for a wigging like this and he was only
trying to protect me. His mouth crumpled in penitence.
I guess he thought it best at that point, baffled and
embarrassed, to strike out on his own. Underground
there he could live among similar oddities, shut from

the world outside with all its annoying strictures. He
gave me one last melancholy look and winged out of the
chamber.

"'<u>Merci</u> <u>beaucoup</u>,' Nemo said, both affectionate and
mocking. He allowed himself that fulsome smile of
his, though on Liam's face, it had an unintentionally
ghoulish cast. 'He's free now, your husband,' he
said, 'freer than he's ever been. He's always found his
fullest joy on the sea, longing for the next voyage,
not knowing what for, exactly. This is his opportunity
to resolve the problem of being alive, human, its lack
of preordained meaning, to live on oceans of space
and challenge the gods without qualm. In spite of his
outward guise, he's complete. This is the life he's
always wanted, not biography but myth.' He raised his
hand as if to pat me on the arm, and then, noting the
pain in my eyes, thought better of it. 'We'll fix the
little blighter,' he said, 'don't you worry' and headed
for the control room. There was no need for further
sophistries or logics. The devil could seemingly be
himself and your da, acquire new acolytes, multiply
himself like a disease, all without a soul of his own.

"The <u>kirpan</u> was a murderous weight. I had the urge to
run the blade through the back of his neck; instead, I
turned to Mama Paris and your da, the accidental monster.
I imagined him in the hollow of that giant carapace, a
wisp of hope and dream, some Platonic idea. Never again
would I feel the soothe of his hand on my back, or his
lips on the pulse of my wrist. Never again would I rest
my cheek on his, tickling him with an eyelash. Never
again. He'd become a horrible abstraction, and to endure
this turn of events, I had to consider them as if we
were creatures in the wild. Whilst not exactly random,
events in the natural world aren't arranged for our
edification. There's no social or moral lesson in them.
There's only experience as bursts of mortal electricity.
'Can he understand me?' I asked the mambo-witch.

"The helmsmonster tipped her into the cargo bay and
she joined me with a shrug. 'He got more'n a crab
wit 'bout him, but ...' Her face fell, and for the
first time in my presence, she dispensed with her usual
self-dramatization. Taking on a quiet seriousness, she

explained how, after the monster had destroyed the remaining <u>zonbies</u>, she'd incapacitated it with her juju powder, how your da came to her in his astral form like a figure in a waking dream, and how, at his request, she'd guided him into the newly-vacated creature. Of course, she'd exhausted her supply of this powder, and lacked the knowledge and means to reconstitute it. Her magickal powers, whatever they were, appeared to be more borrowed than acquired.

"Your da was now an impassive grotesque with a

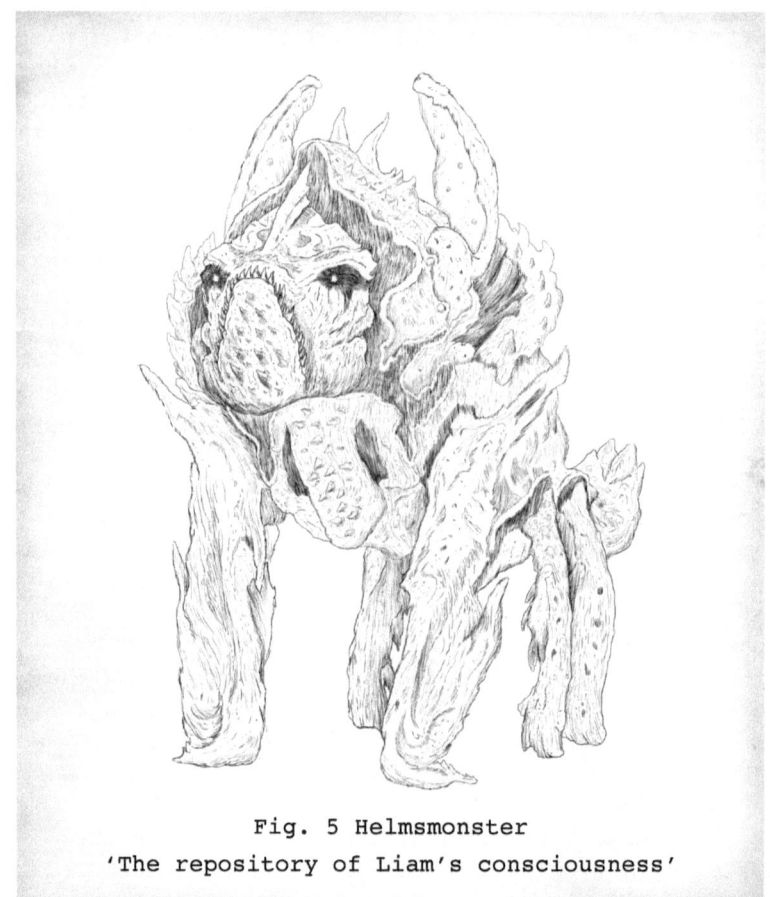

Fig. 5 Helmsmonster
'The repository of Liam's consciousness'

big, low-slung head. I looked in vain for a trace
of recognition. Its eyes were lost in their cavities
and its mouth was a permanent frown accented in wide,
serrated teeth. There was no discernible emotion or
interior life. The creature might as well have been made
of sandstone. I could break its carapace and puncture
its soft insides, I thought, and never get to its vital
centre. On each stab, the monster's essence would
withdraw further and further, eternally in darkness and
ungraspable. I could only hope your da, floating in that
vast elsewhere, would remember himself, remember us.

"Mama Paris dared limp closer. Her eyes had recovered
some of their former colour and intensity. I could tell
she wanted to make a tin can jubilee. She'd played the
mischief with her long-time foes and triumphed. It
was all I could do to stay my hand. The bloody-handed
bedlamite ... She fixed me with a keen gaze. 'He wan' you
tuh know you be his anchor in de drift out dere,' she
said, waving towards the sky. 'He wan' you tuh know you
be his heart o' hearts.'

"A surge of grief came up through my chest and
shuddered into my mouth. I choked on an indrawn breath
and cried. My grief went deep and deeper still. I
worried it might not have a bottom. There could be
nothing grimmer or more unjust than this, I thought.
Given your da's proclivities, I'd brooded on many
direful scenarios, yes, but the difference between these
fancies and his actual loss was incalculable. I wasn't
prepared for the sheer futility of thought itself. My
nerves were vexed to uncertainty. I cramped against the
bulkhead, arms around my knees, and shook, contracting
into sadness.

"Mama Paris waggled her head and doddered after Nemo
and the signal reward for her cunning. I was like a dumb
bird pecking every which way for answers. I'd begin a
thought and stop, stymied by emotion. Searing, cutting,
smothering: all those clichés about grief are real. Try
to recall the jumbled feelings you experienced earlier
today, or any ordinary day for that matter, one feeling
banging into another, shattering, merging, vanishing;
then imagine my upset here, feelings like heaped up slag.
I made an anguish of my hands, dying little by little,

and then all at once.

"Then Jian appeared as a watery blur, and behind him, peering over the lip of the cargo door, the helmsmonster. Jian offered me a linen handkerchief, and I stood to accept it and say farewell to your da. I dabbed my eyes as I approached, defeated before the start. His—its—eyes were so small and lifeless, I couldn't bear to look. My voice broke the whole time I praised his courage and thanked him for his sacrifice, everything ringing false though it were pure-felt truth. I had to pause to let words regain their meaning, and then, the tissue of my throat hardening against my will, I eked out 'love,' a word so short and soft it's prone to get lost on the air. The creature had half-turned away before I'd uttered it.

"Among the sundry regrets and revisions I've contemplated since, I've wondered most about whether he heard and understood that final word. He was an ancient Greek at heart, I tell myself. Whether he heard me or no, he recognized that the gods sometimes ask terrible things of us. He was not unlike Menestratus, who gave himself up to the Thespian Dragon to save his lover and city. Menestratus leapt willingly into the serpent's maw clad in barbed armour. There's a good chance your da proved sacrifice <u>and</u> victor in his case, too, but a world or more away.

"Perhaps I've gone in for too much reverence in speaking of your da in these terms. I worry you're compelled to measure yourself against his achievements. It's easy to treat him as opaque and timeless given how we lost him and, in your case, at such a young age. He died? passed on? before you knew the right questions to ask or what to look for in a father. I know you missed his counsel regarding your 'blood condition.' A few weeks after we'd returned to the estate, I found you collapsed in the library chesterfield draped in one of your da's old dinner jackets, a tie pin through the breast pocket.

"Don't judge yourself against the mythic figure you've conjured up, you know, the one defined mostly by his end; rather, judge yourself by your own philosophy. In French, the word '<u>conscience</u>' translates as 'moral sense' and 'consciousness.' The word conflates the ethical and physiological. Regardless of your blood, you've a distinctly human <u>conscience</u> in both respects. To be human is to be responsible for yourself, for those closest to you, your country, history. To be <u>daimonic</u>, on the other hand, is to be wanton, egoistic, without answer to anyone or any higher principle. Your volunteering for the Royal Irish Lancers showed your humanity in this, the most important sense. No matter how unsettled you feel in yourself, a feeling everyone shares at one time or other, at least be assured of your essential goodness.

"Thoughts of you and my consequent duties belayed the full measure of my agony. There was much to do, quickly and without fail, to affect your recovery. Jian accompanied me to the storage chamber, and to my great relief (more tears, I'm afraid), we found your eyes restored to their honest blue. I hurried to sit you up. Your head lolled in your daze. We disconnected the Gravitator, stoppering your punctured vein with the handkerchief, and shortly thereafter, you convulsed and vomited a slurry of plasma and bile.

"The shock of it returned you to a weakened but ordinary awareness. I hugged you close, slimy as you were, sending hard breaths into your ear, delighted and at once dreading the inevitable questions about your da. I wasn't prepared. How could I be? When you pulled from my embrace, the issue of his absence was behind your eyes. A cruelty on top of everything else.

"I put a finger to your lips before you could give voice to your concern. 'I'm sorry, I'm sorry,' I said in a wheeze and nothing more. My strength of will gave out, and in crushing you to me again, I felt your spine shiver and twist unnaturally. Then your brow pulsed against my temple as if swollen of a sudden, and I jerked back to see Jian chop at your neck, striking the vagus nerve just below the hinge of your jaw, to render you unconscious. He immediately ducked his head in shame and apologized, saying he'd recognized a 'bad spirit' in you.

"I assured him he'd acted properly under the circumstances, and asked for his assistance in removing you from the body-swap capsule. I couldn't brood on your seizure, what it might portend. I was drained of worry: for you, your da, myself. I couldn't remember the last time I'd eaten or rested. Sheer mindless perseverance kept me going. God, the uselessness of that pain ...

"There's not much more to say about the journey itself. The trip home was an overpowering dream. We didn't travel so much as the distance shuddered through us: the ancient cave rock, the unceasing ocean, a sky brighter and bluer than I'd remembered, the sun, perhaps its blinding centre ... It took no time at all by our reckoning. A whelm of sensation, and the rest was aftermath. Like the coronal blurs following a sharp blow to the head.

"Mama Paris emerged from the control room to see us down a hatchway exit. She made a few innocuous remarks. Their substance was lost in my residual anger and distress. I was Persephone garlanded in migraine. I wanted only for you and a familiar landscape and a swansdown quilt. Jian carried you over one shoulder. We descended to the front lawn not more than fifty metres from the manor. I squinted against the astringent light. I couldn't yet take pleasure in the sun, the breath of wind.

"I was loathe to turn and face the helmsmonster. I imagined it shouldering the vessel, the creature and the ship suspended above the earth by whitespace energies. I would've traded any part of me to resurrect it—him. But no one gets to make a choice like that, not even the most accomplished witches. No, I'd said my last to him, however incompletely, and lacked the stamina to try again, especially appraising him from the ground. I felt small enough. My feet ached from all the uneven and unyielding stone we'd crossed. The distance to the manor was endless. The ship vanished with an eerie diminuendo as we neared the portico. The rest you know through living it.

"What else is there to say? I'm approaching the limits of memory, of understanding, even imagination. I suppose those are the limits of any true story. It's difficult making meaning out the thin air of existence ...

"Even after nine years, the house evokes him at every turn, sometimes jarringly so. There are rooms

I can't bear to enter, papers, maps, artefacts I've
left untouched. I find succour in the open air, among
the Scots pine and in the valley fen, what might
be called the firmer heaven or <u>coelom</u> <u>firmior</u>. On a
country stroll, I can cast off the graying nimbus of
mourning, think freely for a time, and at my finest.
Nature inspires thoughts that wouldn't occur otherwise
just as Sunday services offer up words and phrases you
never hear in daily conversation: 'agone,' 'hither and
thither,' 'by-word,' 'go ill.' These walks aren't about
the destination or taking exercise. They're about the
possibility of higher knowledge. Don't worry. I'm not
about to become another Paley. I know first-hand the
universe isn't a rational, pristine unity. 'The horror
of death proves the value of life,' ah, rubbish that.
But there's something to chaotic nature apart from human
desire or presence that suggests a spiritual order.

"If traipsing through an old hedgerow can raise these
notions, how much loftier your da's thoughts must
be, exposed as he is to otherworldly nature? I used
to tease him about having a gyroscope in his centre,
spinning, spinning. Now, when I picture him in that
ship, emm, under it, I see past his outward form to that
gyroscope, radiant, reflecting an impossible colour-field
of stars. Yes, at my most optimistic, I think on him
swifting through space, illuminating the deepest darks
of Creation and beyond.

"It isn't only wishful thinking. Or guilt. Simply put:
your da's not the sort to give up easily on life. So
until there's proof to the contrary, I don't think we
can say the journey is well and truly over. That's small
comfort, I'm sure. We lost him just the same. But I'm
tempted, no, I should, I must, end with an ellipsis ...

PROJECT
NIGHTSCAPE
TO SIN AGAINST OUR MERCIES

Prog Rock Prequel to Early Darkness

Experience the mind-warping horror at the center of *Early Darkness* in mystereophonic sound! This 13-track progressive hard rock concept album features the melodic guitar stylings of Grammy-nominee Tony Gaglio and includes musical contributions from Vinny Appice (Dio), Mirabai Peart (Joanna Newsom's band), Tobin Sprout (Guided by Voices) and Pete Trewavas (Marillion).

"I like Eighties hard rock, I like progressive rock and therefore, I like Project Nightscape. It's a great concept album. For all the lovers of this genre, this album is highly recommended ..." —*Background Magazine*

"... Behind the complicated music there are subtle undertones that link the songs but let them all speak for themselves ... *To Sin Against Our Mercies* is a spectacular concept record! 9/10" —*Musipedia of Metal*

Available at Amazon and
most everywhere music is sold or streamed

NIGHTSCAPE
THE DREAMS OF DEVILS

His Nightmares Corrupt
the Waking world…

Sixteen-year-old math prodigy Case Tannahill has suffered chronic nightmares ever since he can remember. They're so bound up with who he is that he calls them 'threaded dreams.' But the meaning of these night terrors seems forever lost to him.

Until one October morning when Case and fellow high school seniors Kat and Troy are drawn into a neighbor's corn patch by a scarecrow come to life. Investigating further, they're plunged into a shared, life-altering nightmare that threatens to collapse all of reality.

Available at Amazon and other fine retailers